Sic

CAMBRIDGE RED

DuBois Publishing
Cambridge

Published by DuBois Publishing 2019

ISBN: 978-0-9573344-9-6

Cover design: DuBois Publishing ©
Cover photo Kings College Chapel Interior:
By I, Sailko, CC BY-SA 3.0,
https://commons.wikimedia.org/w/index.php?curid=14814557

First published 2012
This edition 2019

DuBois
publishing

www.duboispublishing.com

to Joan, Geoff, Rivers, Clarabella, Bríd

and my thanks to the Cambridge Writers; Group for constructive criticism and encouragement

Contents

Chapter 1 | *Edward*

It was pitch dark when Dr Edward Holroyd's alarm went off on a morning in late September. He was confused. It should be light, because it was only... ah, he remembered, he'd set it for 5am. Today was an important day and he had lots to do before he set off. Edward stretched out a hand to turn off the alarm, but instead of the hard surface of the clock, his fingers landed on something soft and slightly furry. Disconcerted, he sat up, turned on the bedside lamp and looked at the clock. He laughed. A polishing cloth rested in front of it. He turned off the alarm.

Fully awake now, Edward swung his legs over the side of the bed. He picked up the duster and smiled. His cleaner, Eileen, must have been disturbed mid-polish. Eileen was getting rather elderly, but she'd been with him for close on twenty years and he didn't think he could part with her. He often came home to discover wastepaper bins sitting proudly on the sofa, his office chair, or even the toilet seat. Some days when he let himself into the flat, he would see that bright yellow polishing cloth on the hall table, by the phone base. The phone itself would be missing. Eileen liked to chat. If Edward wasn't there to talk to, she phoned a friend. How would she take to the changes he was about to make? Perhaps he should have said something to her, but he'd been away quite a lot during the summer months, and he would be missing again soon for another short while. He should leave Eileen a note. He would do that when he got back from his morning jog.

Dressed in running gear, Edward washed up the mug he must have overlooked the night before, put the sugar bowl into the cupboard, filled a bottle with water and left the flat. It was unusually cold and misty. He shivered in the sudden change of temperature. Cambridge frequently revels in a late Indian summer and it lulls the populace into forgetfulness of the approaching winter. Despite the chill, it was Edward's favourite time of year, this gap between the departure of tourists and the arrival of students. He liked the quietness of the city and the way it gave him a chance to catch his breath and prepare for the coming term. Normally, his mind would be full of academic questions: had he pitched his lectures correctly? Would the new first year undergrads be too in awe of him to challenge the content? Would the second years be difficult to handle on their return from the long vacation? Would those on fieldwork manage without needing constant attention? Could he rely on the fourth years to be sober and diligent as they looked down the barrel of their final undergraduate year? He wasn't thinking of students or his work this morning however, but of his personal life. Perhaps that was why he didn't see the figure hiding behind the stumpy poplars of Coe Fen. He didn't hear the squelching sound of footfalls following him clumsily over the wet grass, nor yet notice the way a half-observed shape ducked out of sight as Edward checked the traffic before running across Trumpington Street, and again as he stooped to re-tie a shoelace near the Judge Institute. Absorbed in his own world, he missed many things. He ran on, oblivious that the step he was about to take would trigger a train of terrible events.

Edward heard music playing as he ran up the stairs to his flat. He turned his head to listen more carefully, as he reached for the spare key which was kept on top of the lintel.

The sound was coming from his neighbour Paul's flat. Edward felt puzzled because it was classical music, but he knew Paul favoured pop. He was moving his hand back and forth searching for the key, which wasn't in its usual place, when Paul emerged to collect a bottle of milk from the doorstep.

'Morning, Edward,' he called. 'Have you had a good run?'

'Not bad. What music are you playing this morning?' he asked, hearing it more clearly now that the door to the flat was open.

'That's Poulenc,' said Paul, standing straighter. 'Roger adores Poulenc.'

'Roger?' echoed Edward, giving up his search and paying more attention to his neighbour.

'I have finally met the man of my dreams,' said Paul, beaming and hugging the milk bottle to his chest. 'Roger is a musician and he's tutoring me on all the great composers.'

Edward dropped his head to hide a tiny smile. Roger's predecessor, who had formerly been the man of Paul's dreams, had been an architect. The pair had spent evenings and weekends redesigning the flat. They fell out over the dining table - Paul wanted wood but Angus preferred glass. Edward wondered how long this relationship would last. Still, he thought, the sound of music was preferable to the sounds of drilling and hammering.

Paul was still hugging the milk bottle. 'Come to supper this evening and meet him.'

'Thanks, but I'm off to Brussels in a few hours.'

'Again!' said Paul, raising his neatly plucked eyebrows Everything about Paul was neat. He was small, tidy, and understated in his dress. His hair was cut close to his head because, he'd once told Edward, it was easier to keep clean, and he couldn't abide dirt of any sort. 'Whatever do you do in Brussels? You spend a lot of time there.'

Before Edward could reply, a tetchy voice sounded behind Paul.

'Do hurry with the milk, coffee's ready.'

Paul smiled ruefully. 'Come and have a coffee with us. I'd love you to meet Roger.'

Edward looked at his watch. He didn't have much time, but Paul became more earnest.

'Oh do come, Edward.'

'Okay, just a very quick coffee, though. I mustn't miss my train.'

He followed Paul into his kitchen. The clean black and white lines reminded Edward of Angus who'd been a minimalist. Paul's cat, Piaf, rubbed against Edward's legs and he bent down to stroke her. She too was black and white.

'Who's this?' growled the voice Edward had heard earlier.

A tall, longhaired man with angry eyes came into the room. Used to towering over Paul, Edward, who was six feet, had to look up for a change.

'Oh Roger,' gushed Paul, 'here is my neighbour, Edward Holroyd. He's a lecturer at the University, and we've been friends for years and years.'

Edward watched a suspicious look cross Roger's face. He'd seen that look in the past, on the faces of many of Paul's boyfriends. Why do some of them assume... He shook his head and leaned down to pick up the cat. 'How do you do,' he said, nodding to Roger as he scratched the cat's ears. She purred loudly.

Roger grunted an ungracious reply.

Piaf rubbed her head against Edward's chin, and then tucked herself under his neck. Her purring grew louder. Roger's eyes narrowed. He seemed to resent the attention Edward was getting from the animal, and that suspicious look deepened.

'I would love to have a cat,' said Edward, resting his cheek against the animal, 'but I spend a lot of time away. Paul allows me to be a surrogate father to Piaf.'

Roger grunted again. He stayed in a bad mood, and Edward cut his visit short, swallowing the coffee quickly and using his trip as an excuse to leave. Paul saw him to the door and gave a cheery wave as Edward reached up for the key once again. He found it immediately, and puzzled fleetingly as to why he hadn't been able to put his hand on it earlier.

The journey on Eurostar was tedious and noisy. The train ambled out of London and never got beyond a canter as it headed down to Dover. A loud-voiced woman behind him began using her mobile, and Edward quickly regretted not booking a seat in first class, which was usually, but not always, quieter. The Chunnel brought a merciful, if short, interval. As soon as they re-emerged, the blasted woman was on the phone again, telling her private business to the entire compartment. Edward tried to focus on work he'd brought with him, but he was restless and his attention kept straying. He looked out of the train window at the passing view, but was caught instead by his own reflection.

Edward rarely paid much attention to his looks, which was one of the reasons he could forgive Eileen's shortcomings. He would glance briefly in the mirror as he dried his face after shaving, just to make sure he hadn't left foam behind, and to tidy his hair. Now he noticed heavy bags beneath his eyes, the result of several sleepless nights. Bad dreams had long been his close companions but he was having more of them recently. He spread his fingers through sandy-coloured thick hair, which was greying now above the ears and smiled sardonically, unsure that he liked this ageing version of himself. A sudden shout of laughter from the woman behind made him jump, and he abandoned his critical self-examination. He hoped she would get off at the next stop, Lille. She did. Edward sighed with relief as the doors buzzed to a close, and nestled more comfortably into his seat. His table companions had also left, and Edward stretched out his legs, enjoying the freedom of being alone.

The train moved off from the grey cavern-like station of *EuraLille*. It picked up speed and Edward began to relax. It was his habit to spend the journey to Brussels working on research as it gave him more free time when he arrived in the city. This was a special trip though, and for once he set his work aside and looked out instead upon the Belgian countryside. It would probably be his last trip for a while, and he realised that he'd never really taken the time to look at the landscape before. Thoughts of work, or pressing publication deadlines usually took precedence over relaxation. Bare fields sped past. The harvest was in. He noticed the thinness of the trees, and the tininess of the villages - each with their own church and spire. The roofs of the houses were mostly red.

Edward felt a lurch in his stomach. He closed his eyes, but opened them quickly as he sensed panic rising. The colour red seemed burnt onto his brain, as though it was a light bulb he'd stared too long at. There were few instances of it in the passing countryside, but his eyes seemed drawn to each one. He took out his mobile and dialled a number. Increasingly breathless, and feeling his heart was beating as fast as the moving train, he almost shouted when the call was picked up.

'Dad,' he called. 'Dad, it's Edward. Dad?'

The voice at the other end kept talking and Edward realised he was speaking to his father's answerphone. He ended the call distractedly, and laid the phone on the table. He was drawn again to the landscape. The red roofs were jumping out at him now, eclipsing the fields that dwarfed them. Edward became more anxious. What had that counsellor said to him? Distraction. He looked along the carriage, at the luggage rack, his fellow passengers, everything, anything, trying to distract himself. All of a sudden, he had the sensation of falling. It felt as though he was sinking through a long tunnel. His ears were battered by the sound of a screaming wind. On and on through the tunnel, he went, drawing closer and closer to a face at the end, which grew larger and larger. It was a woman's face. Her eyes were closed and her skin was paper-white.

Edward began to hyperventilate. He struggled to shut out the picture, but still the face was there. He pressed his hands against his eyes and focussed on noises as he'd been taught. The howling wind quietened and he began to hear the swishing sound of the train. The rhythm was comforting. It gradually became louder and slowly, slowly the woman's face receded. His breathing calmed.

When Edward looked up again, the train had reached the outskirts of Brussels. He made himself describe what he was seeing. House... houses... tall houses... tall and thin... some painted... some painted ... red.

'Anni,' he whispered. 'Anni.'

The train pulled into the *Gare du Midi*. By the time he'd made it through passport control, he was collected again. When he came out onto the concourse, she was there, waiting and smiling. Anni. Lovely, loving Anni.

Chapter 2 | *Anni*

'What are you doing?' asked Roger, coming up behind Paul who had his ear to a glass he was holding against the wall between his and Edward's flat.

'I'm listening. Hush!'

'To what?'

Paul stopped a moment. His eyes were dancing with curiousity. 'I can hear voices. Edward is back from Brussels.'

'Is he talking to himself?' grumbled Roger, who was irritated because Paul usually prepared his breakfast, and he had been left waiting this morning.

'I think I can hear a female voice.'

'So?'

'Edward never has females in his flat! Well I con't count his cousin. He rarely has anyone to stay, except his father and brother. I'm sure this woman arrived a couple of days ago. I wonder what's going on?'

'Why don't you go and ask? After breakfast maybe?'

'Oh I couldn't. That would be nosey, Rog.'

'And what you're doing isn't?'

Paul made a face and withdrew the glass from the wall. 'I suppose you have a point. I do worry about Edward, though. I'm sure I hear noises when I think he isn't there.'

'Doesn't he have a cleaner?'

'Yes, but Eileen makes lots of noise. You can't mistake it when she's there.'

Roger stared at Paul. He didn't like this obsession with what went on in Edward's flat. 'Could we forget Edward,' he asked, 'and focus on my breakfast?'

* * * * * * *

Unaware they were being spied upon, Anni and Edward were in the hallway of their flat. Edward was preparing to leave for work. He pulled on a backpack and smiled at Anni. 'I don't really like to leave you so soon after your arrival, but full term starts today, and I need to be in the Department, even though the teaching term doesn't start until Thursday.'

'I have no idea what you mean by that,' replied Anni, 'but never mind. You can explain another time. I know you're in a hurry.' *Trust Cambridge to make things complicated,* she thought, smiling at her new husband.

Edward was tall and slim, with thick dark blond hair. He was wearing an open-necked white shirt, which set off his tanned skin. He was at least a head taller than Anni. She looked up at him, and decided that he looked good in whatever he wore. She grinned. Her sister, Cécile, teased her mercilessly, but it slid like water off Anni's back. She was happy to admit her infatuation.

Edward seemed to become aware of her approving gaze. He blushed. It amazed her that he could still be shy with her after all this time. She stood still as he reached out to smooth a lock of her hair which had fallen over her eyes. He kissed her fondly.

'Yes,' he said. 'I have a lot of work to do over the next couple of days,' he said, 'but perhaps I had better come back and fetch you this afternoon. I really shouldn't leave you alone so soon. Are you quite sure you can find your own way to the Sedgwick Museum?'

'Of course I can!' she said, pushing him gently away. 'I've travelled the world, remember. Besides, you've given me a map.'

'Oh yes, right, okay. I'll meet you there at 5 o'clock.' Edward tightened the backpack over his shoulder, claimed another kiss, and set off for his office at the Department of Environmental Sciences.

Anni walked into the living room to watch from the windows as he unlocked his bike and began cycling across the fen, into the centre of Cambridge. When he was out of sight, she examined the view. Edward had pointed out the green roof of the Fitzwilliam Museum in the distance, just above the trees. The morning was crisp and sunny and the glass dome was glinting in the sunlight. Her gaze dropped to a group of cows grazing on the common and she shook her head, smiling. It was hard to accept that they were only a mile from the historic centre of Cambridge. Coe Fen, upon which the living room windows looked, was a remnant of the pre-college landscape, with wild marshy fields, scattered trees, and these clumps of grazing cows. Anni wondered if there were any paintings by Constable in the Fitzwilliam - the Fitz, as Edward had called it. She felt herself sinking into the rural look and feel of the fen, lazy, like the cows.

The strident sound of a car horn drew her attention to the road. A cyclist, weaving in and out of a column of slow-moving cars, was drawing the wrath of a driver. Anni smiled. Apart from the universally impatient driver, the contrast to Brussels was huge. She could hardly believe that she was here in Cambridge. It was astonishing that a casual meeting in a tiny museum had led her to a whole new life. She drifted towards the sofa, meaning to sit a while and phone Cécile to reminisce, but a row of suitcases in the middle of the room caught her eye. Changing her mind, Anni put on a CD and went into their bedroom. Sorting her clothes and finding something appropriate to wear for the visit to Edward's office was the first priority. She would phone her sister later.

A track ended as she was sorting through one of the cases, and in the silence, she heard the front door close.

'Edward', she called, thinking he'd returned. There was no reply. Anni walked out to the hallway. No one was there. Feeling sure she'd heard something, Anni opened the front door and stepped onto the landing. A neighbour was going into his flat. That must have been it. She crept back inside, feeling foolish.

Kicking off her shoes, Anni returned to her task, and quickly became engrossed. She drew out a dress and laid it on the bed. What would Edward's colleagues be like? Would they be so absorbed in their research and teaching that they wouldn't notice what she was wearing? Perhaps they were buzzy and up to the minute, involved in the latest scientific breakthroughs and used to noticing and criticising all they saw. She'd often tried to get Edward to talk about the people he worked with, but he'd said very little.

Anni spotted a suit she'd wrapped carefully in several sheets of tissue paper. She uncovered the old favourite; a light woollen fitted jacket and skirt. Holding it against her, she checked her reflection in the mirror. The light green colour of the wool accentuated the hazel in her eyes and set off her long dark brown hair. The neckline was scalloped and it complimented her heart-shaped face. 'Shoes. Now which box are the shoes in? Ah.' Her careful labelling had paid off. She rummaged in the box, and pulled out a pair that matched the suit. Yes, this was the outfit to wear. Anni always felt good in it, and that would offset her nervousness. She knew his work was important to Edward, and these people would probably become her friends.

While shaking the suit to loosen the creases, she was once again disturbed by the sound of a door opening and closing. It was more distinct this time, and she thought she heard a key falling onto the tiled landing floor. Feeling troubled in the unfamiliar surroundings, she ran again to the front door. It was open. How odd, she was sure she'd closed it. The landing was empty but she caught sight of a head through the banister rails. Anni sprinted across the black and white tiled floor, but stood on something sharp. Swearing quietly, in French, she leaned down to remove a small sharp stone from the ball of her foot. By the time she reached the banisters, the stairwell was empty.

'Who is it?' she called.

The only response was a faint echo as her question bounced back from the bare walls and floor.

Chapter 3 | *The Department of Environmental Sciences*

'I can't work out how to use this blessed drinks machine,' said an elderly man as he stood before a vending machine in the staff room of the Department of Environmental Sciences. The room was large and rectangular, with four attractive Victorian sash windows. A big solid door opposite the window wall led to a central stairway. The sun, which had shone earlier on Edward, poured through the windows, lighting up the room and glinting off the vending machine which was set at the kitchen end. A woman, hovering in the doorway, watched the man, who was wearing a tweed jacket that had grown limp with age, and a pair of wide-legged trousers, probably not so much because they were fashionable as because they were wide at the waist to accommodate his girth. A very old-fashioned bicycle helmet hung from one hand, and he held a plastic cup in the other, into which he was staring sadly.

'It's very easy, Professor,' said the woman, pushing large round plastic-rimmed glasses up the bridge of her nose as she walked briskly to stand by him. 'Just follow the simple instructions.'

Professor Potter, known affectionately as Potty, continued to look into his plastic cup. 'I must be doing something wrong Pansy,' he sighed, 'this tea tastes of tomato.'

A bunch of people came into the staff room and Pansy waved an imperious arm at them. 'Gather round, gather round,' she said loudly, and her heavily lacquered hair bounced as she tossed her head. 'I'll give you a demonstration on how to use the new coffee machine.'

'Don't be such a prat, Pansy,' said Dennis Cardigan, a tall middle-aged man with small sharp eyes who had pushed to the front of the group. 'We can manage that without your help.'

Pansy flashed an equally angry look back at Dennis. 'Professor Potter isn't making a success of it!'

Dennis snorted. 'It's pretty disgraceful anyway, if you ask me. Here we are in Cambridge, seat of one of the oldest British institutions and you've seen fit to remove access to another, even more important British institution, namely a decent cup of tea!'

'You can blame the Government for that,' replied Pansy. 'They're the ones who're cutting back funding to Universities. The coffee machine will be a great saving to the Department, since we cannot afford to replace Alex.'

Potty stared sadly into his plastic cup. 'If I'd known that the outcome of Alex's retirement would be a machine that serves tomato tea, I would not have contributed to his retirement present,' he grumbled.

He received sympathetic pats on the shoulder as he walked to his usual seat in the staffroom. The newcomers chose drinks from the machine and drifted slowly towards the chairs. Several grimaced as they tasted their brew, but none seemed willing to complain. At the end of the queue was a woman who glared at the selection, then turned to glare at Pansy.

'There isn't a fruit tea choice,' she said in a southern American drawl.

'All anyone wanting fruit tea has to do is place their *own* fruit tea bag into a plastic cup and press the button which says *Hot water only*. I don't understand why you can't get the hang of such a simple piece of equipment.'

'Well tomato is a fruit. Did *you* want a fruit tea, Potty?' asked Dennis.

'I did *not*. I just wanted ordinary tea. But I swear this is tomato tea.'

'My tea tastes of tomato too,' said one of the newcomers, Chris White, speaking low and tentatively.

Pansy glared at him. Chris was soft-voiced and slightly built. He didn't like getting into arguments. It was brave of him to side with Potty.

'There *is* no fruit tea in the machine!' Pansy repeated.

Poor Pansy. She frequently felt driven to distraction by the stupidity of her academic colleagues, whom she generally considered most undeserving of her continual efforts to make their working lives more agreeable. She opened her mouth to voice her angry feelings, but stopped as the head of Department, Professor Scott, entered the staff room with John York, the technician.

'What on earth is going on?' asked Arthur as he surveyed the collection of unhappy faces.

'Pansy is poisoning us,' replied Dennis, giving his cup to John, who tasted it and frowned.

'They don't know how to operate the coffee machine,' complained Pansy.

John opened the front of the machine and removed a packet from the tea slot. He held it up. 'Someone has put tomato soup into the tea slot.'

Several muffled sniggers were heard. Pansy's face went red. She looked around at her colleagues. Her nose narrowed, her lips tightened, her eyes became small dots behind the lenses of her glasses. 'This is sabotage,' she hissed.

'And we shouldn't be using plastic cups either,' said Dennis. 'Think of the scandal if this gets into the newspapers. I can just see the headline: *Department concerned with Environment uses disposable plastic cups.* Even you must realise that it's not a very environmentally friendly practice.'

Pansy blushed.

'Hmm,' said Professor Scott. 'He's right Pansy. I think we'd better use our ordinary mugs.'

The rush to empty cups of the terrible tea into the sink appeared to wind Pansy up even more. She turned away, and flounced towards the door, but was deprived of her dramatic exit by the appearance of two people in the doorway. It was Sue, from Admin, leading a young woman whose eyes were popping as she watched the drama. Pansy squeezed out behind them, giving Sue a poke in the arm with her bony elbow.

'Everybody, meet Melanie,' said Sue, rubbing her arm and pushing the mesmerised girl ahead of her. 'She started work in the office today. Melanie, this is Professor Scott, the Head of Department, Professor Potter who's a retired volcanologist, Dr Cardigan who's a geologist, Dr White who works on populations... '

Dr White walked over to shake Melanie's hand.

'Chris, call me Chris.'

Sue giggled. 'Sorry, I'm being much too formal. Okay this

is John, our lab tech, Anthony and Victoria are both academics, Maud and George from the Library, oh and this is Harold,' she said, pointing to a man who was turning away from the coffee machine.

Melanie stared open-mouthed at Harold's head. She was treated to a 360° view as he turned full circle to greet her. A long clump of silky, sleek and beautifully groomed orange hair came down to his left shoulder. The rest of his head had been shaved, and rising out of the dark stubble was the word HELL. The H began at the neck, followed by an E over the ear, appropriately, and Ls curving towards the front, ending a third of the way across his forehead.

'Harold is the drummer in a rock band,' said Sue, looking amused.

'And the computing expert when in the Department,' said Maud. 'I am the Librarian. The cross-looking woman who was storming out as you entered is Pansy Mallard, the Departmental Administrator - but you may have met her already.'

Melanie shook her head.

'You'll manage in time,' said Maud. 'It's always tough remembering names on your first day. Would you like a cup of coffee?'

Melanie nodded, continuing to look at Harold's head. When Maud handed her a cup of coffee, Melanie whispered to her. 'Why is he wearing his hair like that? I didn't think coloured hair would be allowed in a University department.'

'Cos it shows I'm different, babe,' said Harold.

'Oh,' said Melanie, blushing.

'Yeah, I'm not establishment like this 'ere dry lot. I make

sounds, babe,' and to prove his point, Harold began to rap on the windowsill.

Dennis snorted again. It was one of his favourite noises. 'Sounds! Huh! You always say you're different to the people who're the same, but really, you're the same.'

'Wot man?' Harold screwed up his forehead. When he did that one of the Ls turned into a V. Melanie tittered. Harold smiled at her, and then turned angrily to Dennis.

'Wot did you say?'

'You're the same as the people who're different from the people who're the same. That makes you the same, not different,' repeated Dennis, speaking slowly and emphasising each word.

Harold stopped rapping and tossed his orange locks. 'Man, I'm different. I...'

'Okay you two,' said Maud. 'You've had this argument before and you know it goes nowhere. Take no notice of them Melanie.'

Dennis frowned at Maud and turned his back on Harold, who went and sat beside Melanie. Arthur Scott came across from the coffee machine.

'Is everything ready for this afternoon, Maud?'

'Yes, Arthur. We've set glasses and plates of nibbles on a table at the end of the Library. John has hidden the wine in my office, so hopefully it won't go missing this year before we get a chance to drink it. I've left Alistair standing guard to make sure the students don't guzzle the food before the party starts.'

'Thanks for setting things up, Maud. Did you get superior nibbles? Edward's wife is probably used to good food.'

'I did,' replied Maud, pulling a face as she swallowed her drink. 'Did we have to get this machine, Arthur?'

'It was Pansy's idea. She's convinced it will save the department a fortune.'

'We still need to replace Alex in other ways. He didn't just make tea and coffee.'

'Alex! He's in Pansy bad books since his set of office keys went missing. He says he handed them back but she says they're not in her office. She's nagging me daily about Departmental security being compromised because there was a master key on the bunch. It will cost a fortune to change all the locks if we don't manage to find them.' Arthur sighed, shook his head and looked down at the floor. 'I suppose I'd better go and calm her down. She was planning to sell the dishwasher to raise funds and I'll need to talk her out of that, as we'll be using our own mugs again. Wish me luck.'

'Before you go, Arthur,' called Dennis, who had been hovering close by. 'Is it true that the Department has been granted funding for a new Chair?'

'Oh, er, yes,' said Arthur, suddenly looking ill at ease. He left the staff room quickly.

'Is the Department badly off?' asked Melanie.

'No more than anywhere else in the University,' replied Dennis, crossly.

'Is it a very special chair?'

'Not really, just an extra Chair for the Department.'

Maud noticed Melanie glancing at the chairs in the staffroom.

'It's not that sort of chair,' she said. Everyone roared with laughter.

'Sorry, Melanie,' said Maud. 'We couldn't help that. The Chair under discussion refers to the head, or professor of a division within the department. We've been granted enough money to pay the salary of a new Professor.'

'Oh,' said Melanie. 'And is the party for the new professor?'

'No, the party is to celebrate the marriage of a member of staff. One of our lecturers, Dr Edward Holroyd, got married during the vacation and he's bringing his wife along this afternoon to meet us. We've turned the beginning of term gathering into a welcoming party for them.'

Chapter 4 | *A taste of Cambridge*

Anni loved exploring. As a freelance journalist, she had travelled a great deal, but often alone. Sightseeing was a way to stay amused. She'd become quite good at it. So, hoping to get a glimpse of Cambridge, she left plenty of time for the walk from the flat to Downing Street, where Edward's department was located.

She had already stored up questions to put to him. Who owned the cattle that grazed on what the map she'd bought called *Sheep's Green*? Which was where she'd looked out on this morning. The sight of cows wandering freely and grazing in the middle of a city fascinated her. She'd never seen that before. Also, she thought there were two rivers running through Cambridge. If one was the Cam, what was the other? Getting her bearings was an important part of settling in.

Having walked across the Fen, and along Mill Lane, she came to a junction of fours roads. Anni consulted her map. Trumpington Street ran left to right, and Pembroke Street, which she needed to take, was directly opposite. 'Trumpington' struck her as a very English name. Anni said it to herself a couple of times, because although she spoke perfect English, she was more used to speaking French. She wondered about the origin of the word. More questions. She chuckled. Poor Edward. Little did he know of what was in store for him.

Anni looked around. The junction was crammed with

interesting buildings. The one on the opposite corner appeared to be Pembroke College. On the far side, beyond railings which were covered with notices, she saw an old church. To her left was a stunning building that looked a bit like a castle. Anni drank it all in. Brussels, where she lived before, has a wonderful centre, but Cambridge seemed to be bursting with architectural delights. It promised weeks and months of sightseeing. *Parfait!* She caught herself thinking in French. Never mind, she would soon get into the swing of thinking in English. Glancing at her map to check where she was going, Anni noticed a '*Trumpington Gate*'. She wanted to know more, but there was an appointment to keep. Nonetheless, as she crossed the road, Anni stopped briefly to look at cakes in the window of a bakery called Fitzbillies. Chelsea buns and fruitcakes filled the display. Her mouth watered.

Anni walked on down Pembroke Street and soon spied a tempting gap set into the buildings opposite Tennis Court Road. It seemed like the entrance to a cave and she couldn't resist walking through the gap. Inside was a collection of structures old and new. People were busily walking or cycling to and fro, and she was struck again by the contrast of pace between Cambridge and Brussels. On the other hand, she had spotted just one café along Pembroke Street, but it only had seating inside. It would have been nice to sit on the pavement over a coffee on such a sunny day, taking in the sights, and engaging in people watching.

As Anni was turning to leave the Tardis-like New Museums site, she spotted a huge skeleton, visible through a long glass window above what looked like a museum. It was set so high, she'd almost missed it. '*Mais qu'est-ce que c'est?*' she said, speaking again in her native tongue.

'It's a whale,' said a man, as he passed.

Anni laughed, amused that a random stranger had both understood French, and knew the answer to her question. There was so much to see. She checked her watch. Still a bit of time, so she left the site and walked to the top of Downing Street, lured by the entrance to what she discovered was Emmanuel College. Anni stepped cautiously into the college grounds, glancing timidly at the porters in case she was ordered out. They took little notice, seeming as relaxed and cheery as the fire she saw burning in their lodge. Once again, the buildings were tantalisingly interesting, tantalising because she realized there wasn't time to ask what they were, or to peep inside. What fun she would have, seeing more of Cambridge when Edward was less busy.

Checking her watch again, she headed back along Downing Street and crossed by a modern hotel, which seemed out of synch with its older neighbours. Anni didn't notice the cycle lane heading, unexpectedly, in the opposite direction to the traffic, until the sound of a bell being rung vigorously made her jump out of its path.

'Bloody pedestrians,' shouted the cyclist as he sped by.

Regaining her composure, Anni made it to the Sedgwick Museum without further incident. 'Consider yourself lucky,' she said to Edward, when he arrived at their meeting place.

'Hmm?' he asked, distractedly.

'You might have been a widower by now if an encounter with a speeding cyclist had turned out differently.'

Edward laughed and drew her arm through his. 'Darling, you must let me warn you against walking, cycling or driving near lecture theatres first thing in the morning, before lunch, after lunch and late in the afternoon.'

'That covers a lot of time.'

'Students cycling to and from lectures cover a lot of space! In fact, they often take over the entire road. I've seen them stop the traffic as they pedal desperately to make it to their lectures in time. And, believe me, the last place you want to be is in the middle of that mêlée. For students, manners, rules of the road and the rights of anyone other than themselves fade into oblivion in the face of what appears to be the urge to learn. Of course, it's worse in the Michaelmas term - I mean the first term of the new academic year.'

'Michaelmas? What's that?'

Edward laughed. 'Oh, you'll get used to the Cambridge jargon, not to mention the cyclists. And now, as punishment for having married a crusty old academic, you have to run the gauntlet of his entire department as they gather to, ahem, welcome you.' Edward smiled. 'Well, some of them will be welcoming, but I suspect many others are simply waiting for an opportunity to size you up. I hope you've worn your thickest skin, darling.

He raised her hand to his lips. Anni noticed it was shaking slightly and she felt that his efforts to be light-hearted were hiding nervousness. Were his colleagues so fierce as to worry him? Surely not. But his nervousness communicated itself to her, and she found herself pulling her jacket into place, and wondering if the soft breeze had made her hair look messy.

'First port of call is the Head of Department's office for a glass of sherry,' said Edward, leading her through the crowded Downing site.

Chapter 5 | *Meeting the colleagues*

The Head of Department, Professor Arthur Scott, was smiling broadly beneath his thick untidy white hair as Edward introduced Anni. He had been wondering what the woman who had tempted his bachelor colleague into marriage would look like. She was lovely. At six feet, Edward was tall, but the top of Anni's head came to his chin, so she was tall for a woman. She was also slim and shapely. When he'd discovered that Edward had married a Belgian, he worried that she might not have a sense of humour, but the sparkle in Anni's eyes reassured him. Her face was framed by hair that was neither curly nor straight. Arthur stored up all these details because he knew he would be in trouble with his wife later, when she pressed him for specifics. Yes, Edward's new wife was lovely.

Arthur poured a very large sherry and offered Anni the most comfortable chair in his crowded office. He and Edward sat on two straight-backed chairs by a table piled high with files and papers. 'My dear,' he said, 'I'm relying on you completely for a few sentences with which to introduce you to the department. We've all been astonished by Edward's news, and no one has managed to discover much about you.'

Arthur noticed the way Anni cast a puzzled glance at Edward, who squirmed a bit in his chair, and avoided her gaze.

'The way Edward pronounces your name, for example, in two syllables, Ah-nee, makes it sound foreign, but you speak perfect English.'

Anni smiled. 'It's simply Annie in a French-sounding way,' she said. 'My father was Belgian and my mother English. My sister and I went to the English School in Brussels, and we spent many holidays in England, with our grandmother. She worked hard to perfect our English.'

'My dear, I'm very glad to hear that. Being familiar with the country means you're already aware of the difference in cuisine and refreshment,' Arthur chuckled. 'I did, however, pull the better wine out of the basement in your honour. We're a pack of Philistines here, and happily knock back plonk as and when it's offered.'

Anni's grimace as she swallowed a mouthful of the sherry worried him. He slid open the bottom drawer of his desk, and glanced at the label on the bottle. Harvey's Bristol Cream. It tasted fine to him. Perhaps she had toothache.

'I need to update my ideas about Cambridge,' said Anni, looking around at the rows of books which covered most of the wall space in Arthur's office. 'I imagined you sitting in ancient halls, drinking superior wines and ports.'

'Ah,' said Arthur, sighing, 'those days are gone. There are far too many people in Cambridge now and if the colleges offered their good stock to everyone, the cellars would soon be empty.' He glanced at his watch and rose, smiling mischievously. 'Time to join the others.'

Arthur led the way along deserted corridors, apologising for the strong smell of paint. 'The redecoration should have been finished before term started but Alistair went off on holiday.' He shook his hairy head. He did not approve of Alistair taking a holiday at this time of year. 'The students are having an awful problem finding their tutors and supervisors.

It's absolute mayhem. We did try taping sheets of paper to the carpet in front of each door with the name of the occupant, but some practical joker switched them around, causing even more chaos, so we had to remove them.'

He didn't notice Anni bite her lip to prevent herself laughing, or the way she and Edward glanced at each other and squeezed hands sympathetically.

Anni looked around as Arthur led them down a wide staircase and into the Library. Instead of a big grim place, it was small and cosy. More like a private library than that of a teaching department, she thought. The room was packed with people. Somebody spotted them enter, and the buzz of chatter faded to a whisper, which slowly rippled to the back of the room. She and Edward followed Arthur along the central aisle to the top of the room, where he turned to address the assembly.

'It is my pleasure, on behalf of the Department, to welcome Edward's wife, Anni, to Cambridge. Mrs Holroyd,' he turned to her, 'you must forgive us for making such a fuss of the event, but Edward has taken us completely by surprise. When he went off on vacation at the beginning of July, we had no idea that he would return in the autumn with a wife. Edward has always been a confirmed bachelor. We're astonished that he's brought such a lovely bride into our midst.'

Anni blushed. Inwardly, she was taken aback. Why had Edward kept her a secret?

Arthur was still talking. 'I guess this will be the end of his company on field trips for a while. Well, he was generally useless anyway. Whenever it was his turn to take the undergrads, we found he'd disappeared into a nearby forest, up the side of a mountain, or somewhere equally unreachable, claiming he was reconnoitering for project work.'

Anni listened and laughed politely as Arthur told stories of Edward's academic life. Sometimes she recognised him, and sometimes it seemed as though Arthur was describing a stranger. The anecdotes all featured him as a single man. She thought she detected a hint that he was a loner. Finally, Arthur raised a toast to her and Edward, and ushered them into the arms of those who rushed forwards to introduce themselves.

Who they were, what they did, where they worked, it all passed in a blur of quick introductions and attendant confusion. Some asked where she and Edward had met. What field was she involved in? They were surprised to find she wasn't an academic and Anni was amused to think that for some of them, a life outside academia hardly existed. How had Edward met her if she wasn't an academic? Most were surprised to hear that they'd met in Belgium. Edward hadn't mentioned being in Belgium! Most of the people she spoke to were amazed to discover she and Edward had been involved for three years. Then someone in the group remembered that Edward often attended EU funding and research meetings in Brussels.

Anni found it hard work at times, satisfying people's curiosity while trying to maintain her own and Edward's privacy. She was continually reminded that he'd told his colleagues nothing about her. She wondered, loyally, if he had a particular reason for keeping quiet and decided to be economical with replies until she had a chance to talk to him in private. She'd lost sight of Edward eons ago. He seemed to have been spirited away, leaving her to parry the interminable questions alone.

Among the curious faces, she became aware of a quiet, friendly one. This woman didn't push forward to grill her. She seemed content simply to smile sympathetically. Anni had an impression of something familiar in her face, something that reminded her of Edward's brother, Richard. She wanted to stop and speak to the woman, but Arthur insisted on introducing her to more people, and she found herself whisked out of one group only to be deposited into the centre of another. Here, mercifully, the direction of the talk became less personal and more academic. Here, at last, Edward joined her. Anni blushed to see the grins Edward's colleagues turned on him. She suspected some of them would have winked at him or nudged his arm, if she hadn't been standing nearby. Honestly. Edward appeared embarrassed but he nevertheless managed slowly to turn the conversation to academic matters. People came and went, and as the room became noisier, it was difficult to focus on much beyond brief outlines of individuals' research interests. Anni became separated again from Edward. Arthur was called away and she found herself on the edge of the group, giving a potted biography to yet another person, a tall, grey-haired, large-nosed and very loud man.

'Environmental journalism!' said he, repeating what Anni had told him, and looking aghast and disbelieving all at once. Anni opened her eyes wide at the ill-mannered response. The man didn't notice. He sucked in his nostrils as he looked down at her and Anni noticed the hairs of his nose quivering. She smothered a laugh.

'Absolute rubbish,' he said. 'Lay people know nothing of environmentalism. Only an academic can produce any sort of informed discourse on the subject.'

Anni raised her eyebrows, but the movement went undetected by her companion. Neither did he notice the group around them turning to look compassionately at Anni. Her critic poured a bit more wine down his throat.

'I was the first in the field, you know, he boomed. 'I pushed the concept when it was double Dutch to everyone else. I am the Father of Environmentalism. Oh yes, I...'

'Excuse me, Professor Booker, I must take Mrs Holroyd to meet a latecomer.' Anni had noticed the woman with the friendly, Richard-like face pushing her way through the group. She heaved a silent sigh of relief and allowed herself to be drawn to the far side of the room.

'I couldn't bear to see you being lectured at by that old phony,' said the woman. 'He's as full of himself as it's possible to be. Most of what he says is made up. Once he retired, he spent his time developing a fictionally rich and interesting academic career and now he comes along to every function, concentrates on the new faces, and bores them to tears.'

Anni laughed. 'I'm very grateful to you for rescuing me. He did seem keen to lay down the law. she paused. 'I don't think I've met you yet, but please forgive me if we have been introduced. I've met so many people this evening that my head is buzzing and I doubt if I will remember half of the names, not to mention which belongs to which face.'

'I'm Maud! Maud Cadogan!' She said it in such a way that Anni felt she ought to know who she was. But she didn't have a clue. Extracting information about his life in Cambridge from Edward had always been a bit like pulling teeth, and Annie had long since given up the struggle. She mentally added asking who Maud Cadogan was to her ever-growing list of questions for Edward.

'I have every sympathy with you,' said Maud, and she didn't seem to mind Anni's ignorance. 'These gatherings are always an ordeal for the person at the receiving end and I imagine it has been even worse for you, for all that you are familiar with the general trend of the department's research, albeit from a lay point of view of course!'

They both laughed at the reminder of Professor Booker's criticism.

'Oh dear,' said Maud, and Anni saw her looking at a young man who was heading in their direction, 'that's Dr Black. Let's avoid him. Quickly, this way.'

Caught up in the spirit of the moment, Anni was happy to oblige. She'd had her fill of small talk for one evening. Off they ran, like a pair of schoolgirls, giggling as they went.

'This is my office,' Maud said, ushering Anni into a room. She turned on a desk lamp, which shone softly, adding to the cosy feel. The large desk was tidy, but boxes and stacks of books lay in piles on the floor surrounding it. 'I'm the Librarian, but you probably knew that already. If Dr Black pursues us, I shall shove him out and lock the door. I know it's unprofessional, but I simply can't stand him. I don't normally run away from people.'

Anni was highly amused. Oh good, office politics. There's nothing like a bit of intrigue, she thought, wondering what Dr Black had done to annoy her new friend.

Maud led the way to the far side of her office, weaving a path through the piles on the floor. They sat on the broad window seats. Anni was charmed.

'What has Dr Black done to you?'

'He's plaguing me with a huge book list, and the fact that this is a social event won't stop him. He's insisting that I spend half my annual budget buying him a number of obscure titles, which, he keeps telling me, are essential to his research and which he can't get from the University Library. That has to be a lie, because it's a copyright library. I, in turn, keep insisting that I have other people's needs to satisfy, and that he can't have all of my resources. It's like a game of financial ping-pong. I'm not getting through to him. Pestilent man!'

Anni smiled. She was enjoying the picture Maud was painting of an academic world she hadn't imagined. But she ought to have realised that academics were human, with the same concerns as the rest of the world. Somehow, she'd built up a picture of Cambridge where all people did was research and teach. Silly really. The more she found she was wrong, the more she began to enjoy it.

'Now,' said her companion, 'I'm sure you're tired of talking, and even more of listening. Edward shouldn't have put you through it, though I doubt he could have managed to put the party off. You must realise that you've been the main topic of conversation all week. No one ever dreamed that Edward would get married and now we find that he's been conducting a successful relationship behind our backs. Disgraceful! We should have been given all the details, you know and since *he* hasn't told us, and doubtless won't, we have no choice but to try and extract them from *you*!'

Anni laughed again, enjoying Maud's light-hearted humour and easy manner, but she felt a prickle of unease beneath the laugh.

'Don't be concerned,' said Maud. 'I won't subject you to anything difficult. Instead, may I suggest that we meet for lunch sometime soon? I believe you've never been to Cambridge before and I would be happy to give a bit of background to the city, not to mention the department.'

'Oh, thank you, Maud. I'd love that. Edward has only given me a very quick tour of the city – actually it was a ten-minute lecture from the tower of Great St Mary's.'

'Good heavens, did he drag you up all those steps?'

'He did. The view was amazing, but I would appreciate seeing the city at ground level.'

Maud laughed. She really was cheerful, and she made Anni feel good. 'I'll phone you,' Maud said, 'and we'll arrange a time to meet. Okay?'

'Please do.'

Anni caught sight of Edward in the office doorway. She hadn't heard the door opening.

'There you are,' said Maud, and her tone sounded accusing. 'What have you to say for yourself?'

Edward looked embarrassed. A bit, thought Anni, like a naughty schoolboy who'd been found out. He stayed in the doorway.

Maud shook her head at him. 'Never mind,' she said, 'we can catch up later. Will you be in the Department tomorrow?'

'Yes, though not until late afternoon. I'm supervising at college. I'll give you a ring when I'm through.'

Maud and Anni left the window seat and joined Edward. He turned and put his arm around Anni, giving her a squeeze. 'Do you mind if I whisk Anni off to dinner, Maud? She has certainly earned a break.'

'No one could argue with that.'

They left the department, and Edward took Anni through a side entrance out of the Downing site and into Pembroke College grounds. A cat strolled out in front of them as they passed the Dean's Garden. Anni stopped to stroke the friendly Burmese, who purred and rubbed against her legs. She looked up at Edward.

'Why didn't you tell them about me?'

Edward stood with hunched shoulders, making no effort to stroke the cat.

'I'm sorry,' he said, hesitantly. 'I realised I should have done so as soon as Arthur began turning you into a mystery woman. But, Anni, you know I'm a reserved sort of chap.'

Well yes, she thought, but not that reserved. There must be something else going on here. She stood up and they walked on through the gardens. Anni stayed silent, and eventually Edward spoke again.

'I kept quiet about you in the beginning. I was concerned that the relationship might not last. It's just, well it became more and more difficult to raise the subject as time went on. I knew they would question me mercilessly and I couldn't face it. I put my head in the sand.' He stopped and put his arm around her.

'I hope they haven't given you a hard time?'

'No,' said Anni. 'They were mostly charming, with the odd exception.' She told him of the encounter with Professor Booker. Edward laughed, saying Booker wasn't the only oddball in the Department. His laugh sounded nervous. It didn't dissipate the tension between them, but it lightened it. Anni looked reflectively at her new husband. There was a lot she didn't yet know about him.

Chapter 6 | *Catching up with Céc*

'None of them knew anything about me, Céc.'

Anni heard her sister's intake of breath. 'He didn't tell anyone he was getting married?'

'Apparently not. He gave me a vague explanation, but it sounded lame. It's not that I disbelieve him; I know he's a private person, but he must talk to someone, surely. I met a woman called Maud who seemed to know him quite well. At least well enough to tease him.'

'I don't know what to say, Anni, except that you need to give it time.'

'I know, I know.' Anni fiddled with a button on the dress she was wearing.

'And don't go getting suspicious,' said her sister. 'He's your husband now. Believe in him.'

Cécile always stood up for Edward. She was a very fair person. Anni really needed to be more like her. She knew she was jumping to silent conclusions, even about friendly Maud. 'I'll do my best,' she sighed. 'But there is so much that he didn't tell me! For example, I didn't know he had a cleaner. We came back last night and I found bits and pieces moved around, and no sign of the phone. It was a bit freaky. *'Oh,'* he said, *'that will be Eileen.'* I wondered who on earth he meant, especially after what had happened at the party. *'Who?'* I asked. *'She's my cleaner,'* he said. Imagine not telling me about that, Cécile? For goodness sake, I live here now!'

'Ah, um, yeah. I think he should have mentioned that. I'm jealous now. Think of all the more artwork I could produce if I had a cleaner.'

'But he should have said!'

'I know, but how much did you ask him before you got to Cambridge?'

'I didn't think to ask about things like that, and you know there wasn't time. I don't want a cleaner. I can keep the place in good shape myself. Far better than Eileen, in fact. The bathroom bin was sitting on the toilet seat!'

'Sounds like she moved it to wash the floor,' said Cécile, laughing.

'So why not put it back down afterwards.'

'She was waiting for the floor to dry? I don't know. Listen, Anni, have you spoken to Edward about letting this Eileen go?'

'I mentioned it last night. He won't hear of it. She's sixty-something and he says he's very fond of her.'

'There are people who would love to have a cleaner, but I think I understand what's upsetting you. Someone you don't know is coming into your home and it limits your privacy. You've lived alone for too long, *chérie*. Make the best of it.'

'Okay, okay! I'll give you a ring in a couple of days, Céc. *Au revoir*.'

'*Au revoir, chérie.*'

Anni replaced the phone, and walked around the flat. Her sister was right, but Anni wondered how Cécile would feel in her shoes. She was certain some of her suitcases had been opened and the contents examined. But when she'd mentioned that to Edward, he'd said Eileen probably had to move them to hoover. Well maybe, but she shouldn't have opened them and looked. That was nosey.

The phone rang.

'Anni? It's Maud. Are you free for lunch today?'

'Why yes,' answered Anni, pleased that Maud had remembered her. Getting out of the flat was just what she needed.

'Could you make it to the Department by 12.30?'

'Yes, I can. Thank you, Maud.'

'Good. I'll meet you on the steps of the building.'

Chapter 7 | *The gossip*

Maud had been prompted to phone Anni after overhearing a conversation in the staffroom earlier that morning. Some of the Admin staff were sitting in a huddle at coffee time. They were talking, unsurprisingly, about Edward and Anni.

'What age do you think she is?' asked Becky, who worked in the office with Sue and the new girl, Melanie.

'Mid-thirties, at least.'

'Really? But she wears her hair long!'

Maud noticed Sue smirking. Sue was thirty-something with shoulder-length hair. Maud caught her eye and shook her head.

'If I was in my thirties,' said Becky, 'I would keep my hair short, especially if it was just plain dark brown. That's so boring! Long hair doesn't suit older people.' Becky tossed her long, blond, bottle-fed locks.

'And how old do you think Edward is?' asked Melanie.

'Let's ask Maud, she'll know.'

Maud decided she didn't want to be drawn into that conversation, and so she made a sharp dive past the group and headed for the vending machine. She pushed a few buttons and ended up with a half-full cup of coffee. Turning back to the room, Maud noticed that Dennis Cardigan was dominating the second huddle.

'Well I think it's pretty certain that Arthur has got the V&A lined up for the position,' he was saying.

'The who?' asked Melanie, overhearing.

'V&A,' said Potty in a chirpy voice. 'Code for Victoria Angelo-Montgomery. Dennis believes that Arthur intends to support her application for the new professorship.'

'Oh,' said Melanie, puzzled.

Dennis was clearly irritated by the distraction. He pursed his lips and hunched his shoulders. 'Now look chaps, are we all agreed? We simply can't have this. The woman has hardly been in the Department for five minutes. There are plenty more suitable candidates for professor.'

'Such as yourself, Dennis?' asked Maud, sitting down beside Potty.

'And why not?' Dennis glared at her. 'Right, let's agree that we'll go in a body to the Head of Department and protest about...'

'Shush,' said someone.

Maud looked up as the woman under discussion walked into the staffroom, carrying her mug and a fruit tea bag. Victoria Angelo-Montgomery seemed specially designed to annoy Dennis Cardigan. She was energetic and enthusiastic, where he was laid back and lazy. She was an American who'd researched her PhD at the University of California. Dennis had studied in Cambridge. Victoria had worked her way across the US, ending at Columbia University in New York, before taking a post in the Department. Dennis had been awarded a post-doc in Cambridge when he finished his PhD, and three years later, accepted a post in the Department. The most time he'd spent away from Cambridge was a three-month sabbatical in Southampton, and even then, he'd been obliged to return to Cambridge every weekend because his mother insisted he should still do his jobs around the house. Victoria had variety in her background that he would never achieve, and it irritated him.

Victoria pressed the 'hot water only' button and was rewarded with a half mug-full of water. Aggravated, she thumped the button again. This time the water flowed over the top of her mug. She growled. 'Isn't anyone gonna do anything about this goddamned machine?'

'I think we should. I, I, I really do think we should take that in hand, Victoria,' said Dennis.

'What's the matter with you, Dennis? Your face is red.'

'Oh, just had a slug of extremely hot coffee,' said Dennis, tittering.

'Well it can't have come from this machine. The hot water isn't even at body temperature.' Victoria looked across at Chris White, who was blushing.

'Two red faces, huh! Are you helping Dennis stab me in the back, Chris?'

Victoria marched off, dripping fruit tea as she went. Once she was out of earshot, Chris turned to Dennis.

'I'm not going to be any part of this!' he said. 'Surely Arthur will only promote the best man, er, or woman.'

Maud was surprised to hear him speak so emphatically. Chris was normally so timid.

'Don't be such an innocent booby, Chris,' replied Dennis. 'Academic records go out the window in these situations and politics rush in. He'll give the chair to her just because she's a woman. I know it.' Dennis drew his thin lips into a sharp line and nodded his head for emphasis.

'Her academic record is quite brilliant, Dennis,' said

Maud. 'I think you should give her a break. And anyway, if you continue to annoy her like this, she may take revenge if and when she is appointed!' Maud enjoyed the horrified look that appeared on Dennis's face.

'I agree with Maud,' said Anthony Macmillan.

'Huh, what would she know,' said Dennis, and he got up and left the room.

'He doesn't care much for you, Maud, does he?' said Anthony.

'I don't think Dennis likes any woman.'

'He loves his mother,' put in Potty. 'Love and loyalty can be the only reason for wearing the dreadful cardigans she knits for him.'

'Well if he keeps behaving this way,' said Maud, 'she'll be the only one left who loves him!'

The group laughed.

Chapter 8 | *Maud*

Anni sat opposite Maud in the Arts Theatre restaurant. Having been entertained by a series of lights embedded into the stairwell walls that crackled and flickered as they passed, she found the large bright and airy room architecturally disappointing. It had more the air of a canteen than a restaurant. It was clearly popular however, as it filled quickly and the room soon resonated with the chattering of diners.

When they'd given their orders, Maud tidied her bag away in a business-like manner, sat up straight and smiled at Anni.

'Do you mind if I ask how you and Edward met?'

Anni smiled, remembering Maud's comment at the party about relying on her for information. She had expected the question, and because she had warmed to her companion, she was willing to talk.

'We met in Bouillon in the south of Belgium. My sister has a house there. Do you know it?'

Maud shook her head.

'It's a very old town in the Ardennes, just by the border with France. Cécile paints and travels a lot. That summer, three years ago...'

'Three years ago!'

Maud's eyebrows shot up. It seemed quite a strong reaction, and Anni felt something was amiss, but she couldn't quite grasp what. If Maud was just a colleague, why had she reacted that way to hearing that Edward and Anni had been seeing each other for such a long time? Oh dear, she thought, was she a former girlfriend? That would account for Edward's embarrassment yesterday evening. Now Anni felt nervous about what to tell Maud. Was she fishing for information? Would Edward object? Having begun, however, it was hard to pull back. Besides, if she gave a bit, she might get more back.

'Cécile had come back to Bouillon for August,' she said, 'and I spent the holiday month with her as usual. I met Edward in the little museum there. He was trying to read a history of the region from a poster and I watched him search diligently through a dictionary for almost every word. I took pity on him and translated. It's not a very big exhibition and I suggested we walk around it together. Afterwards, he bought me a coffee. We chatted about the town and the region. We talked mainly about the Crusades and local history. Unfortunately, he had to dash off - he was meeting his brother in Paris, he said - and I thought it just my bad luck to bump into an interesting man who lived in a different country. I never thought I would see him again.' Anni was relieved to notice that Maud was smiling, and not looking at all jealous.

'Typical Edward,' she said, 'not to think of asking for an address or phone number.'

Anni relaxed a bit. That was an accurate description of Edward. Maud obviously knew him well. Encouraged, she continued to tell the tale.

'But we did meet again, in the autumn, at a conference on climate change in Dublin. I went along at the last minute - one of the magazines I write articles for asked if I would stand in for another journalist who was ill. Climate change wasn't really my area of environmentalism, but of course I knew a bit about it, and I was prepared to go at short notice. Oh the joys of being freelance! I had just a couple of days to read up on atmospheric chemistry, the hole in the ozone layer, aerosols, and the Montreal Protocol, before flying to Dublin. I remember that I was standing in the lobby checking who would be presenting papers in the morning session when I noticed that one of the speakers was Edward Holroyd. As I wondered if it could be the same person, I heard my name called. I turned around, and there was Edward!'

'Ah,' said Maud, opening her eyes wide, 'the coincidences of life.'

'Yes, isn't it extraordinary? He was surprised to see me, as although I told him I was a journalist, I hadn't mentioned my specialism. Anyway, we saw quite a bit of each other from then on, in between work commitments. Edward was very helpful at the conference. He proof-read my work and I wrote quite a decent article. I was asked to cover the Kyoto conference the following October on the strength of it. Edward was there too. In terms of getting to know each other however, that summer in Dublin stands out. We sat for hours high above Killiney Bay, talking and gazing down at the sea. That was the spark for the relationship. Going to Kyoto cemented it. Edward began coming to Brussels frequently for EU research and policy meetings, and we spent more and more time together.'

'I hadn't picked up on him going so often to Brussels,' said Maud. 'I should have been suspicious!'

She waved a finger about and Anni had a qualm as the waiter served their dishes, though the gesture seemed more like the sort of thing Cécile would do, than censure from an ex-lover.

'What made you decide to marry?' asked Maud as she speared a pile of salad.

'You're very direct,' said Anni, taken aback.

'Sorry. Do you mind?'

'Yes and no, but I guess I may as well tell you some of the things Edward has apparently kept from everybody. I'm no mystery woman. I don't understand why he never told the people in the Department about me.'

Maud laid down her cutlery and leaned across the table. She laid her hand on Anni's. 'He can't help it, you know. He's just very reserved. I've known that for a long time, Anni, but clearly, he's even more private about his personal life than I realised. Don't be upset with him.'

Anni felt close to tears. 'I am exasperated with him, though. I don't understand why he kept me such a secret.'

'Don't tease yourself about it. Get your own back by telling me everything.'

Maud's grin was infectious.

'Okay,' said Anni, cheering up and laughing. What was it about Maud that made her feel like a co-conspirator? She launched into the rest of her tale. 'Well the decision to marry was very spur of the moment, though I must say the long separations were beginning to be a strain. Edward never invited me to Cambridge. I'd suggested coming over several times during the first few months of our relationship, but he always insisted that he was much happier coming to Brussels, or, that Cambridge was dreadful in the summer because it was so full of tourists or, dreadful during the rest of the year because it was so full of students. He gave it such bad press at times!'

'Well,' said Maud, 'there is a certain amount of truth in what he said. It's hard to move here in the summer because of the number of tourists and foreign students - I mean those who come to learn English. These last few years the numbers have grown and grown and, as you doubtless know, Edward can be quite anti-social at times.'

'That does sound like Edward, but I was sure Cambridge couldn't be so bad, Maud, because, after all, he continued to live here. Eventually, I began to wonder if he was married.'

Maud looked up and chuckled. 'Did you?'

'Well I did wonder if perhaps he was leading a double life: wife in Cambridge, mistress in Belgium. When I challenged him, he laughed. Then he became serious and asked how I thought he would manage to disappear for months on end if he was married, or phone me and receive phone calls from me if he had a wife in the flat.'

'Good points,' said Maud.

'Oh, he spent a lot of time telling me how much he loved me and only me. I could no longer doubt him. So, I carried on. I felt too involved at that stage, I simply couldn't give him up.'

They ate in silence for a bit. Maud cleared her plate. Anni glanced at her from time to time, and noticed a frown. Urm, she thought, am I going to hear something I won't like? Finally, Maud laid the cutlery neatly on her plate and spoke.

'We had begun to wonder where Edward was going to during term breaks. He was adept at dashing off before we could prise information out of him. His absence became even more noticeable during the past year. He dashed off for several weekends during Michaelmas and he was away for Christmas. He went missing again during Lent term, and I noticed him winding up his teaching as quickly as he could last May, before vanishing in June as soon as exams were over. He was gone for the whole summer. His father phoned me to ask where he was.'

'You know Edward's father?' Anni hadn't expected that!

'Of course I know Robert,' said Maud. She gave Anni a puzzled look. 'You know that Edward and I are cousins, don't you?'

Anni dropped her own cutlery with a clang and stared at Maud. 'Cousins!' Then she remembered the likeness to Richard. 'Cousins!' she said again.

'Second cousins, really, we've known each other all our lives.'

'Maud, he never told me. I know almost nothing about his family or friends.'

'Oh, Edward is exasperating,' said Maud, looking fierce. She asked if Anni knew that his mother was dead. Anni said he'd told her that much. 'I really think he's turned more and more in on himself since his mother's death. I have noticed him withdrawing from social functions over the years, though lately he has begun to improve. Your softening influence, I guess,' she smiled. 'But it really is ridiculous that he didn't tell you we're cousins. For goodness sake, you're married to him!'

'Oh,' sighed Anni, 'his lack of openness about so many things, but especially about family, does bother me at times.' She looked down at her plate and pushed a cherry tomato from one side to the other. A happy thought cheered her up.

'Never mind. You can give me lots of the missing background, Maud. How wonderful to have someone to ask. I'm delighted to find you're a cousin. I have spoken a little to Richard, and he's a lot of fun, but men are never quite so good at spilling the beans as women, are they?'

'No,' said Maud, giggling again in that way Anni warmed to.

'So, you've met Richard.'

'Yes, he and Cécile were witnesses at our wedding. I like Richard. He seems very easy-going and amusing.'

'Yes, he is. Edward takes more after his father. They do have a sense of humour, but sometimes you have to dig deep to find it.'

'Well, I thought Richard and Edward's father behaved very well considering Edward sprung the marriage on them. In fact, I did wonder how much he'd told them about us. Robert seemed uneasy at times, but I guess it may have been anxiety that we were rushing into marriage.'

'You thought Robert was uneasy?'

'I got that impression, but you see everything happened in the space of a fortnight and even I hadn't expected such a turn of events. Edward had been getting more and more restless as the time for him to return to England drew near. He disappeared for hours one day and when he came back, he asked me to marry him. I was shocked and surprised, but I agreed. There was barely time to organise a licence, for me to close up my flat, to gather our family and friends and get married before rushing to Paris for a brief honeymoon, and back here in time for the beginning of term.'

'Ah,' said Maud, 'that explains why I didn't hear! I was on holiday myself and found a message from Robert on my answerphone when I returned. He said there was news but would leave it to Edward to tell me, as he was going over to Ireland to stay with Richard. So, in a way, I wasn't surprised to hear the announcement. I'm stunned to discover you've been together for three years, though. Wait until I get hold of Edward. He's wicked to have kept you secret from me.'

Anni felt embarrassed and hurt, and even angry. She would have to confront Edward. Still, for now she must be loyal to him. She changed the subject.

'Have you always lived in Cambridge, Maud?'

'No, I was born in Ireland, in Wicklow. My grandfather and Edward's maternal grandmother were sister and brother. He and his family often came to spend summer holidays with us. Richard, as you may know, moved to Dublin quite early on, and because I lived in Dublin then, I saw a fair bit of him. Edward and I fell out of touch somewhat, apart from rare meetings at Richard's house and the very odd trip to London on my part.'

Maud chatted on, giving Anni a chance to finish her lunch.

'I contacted him when I decided to move to England after my mother's death. That was almost twenty years ago. I lived in London for many years, and moved up to Cambridge about eight years ago. Indeed, it was Edward who told me about the librarianship in the Department. I've spent Christmas with his family ever since I've been in England.' Maud stopped talking and shook her head. 'I still can t believe that he hasn't mentioned me to you, especially as you were coming to Cambridge! Whatever must you think?'

Anni felt a stab of guilt. She'd been running Edward

down. It was time to show a bit more loyalty to her husband. 'Perhaps it was because he and I didn't live together all the time. It really did feel like a holiday when he was in Brussels, and I guess we didn't spend much time talking about families and day-to-day things.' But Anni's explanation sounded lame, even to her.

'Anni, you will not excuse him,' said Maud, and a stubborn fierce look crossed her face. 'Does he know about your family?'

'My parents and grandparents are dead, but yes, he does. Oh, I don't know, sometimes I get the impression that he's afraid of something, but oh I guess I 'm just being fanciful.'

Maud fell silent. Anni watched the departure of diners at the next table. Maud glanced at her watch.

'I should get back. Will you come with me? I have several old photographs in my office and Edward looks pretty dreadful in them. Would you like to have a look? You may yet regret marrying him when you see what your children might look like!'

They left the restaurant laughing, with Maud painting pictures of lanky boys with big ears.

Chapter 9 | *A burglary*

Muffled sounds of shouting greeted the women as they entered the Department. Maud paused on the stairs. 'It's that dreadful Dr Black,' she whispered, 'I'd know his voice anywhere. But what's he shouting about? And he's in Arthur's office. I wonder what's going on?'

The Head of Department's office was a couple of doors along from the staffroom. Maud noticed Harold's unmistakable head poking out of the door. She drew Anni into the room. A group had gathered, and they were listening to the rumpus from Arthur's room.

'What is Dr Black so steamed up about?' asked Maud.

Anthony Macmillan was about to answer but Melanie beat him to it.

'You have to ask Harold. He knows *all* about it.' She turned a beaming look on Harold, who beamed back.

Maud saw the angry look Anthony shot at Melanie, but the girl didn't notice. Then Maud noticed Anni staring at Harold. She smiled. He really was a splendid vision, and it looked like Anni was as struck with his hair as Melanie had been on her first encounter. She wondered how Anni had managed to miss seeing him at the party. He was the centre of attention now, as he walked into the middle of the group.

'Dr Black's office was burgled,' he said.

'Burgled!' Maud was astonished. 'Good heavens.'

'Yeah, and like the way he's going on about it, you'd think he had state secrets in there.'

'Yes,' broke in Melanie, 'and poor Becky was attacked by the burglar and she's not causing a commotion.'

Maud looked over at Becky, who was sitting quietly, sipping a cup of tea. She looked pale.

'The burglar pushed Becky against the wall when he was running away,' explained Harold. 'And, like man, we'd hardly picked her up when Dr Black was shoving his way into Arthur's office to complain about security. Then, of course, Pansy was called in and that's when the shouting started.'

'Pansy's in there?' said Maud. 'No wonder there's a lot of shouting. What did the burglar take?'

She noticed that Anthony was frowning and shaking his head at Melanie, who'd opened her mouth to speak. Anthony was very 'old school' and Maud knew he'd soon be complaining about people who took outrageous liberties when they'd only been in the place a few minutes. Melanie took the hint and backed out of sight behind Harold.

'As you know,' announced Anthony, 'his office is next to mine, and we returned from lunch at the same time. Why would a burglar target *his* office? And why would Dr Black make such an incredible fuss? Something stinks if you ask me.'

'Hmm,' said Maud, 'it is strange.'

Remembering Anni, Maud turned back to her. Anni was watching several people re-arrange pot plants into a cluster. Maud followed her gaze. The group stood back to admire their handiwork. The plants looked well, assembled in a semi-circle in the far corner of the room, but why move them at all?

Potty edged around the cluster. 'Can you see me?' he called.

'No,' came the chorus of replies.

He re-emerged, grinning and rubbing his hands together. 'Jolly good. Now, I'll bring in a kettle tomorrow and we can organise tea, coffee and biscuits from the Coastal Defence Slush Fund. Who's going to buy the milk?'

'I'll buy it on my way to work,' volunteered Sue.

The sound of a door closing hushed everyone. Pansy appeared. She had red spots on her cheeks and was holding her head very stiffly.

'I'm off to talk to University Security,' she said, looking around the faces by the door. 'You're here, Harold. Good. I don't have to search for you. Go and check if Dr Black's computer has been tampered with.'

'Wot?' said Harold. 'He never lets me near his machine. He'll go spare if I touch it.'

'Arthur says you're to look at it,' replied Pansy, firmly.

Harold opened his mouth as though to protest.

'Arthur says,' growled Pansy, 'and since it's a departmental machine, Dr Black will just have to do as he is told and let you check it!' She heaved a huge sigh. 'The trouble that man has caused.' She left the room, still sighing.

There was silence as she descended the stairs heavily. As the sound of her footsteps faded, the plant-movers giggled. Pansy hadn't even cast a glance in their direction.

'Alternative tea and coffee arrangements are now in

place,' said Potty. 'But we must be careful not to draw Pansy's attention to us.'

Maud laughed. 'You won't fool her for long, you know.'

'Probably not, but we'll do our best.'

Still chuckling, Maud shepherded Anni back downstairs and over to the Library. She chatted to Anni about Pansy and the coffee machine as she led them to her office. As she went to insert the key into the lock, the door opened inwards. 'How odd. I always lock the door when I leave.'

Maud pushed the door open and walked into the room. She stopped abruptly, and Anni, who was following closely behind, bumped into her.

'Oh my God! What is it? Look at the blood! It's everywhere.'

Startled, Anni looked over Maud's shoulder.

'Do you see it?' she asked.

Lying on the desk was what looked like a heart from which blood was seeping. Maud stood still just inside the door, clearly too shocked to move. Anni went over to the desk for a closer look. 'I think it's a cow's heart,' she said.

The colour had drained from Maud's face. 'But what is it doing on my desk?' she asked. 'Who could have put it there?'

Chapter 10 | *An Inspector calls*

Arthur Scott had been resisting Pansy's demands to call in the police after the burglary, but he capitulated when he heard of the unexpected deposit in Maud's office. 'Very nasty,' he said, 'go ahead and call them.'

Inspector Grant, from Parkside, came promptly. He was accompanied by his new Detective Sergeant, Harry Meredith. Pansy met them at reception. It was the first time she'd met a police inspector, and she examined him carefully. He was tall and thin, as far as she could tell, because he was wearing a long trench coat. It reminded her of films she used to watch with her mother, when she was a child. He didn't wear a hat, however, but then he did have a good head of hair. Pansy beamed at him, ignoring his junior companion, and swept him away to her office, out from under Becky's, Sue's and Melanie's twitching noses. She ushered him along with a proprietorial hand under his elbow, filling him in on the burglary, and the 'incident in the Library' as she called it. He listened to everything she said, nodding and asking DS Meredith to take notes. Pansy thought Inspector Grant was charming. She led him to Dr Black's office.

She could see that Inspector Grant wasn't happy with Dr Black's protestations of innocence. The detective continued to question him about minutia long after Pansy thought he'd extracted all he could from him. But she knew the character of the man being interviewed and she was very suspicious. Dr Black was unusually passive behind a seemingly stubborn determination to say little or nothing. Inspector Grant's nose twitched. The faint whiff of something not quite right was in the air, and years of experience had clearly taught the Inspector to stick with his quarry until they let their defences down. He couldn't move Dr Black, though. He followed Pansy back to her office, which she kindly offered as an interview room. Inspector Grant consulted his list of witnesses and settled into Pansy's chair.

Next to be questioned was Becky, who had been knocked over by the burglar. The promising sighting of the intruder turned out to be a red herring. Becky felt sufficiently cowed by the Inspector to tell him the truth. A student called Michael had called to the office and apologised for crashing into her without stopping. Michael, in turn, was brought to see Inspector Grant. He was a new 1st year, tall, gangly and very nervous about being called before the police. His story was simple: he went to Dr Black's office for a tutorial and found it in a state of disarray. Concerned that he would be blamed - Dr Black had quickly established a reputation for flying off the handle with students - he simply ran away, bumping into Becky as he went.

Maud and Anni were weary of waiting by the time the Inspector came to see them, and puzzled by the direction of his questions.

'How well do you know Dr Black?' he asked Maud.

'I guess I know him as well as most people here do, but I have to admit that means not very well at all,' she replied.

'Can you think of any reason why his office should have

been the target of a burglary?

'Well, em, no. He's just a researcher. I mean... I mean,' stumbled Maud, intimidated by the raising of Inspector Grant's substantial eyebrows. 'It's not as though he was leading a team or engaged in, well, cutting edge research.'

'Hmmm, why don't you know him very well? He's been in the Department for six months.'

'I don't have much to do with him.' Maud blushed.

Anni, sitting quietly by, examined the Inspector and his companion. DS Meredith, she thought, must be new to the job because he was concentrating firmly on taking notes, and looking now and then to his superior for direction. The Inspector reminded her a bit of *Maigret*, partly because of the trench coat, which he'd laid over the back of a chair, and partly because he was so self-contained. She expected him to pull out a pipe and nod his head, saying, *Cherchez la femme*. The Inspector turned suddenly to her.

'And you, Miss? How well do you know Dr Black?'

'Not at all, Inspector,' replied Anni, resisting an urge to break into French.

'Do you work here?' he asked flicking through the list of staff Pansy had provided.

'No.'

'Then why were you here?'

Anni was tempted to get angry - he was quite offhand - but she swallowed her ire and replied. 'I was having lunch with Maud and returned with her. I was following behind when she walked into her office and found the heart on her desk. This is why you're interviewing us, isn't it?'

'Hmmm,' said the Inspector. He gave Anni a long sharp

look, as though he expected her to break down and admit responsibility for one of the crimes. She smiled at him, because he didn't know she was a journalist who'd long since learnt to hold her own with angry and challenging people.

Inspector Grant turned back to Maud. 'Do you think there is any link between the burglary and the object left in your office,' he snapped.

'Why Inspector, I can't see that there is any connection, except that something was stolen from Dr Black's office and something was left in mine. Do you see a connection?'

'Not yet, Miss Cadogan. Can you tell me who Dr Black's particular friends are?'

'No, I can't.'

'You can't,' he repeated. 'This is a small department. Surely you've seen him speaking to some people more than others?'

'No, I haven't. Dr Black is a difficult man, prone to falling out with his colleagues and most of us avoid contact with him.'

Maud stopped suddenly. Anni suspected she was aware that she might have said more than she should have.

'Do you know of anyone who might have a particular grudge against him?'

Maud shook her head. 'No. He hasn't been here very long. We may not love him, Inspector, but I don't think anyone feels strongly enough about him to have developed that serious a grudge. He does his research, deals fairly civilly with those people with whom he's involved and, and... well that's just about it, really.'

'And does anyone have a particular grudge against you?'

Anni thought Maud was taken off-guard by the sudden switch in questioning, but she seemed to recover quickly. She shook her head, saying she got on very well with most of the staff.

'And yet I hear that you and Dr Cardigan had a disagreement in the staffroom this morning.'

Maud raised her eyebrows, and Anni knew she was wondering how he'd come across that piece of information.

'Dennis Cardigan and I have been rowing for years, Inspector. That's Dennis. He's a grumpy person.'

'Grumpy enough to leave a nasty calling card on your desk?'

'Oh no. He wouldn't do that. I'm sure he wouldn't. He hasn't the imagination for it, apart from the courage, and where would he get hold of a heart? His mother does all the shopping.'

Her attempt at humour was lost on Inspector Grant who continued to look grim, but Anni had to work hard to stop herself from laughing out loud.

'Miss Cadogan, I would say that the placing of such a particular object upon your desk does imply a personal motive. Are you quite sure that you know of no one who might wish to cause you distress?'

'Truly, I can't think of anyone. I'm sure I would be aware if I had upset someone, certainly to the extent that they would be driven to put a bleeding cow's heart on my desk.'

Inspector Grant turned away towards the window. Perhaps he didn't like being given spirited replies. He swung back round to face Maud.

'Most of the students come into the library, Miss Cadogan. Can you be sure that you haven't alienated one of them?'

'I can't be sure of that, but they seem quite sane, for students. All they want is access to books and information. George and I hand out each freely. How could they feel aggrieved? I can't explain this. Surely it's linked to the burglary in Dr Black's office? Did the burglar leave a calling card there?'

'We've found nothing,' he said. 'Thank goodness you had the sense to leave things undisturbed. We've little chance of collecting clues from Dr Black's office because he tidied up after the intruder.'

Inspector Grant's moustache drooped. He thanked Maud and Anni grumpily, and the two policemen left.

Despite further questioning, the police could neither extract a satisfactory explanation from any of the staff, nor offer one themselves. They took lots of fingerprints from Maud's office and, thankfully, the heart.

'Why did he ask you so many questions about Dr Black?' said Anni, when the Inspector had departed.

'I don't know, unless he suspects him. What I'd like to know is who told him about the tiff Dennis and I had this morning!'

It was past five o'clock when the police left, and Anni and Maud had returned from lunch shortly before two. Anni wondered if Edward was in the Department. She mentioned to Maud that he had been lecturing at the Judge Institute that morning. Maud doubted whether he would have come back, but suggested they check his room. They wandered slowly through the silent corridors, past Dr Black's room and on to Edward's, which was at the end of the corridor. The door was locked.

'I suspect he's doing supervisions in college,' said Maud. 'They could run on because the system is new to the 1st years and Edward always spends extra time with them.'

Maud accompanied Anni to the main door of the building, and then headed back to her office, stopping to collect cleaning materials from the staffroom on the way. She was still there, talking to Anthony and Chris, when Edward walked in a short while later.

'Are you considering a change of profession?' he asked, looking at the bucket Maud held.

They told him what had happened.

'Ah, I wondered why you were carrying that.'

'I have a bone to pick with you,' said Maud. 'Come and help me clean up my desk.'

It was dark by the time Anni let herself into the flat.

'Hullo,' called Edward, coming into the hall. 'I was beginning to wonder where you were.'

'I just went for a walk,' said Anni. 'I needed to clear my head. Did you return to the Department?'

'Yes, and I know about the object in Maud's office.'

'Oh Edward, it was horrible! Who would do such a thing? Does someone hate Maud?'

'I can't explain it. Maud is very well liked, she always has been. Dennis Cardigan doesn't like her, but I'm not sure he likes anyone.'

They went into the living room and Anni sat on the sofa. Edward joined her and drew her close.

'I have just the tonic to put it out of your mind,' he said. 'Paul is panting to meet you and we've been invited to dinner.'

'Oh, could we put it off, Edward? There are things I need to discuss with you.' The reason she'd been late back wasn't entirely due to the discovery in Maud's office. Anni was troubled that Edward had told her so little - especially about Maud. What could be the reason for keeping that a secret? She'd walked for an hour or more, tossing the matter around in her head. She had to challenge him. What else hadn't he told her?

But Edward drew away and stood up. He began to fidget with ornaments on the mantelpiece. 'May we talk another time, sweetheart? I've been promising to introduce you properly to Paul and he's been preparing dinner all afternoon. He's a marvellous cook.'

Anni knew she could make a fuss, but he was clearly reluctant to talk, so what good would it do? She gave in, she was tired after the long day. Cécile's advice echoed in her mind. Best not to rock the boat. Yet, she added, in her own mind.

Chapter 11 | *The neighbours*

'Come in. Come in!' said Paul, grabbing Anni's hand and dragging her along the hallway in the manner of an excited child. She cast a glance over her shoulder at Edward, who was smiling as he closed the front door and followed them into Paul's kitchen.

'I must show you everything, Anni, and get your opinion. French people are superior cooks but... ' He stopped talking, probably noticing the look on Anni's face. 'Belgian, Belgian!' he shouted, putting a hand across his mouth and giggling. 'Sorry Anni, I forgot.'

Anni laughed.

'He's a scatterbrain,' said Edward. 'I'm often surprised at how well he manages his hairdressing business.'

'I never forget a client's head,' replied Paul, fingering Anni's hair. 'Lovely condition.' Anni laughed, but she felt a bit disconcerted by the close attention.

Anni looked over at Roger, who was standing in the doorway between the living room and kitchen. If the look on his face was anything to go by, he was already exasperated by the guests. Edward had given Anni a potted biography of Paul and his new boyfriend, before they left their flat, commenting that he'd yet to see Roger looking happy. He already thought that Roger and Paul were as much of a contrast to each other as the black and white colours of the kitchen.

Paul began lifting lids on pots and giving Anni chapter and verse on what he was cooking for dinner. The smells were good enough to tempt Piaf, the cat, from her usual perch in the living room. She rubbed past Edward and jumped onto the lid of Paul's spotless stainless-steel bin.

'Oh naughty P,' he said, lifting her carefully off, and checking the surface for scratches. 'I'll have to find a bin with a sloping top. She keeps sitting on this one.'

'I'll go into the living room,' said Edward, 'she might follow me.' He eased past the belligerent Roger and sat on the sofa. Piaf leapt from Paul's arms and followed.

'I'll leave you to cook,' growled Roger and followed Edward into the living room.

'Rog the Dodge,' whispered Paul to Anni. 'That's what I call him. He always leaves the cooking to me.'

'I suspect you're better at it,' she whispered back, diplomatically.

'I'm glad he's gone; we can talk away in private now. Girl, there's so much you have to tell me. Do you realize you're the only woman I've ever seen Edward with? I've known him for years and years and years. Come under the light here, I should check you for wings.'

He turned Anni round and round, and she laughed.

'Nothing.' He sounded disappointed. 'Hmm, I'll look another time, you might have left them behind just to fool me.' Paul chatted away in a light-hearted gossipy way. Anni warmed to him. They pottered about the kitchen together, in almost perfect harmony.

In the living room, Edward sat on the sofa, listening to their happy burbling and stroking Piaf who was sitting gracefully on an arm of the sofa. Roger stood with his back to the window, keeping a sour and watchful eye on him. It puzzled Edward that Roger continued to be suspicious of him, especially now that he'd met Anni. Edward had begun to notice how often Roger tried to control what Paul did, and whom he saw. It bothered him but he planned to stay well clear of any differences between them. Roger might not be aware that he was just the latest of Paul's many boyfriends. Edward had seen them come and go over the years.

Roger came towards the sofa. Piaf hissed as he passed and shot out a spiky paw. Roger moved out of her way quickly, impressing Edward with his speed.

'Do you work out?' he asked.

'I go to a gym,' replied Roger.

'I guess you need to keep fit, as a musician.'

'Yes.'

Piaf filled the silence that followed with loud purring as Edward tickled her ears and chin. Eventually, Paul and Anni came through carrying the starter.

'What a wonderful table,' said Anni, as she laid the dishes on it.

'It's too big,' said Roger.

The table was long and wide. When the chairs were drawn out, it took up a good half of the big living room. It was laid with meticulous care. Edward knew that Paul had measured the distance between each set of cutlery so that every setting looked exactly the same. He must remember to tell Anni that. Paul was obsessive, but he was also impishly funny, and that quality softened the edge of his neurotic side. He'd written out place cards, and Anni and

Edward obediently took their places either side of the table. Roger immediately sat down and began to eat while they waited politely for Paul to join them. Throughout the meal, Anni helped him remove each course and set the next. Paul didn't relax until the main course had been served and removed, and he'd laid out their dessert. He put on a CD and began chatting to Anni as he sat back down.

'Roger is tutoring me on all the great composers. We've covered Poulenc and Lulla.'

'Lulla? Repeated Anni, looking puzzled. 'Do you mean Lully? Who composed Armide?'

'That's the one,' said Paul. 'It's tragic, isn't it?'

'Yes, it's a tragedy.' Edward noticed the light in Anni's eyes. She was trying not to laugh. He stretched out his foot to tip her under the table. She looked over at him, and two huge dimples appeared in her cheeks. Yes, she was trying not to laugh, bless her. 'What do you think of Beethoven and Mozart?' she asked.

'Roger says they're over-rated. Don't you?' He looked over at Roger who was scraping the last of the dessert off his plate. He didn't look up.

'Yes,' was his brief response. He seemed bored.

'Oh, right, em,' said Anni. 'I think they're worth listening to because they were outstanding composers. It's great that you have someone to guide you along the way. Have you listened to Tchaikovsky?'

'No, because Roger says he's tat. This week's great is Duprat. I remember the name by thinking of 'do' and 'prat'!'

Edward laughed. Anni took her cue from him and laughed too. Roger's face grew dark.

'I confess I haven't heard of him,' said Anni, 'but there is so much to learn, really.'

'You must have heard of him, Anni, he played the French horn!'

Anni smothered a giggle. 'Remember Paul, I'm Belgian.'

'Oh, I forgot again, sorry.'

Anni turned to Roger. 'Who is Duprat?'

'It's Dauprat, actually. Paris. Eighteenth century.'

Anni waited a few moments to hear more, but Roger didn't speak again. She gave up discussing music, giving in to more pressure from Edward's foot. They listened to Paul chatter on. The food was delicious and so was the wine. Paul and Edward carried the conversation for the rest of the evening. Roger confined himself to eating, drinking and casting stony looks at Edward.

Anni felt like a naughty schoolchild, trying to hold in her laughter until Edward had closed the hall door of the flat.

'What is Roger up to?' she asked. 'All the composers Paul mentioned are obscure. Well, Poulenc isn't, but you'd hardly call him a major composer.'

'I don't know what he's up to. I don't trust him, but it's best to let the relationship take its own course. I've known Paul for many years and seen the same pattern repeat over and over. Roger is just the latest in a very long line. He'll disappear like all the others. Piaf is a good judge of character. I watch how she takes to people and base their lasting power on that. She's more anti Roger than she's been with any of the others. I'd give him a month at most.'

'He doesn't like you! He seems to be jealous. Can he

really think you'd run off with Paul?'

Edward pulled Anni close for a hug. 'The man is blind. One look at you should have been enough to reassure him.'

They went off to bed giggling.

Chapter 12 | *Visit to London*

They woke the following morning to the sound of the phone ringing. It was Edward's father, who'd returned from Ireland. The conversation was brief but Anni noticed it brought about a change in Edward. From the smiling happy relaxed man of yesterday evening, he became jumpy and distracted. She sighed. She'd seen brief episodes of nervousness in him before. When she didn't know him so well it seemed presumptuous to try and draw him out about the cause, and he always settled down within a couple of days of arriving in Brussels. As time went by, she learned to manage the episodes, mostly by means of long walks in the countryside. He also suffered from headaches and nightmares. The headaches also subsided after a couple of days. When Anni asked him what the nightmares were about, he would say he couldn't remember. Anni never told him that he talked in his sleep. She'd paid little attention to begin with, but over time she became aware that the disturbances related to his mother, whom he rarely spoke of when awake, to someone called Lucy, and to a third person whose name he never mentioned, but who disturbed him more than anyone else. She sighed again. Oh dear, how much of this was her fault? Should she have pushed him long before now to talk about what was bothering him? In a way, she'd been deliberately blind, probably because she didn't want to upset him, or drive him away. But something was troubling Edward at a deep level, and now that they were married she would no longer be able to shrug the problem off. But it wouldn't be a good idea to push him to explain just now. Later, she thought. When he's in a better mood.

Still distracted, Edward left for work. He went out the door but returned almost immediately to ask Anni if she'd like to go to London with him the following day to see his father. Surprised but pleased, she agreed.

Once he was gone, Anni quickly regained her equilibrium and became absorbed in reading for a project of her own. She looked forward to the independence a piece of work would bring. Mikhail Gorbachev was coming to Cambridge and Anni had been asked to cover the visit. It wasn't in her usual line of journalism, but she'd agreed to take on the assignment because it was connected with his work for the Green Cross. Anni had already written several pieces on Green Cross's work in Eastern Europe, where they were trying to undo environmental damage built up during the communist regime. It was becoming clear to her that contracts in and around Cambridge would probably be few and far between because the city was full of experts with whom it would be difficult to compete. She would have to review her line of work sometime, but for the present, her main concern was to make a success of her impetuous marriage to Edward. Work would have to take a backseat for now.

The visit to Edward's father was brief and puzzling. Anni was still mulling over it as they emerged from the Underground at King's Cross railway station on their way back to Cambridge. Edward looked up at the screen showing train departure times and platforms.

'Run, Anni, RUN,' he shouted to her. 'We'll just about

make it.'

Anni ran after him, dodging people dragging bags and cases, and almost knocking a cup of coffee from the grasp of a man who'd wandered into her path. She turned back to apologise, then realised she could no longer see Edward. A hand appeared through the crowd and pulled her onto the platform.

'In here,' said Edward. 'Jump!'

The train moved off almost immediately and they collapsed into seats, laughing.

'Crusty old academics aren't supposed to run after trains,' she gasped, giving him a playful dig on the arm, 'and they shouldn't force their wives to follow their example. Ooh, I might have had a heart attack.'

Edward laughed. 'I knew you could do it.'

'Well I didn't!'

Anni laid her head on Edward's shoulder and looked out at north London passing swiftly by. The visit to Robert was uppermost in her mind. Their busy wedding day had left few opportunities to examine her in-laws, so Anni had welcomed this chance to get to know Robert better. He was almost as tall as Edward and the family resemblance between them was strong. She had watched them as they stood by a window at the far end of the living room, talking together in low tones. Edward looked like a clone of his father. Same height, same type of hair, though Robert's was grey now. She also noticed that they shared certain mannerisms, such as pushing back locks of hair, though neither's was long enough to fall over their face or eyes. It seemed more of a nervous gesture.

Anni had picked up a photograph of Edward standing,

she presumed, beside his mother. It wasn't sitting quite right in the frame, and she realised that part of the photo had been cut. There was a line of someone standing the other side of Edward. It piqued her interest and she was going to ask about it, but when she looked up, father and son were deeply engaged in conversation. Anni replaced the photograph on the sideboard. The afternoon had been pleasant, but she had a nagging feeling that something was wrong. Robert said little, and in retrospect, she thought it would have been better if Edward had gone alone.

'Your father seemed ill at ease this afternoon,' she said. 'Did you notice? Is he normally reserved?'

'Em, no,' said Edward.

'Obviously, I hardly know him, but I thought he kept the conversation very general. I was surprised he didn't ask any questions about my background or family. After all, I'm his daughter-in-law. It would be natural to be curious, and there was very little time for talking at the wedding.'

Edward didn't reply.

'It wasn't that I felt he disliked me,' said Anni, struggling out of their embrace and turning to look into his face. 'Indeed, he smiled at me, but sometimes the smile would, well sort of die and then a worried look would take its place. You must have noticed.'

'Oh he's like me,' said Edward, finally, 'he's quiet and just a bit unsure of people's reactions. Maybe he was worried that you won't like him. We did take him by surprise, marrying so quickly.'

'Hmm, perhaps. Oh well, I like him regardless, and I'm sure we'll enjoy each other's company in time and be good friends.'

Anni turned again to look out at the passing scenery. There didn't seem to be much more to say, and she didn't feel reassured by Edward's reply. Far from putting her mind at ease, it seemed that every new event or encounter raised more questions in her mind. Why hadn't Edward told his family about her prior to their marriage? And why hadn't he told her about them? For a long time, she'd thought he was an only child and that his parents were dead. With just one sister of her own, she'd been delighted to discover, just before the wedding, that he had a father and a brother. And now there was Maud. Anni loved family. She hoped she and Edward would have children. And that was another subject she didn't dare raise, especially at present. What was the secret in his background? It must be bad to give him nightmares. Why wouldn't he tell her about it? Didn't he trust her?

Edward slipped his hand into hers. She felt a sudden rush of affection for him. He was gentle, undemanding and affectionate and they were good friends as well as lovers. Surely the marriage would work. Surely Edward would begin to trust her more as time went by. Surely he would confide in her.

Chapter 13 | *A petition*

Back at the Department of Environmental Sciences, the police were making slow progress in identifying the intruder. They'd collected numerous fingerprints from Maud's office but as Dr Black had cleaned the surfaces in his, they were unable to isolate a match.

The Departmental staff room buzzed day after day with speculation on motives behind the dramas. Dr Black was the main subject of conversation. As people talked about him, conflicting stories about his background emerged. The most commonly held belief was that he was from the Midlands, but someone remembered that he'd grown up in Devon. A research group who'd been discussing a field trip to Dartmoor found Dr Black surprisingly knowledgeable about the area, and this was the explanation he'd given. Why would he lie about his background? Nobody cared where he came from. What did it matter to them if he'd been born in Timbuktu? Questions were asked about these inconsistencies and conflicts. What was he hiding from the police? What was he hiding from the Department? Pansy was especially interested in these discussions, but as people didn't trust her fully either, they were inclined to clam up when she was nearby. Pansy found that very frustrating.

The greatest mystery was the appearance of the heart in Maud's office. This was puzzling. She was popular, and her sense of humour and practical approach generally meant that, unlike Dr Black, she made friends rather than enemies. As Maud wouldn't discuss the matter with anyone other than Arthur Scott, her colleagues were left to wonder. Inevitably, someone suggested that Maud had a secret lover. Becky was probably responsible, encouraged by Melanie. They were often seen huddled together in a corner of the staffroom, whispering to each other. They decided it was a desperate gesture from a rejected lover. They lamented that it hadn't happened on Valentine's Day. That would have made the whole thing so much more intriguing. While Becky and Melanie lingered over discussion of their pet theory, the rest of the staff tended to avoid them.

Inspector Grant, or other members of the police, had questioned everyone who'd been in the department that morning, but no one admitted to seeing anything unusual. That was hardly surprising. The incident had occurred right at the beginning of term, when the Department was teeming with people. It would not have been difficult to blend in with the hoards of staff and students, as they dashed up and down the stairs running from lecture, to seminar, to tutorial or supervision. Groups of students sat in clumps either side of the stairs in between lectures. Pansy did her best to shoo them away whenever she passed, but they drifted back as soon as she was gone. The staff had to pay particular attention to where they put their feet. Apart from Dennis, that is. He took great delight in standing on fingers or feet, and listening to the students squawk in pain. In such circumstances, it would have been all too easy for someone to make their way unnoticed to Dr Black's room, or to Maud's office.

Arthur Scott warned the staff and researchers to lock their doors while out, insisting they do so even when visiting the toilet. Many resented this restraint on their freedom. The happiest group in the Department was the one who'd formerly complained the loudest. The lowly research assistants, whose working area was a dark narrow basement room with twenty of them crammed into a space suitable for five or six. They never needed to lock up. There was always someone left in the room.

Eventually, interest in the burglary diminished. Melanie slowly deserted Becky and was more usually seen listening intently to whatever Harold might be saying. Anthony became more and more irritated with her, especially as she began repeating Harold's comments, turning him into a sage.

There was a lot of activity behind the plant screen during morning breaks, with most people managing to secure their drinks before Pansy's regular time for coffee. The contented looks and smiles on their faces encouraged Pansy to decide that the coffee machine had been a success. She collared Arthur Scott one morning.

'Have you noticed, Arthur, how everyone is drinking their tea and coffee with gusto? They're clearly enjoying it. Now you must admit that it was very clever of me to have thought of installing the coffee machine. I'm certain it's saving the Department a fortune. Tea and coffee are instantly available, and people can get back to their desks much faster! I have several more projects in mind. I'll come and talk to you about the photocopiers shortly.'

Arthur smiled weakly and left the room as soon as he could. When he was gone, Dennis began approaching the academics and presenting them with a letter. Anthony cut him short and left the room. Dennis stood in front of Chris White, who listened red-faced and silently polite. Those nearby who overheard what Dennis was saying, slipped quietly out of the staff room fearing they would be approached next. At the finish of his monologue, Dennis turned around to find that no one else was left in the room. Chris was driven to behave uncharacteristically. While Dennis's back was turned, he stood up and left. Dennis saw him slide out through the door. He shrugged his shoulders, left the staff room, and set off for the Library.

Maud was helping a young Japanese student as he pushed his way to the issue desk. The timid student melted away before him. Dennis didn't even notice.

'Maud, I want you to...'

'Just a moment, Dennis,' cut in Maud, going after the disappearing student and directing her determinedly to the periodical stand. When the girl had spotted what she needed, Maud turned back to Dennis. 'You really shouldn't treat the students that way. Come into my office if you have something to say.'

'Uh,' he grunted as he followed her, 'students! We're wasting our time on them. They don't come here to study; they just want to make trouble. Have you seen the latest poster on their notice board? The one asking for volunteers to go up to Scotland and demonstrate outside a nuclear submarine base?'

'I never look at their noticeboard, Dennis.'

'Well maybe you should!' he said, dropping heavily onto one of the low chairs in Maud's office. 'It invites anyone with bolt-cutters to bring them along, saying the ringleaders will ensure no one gets arrested. That is a blatant invitation to perform a criminal offence! Last week, they had a poster inviting students to demonstrate against the G9 meeting in Birmingham. *Dress Smart* it said, *that way the pig police won't harass you*. They're all out to cause trouble. Why should I care for any of them?

'Honestly, Dennis. And do you bracket Nami in that category?'

'What?'

'Not what, who! Nami is the student you just pushed aside at the desk.'

'Huh. That's not the point, Maud. These students are dissidents and troublemakers. You have to try and keep them down. It's frightening to think what they might get up to next.'

Maud sat back into her chair. She despaired of Dennis at times. 'Why did you consider teaching as a career, Dennis? You never have a good word to say about the students.'

'You know my mother thought it would be a secure career for me. Permanent, pensionable and all that.'

Maud couldn't resist a wry smile. 'So, you didn't decide to become a lecturer because you liked the profession?'

'I certainly did not. I hate teaching.'

Maud sighed. 'What did you come in for, Dennis?'

'I'm collecting signatures on a letter to Arthur about the new professorship. If we don't put pressure on him to appoint in order of seniority, he'll give it to that blasted American.'

'We?'

'Well, em,' Dennis wriggled on his chair. 'I'm asking all the academic staff and I'm sure most will give it their backing.'

'You don't have any signatures, do you? You won't get them, Dennis, and you're dreaming if you think that Arthur will propose you for the position because you're the longest serving member of staff not yet holding a professorship. You haven't written a new paper for years, not to mention publishing a book. It's on the basis of research, Dennis, not seniority.'

Dennis scowled blackly at Maud. 'You've always been far too free with your opinions, Maud Cadogan. I'm not surprised that someone felt strongly enough to leave that cow's heart on your desk. You don't really have a heart, and are clearly in need of one. If you did, you would back me up in this. We've known each other for many years and I think you should stand by me.'

Maud stood up. She was angry. 'I think you're wrong in what you're doing, Dennis, and I won't back you if I believe what you're doing is wrong.'

'You're a traitor, Maud,' Dennis too stood up, 'and you'll get your just desserts one of these days,' he shouted, his face redder than ever, 'and I, for one, will be only too glad to watch when that happens!'

Maud's colleague, George, must have overheard the exchange. He came into the office, and found Dennis standing over her. 'Don't threaten Maud, Dennis. It won't help your cause.'

Dennis backed off angrily, sidling around George and slamming the office door behind him. He left the Library with the unsigned letter still clutched in his hand.

'What an idiot,' said George. 'He's determined to cause trouble this time. I've never known him to pursue promotion with such vigour.'

'Thanks for intervening, George.' Maud sat back down. 'I expect he wants the bigger pension that goes with the job. Poor Victoria, it must be difficult for her to continue without being upset by his conspiracy.'

'Don't worry about her. She's tough in her own way. She'll certainly need to be if she does get appointed. Dennis will make her life a misery afterwards.'

Chapter 14 | *Tour of Cambridge*

Anni was aware that Edward was trying to distract her from dwelling on the unpleasantness she'd witnessed with Maud. He kept talking about the uniqueness of the city and its history, the gems that he was looking forward to showing her, and it was obvious he was worried that she might be developing a negative view of Cambridge. Anni knew she was far more resilient than he realised, and that Edward was mistaken in thinking that her growing anxiety was linked to the city. Part of the frustration she felt was due to her own failure to tackle him on his lack of openness. She feared Edward might be neglecting his work, as he had taken to rambling home for coffee breaks or extended lunches with her. One evening, he announced that he was going to take her for the long-promised tour of Cambridge.

Anni was up before him the following morning, looking forward to the day. As she headed to the bathroom, she noticed the post had been delivered, and an upturned postcard caught her eye. It was addressed to Edward, and contained just one word in the message section: Minnie. '*Someone else he hasn't told me about,*' she thought, and carried on to have a shower. When she re-emerged, Edward had picked up the post and laid letters for her on the hall table, as he usually did. There was no sign of the postcard and he didn't mention it over breakfast. He talked instead of his plans for the day, and as she listened, Anni added the name 'Minnie' to the growing list of mystery people connected with her husband.

'I thought we might go quickly round some of the colleges,' said Edward, carrying the coffee pot to the table. He poured cups for both of them, and then added three spoons of sugar to his. Anni, who didn't take sugar, was about to suggest that he should cut down on his intake, but she noticed the way his hand shook as he spooned the sugar into his coffee. She bit her lip. Anni watched Edward fuss about the kitchen, clearing and tidying. He was making an effort to appear normal, and she puzzled about what could have made him so nervous. He'd been fine when they woke.

'We can visit them properly another time,' he said, stopping by the window, then quickly backing away from it. 'I thought you might like to spend an hour or two in King's College Chapel. The stained glass there is really fine and it's historically interesting because of its connections to royalty and events at the time it was being built.'

'Oh, great,' said Anni, rising and pausing by the window as she made her way to the sink. There was nothing unusual to be seen, at least nothing that she could see. Why had Edward ducked out of sight?

'We could have lunch in one of the chic new places that are springing up in the city, then afterwards we might wander up Castle Hill before visiting Kettle's Yard,' said Edward drawing her out of the room. Anni suddenly felt tired.

'What's Kettle's Yard?' she asked, wondering why she had to make an effort to be interested when she'd been so eager earlier.

'It's an art gallery, a most unusual one. I think you'll like it.'

They left the flat and walked across Coe Fen to the city centre. The fresh air and crisp sunny morning restored some of Anni's energy and it seemed to soothe Edward. When they reached the busy pinched exit from the fen, by the Mill Pond, he stopped and told her some of the history. 'It's called Lammas Land or Sheep's Green,' he said.

Ah, Sheep's Green. That was on her list of questions about Cambridge. 'Lammas? Is that spelt like 'lamb' as in 'sheep'?

'No, it's *Lammas,*' Edward spelled it out for her. 'It's got to do with people having the right to pasture their animals on the land in between harvest and planting a new crop. It's a bit like the notion of common land, which belongs to everyone, but Lammas day is on the 1st August, and there was just a window of time for people to use the land.'

'I notice there are lots of green areas in Cambridge.'

'Yes, and much of them are common land. We must take a tour of them someday - perhaps we could cycle around. Have you cycled much?'

'As a teenager.'

'Oh, right. Okay we could get some practice in. Cambridge is a perfect place to cycle in because it's so flat. Now look here below us.'

Edward pointed down to Scudamore's punt yard, whose offices were on a raft at water level. Rows of punts were lined up against a boardwalk and it looked like the sunshine was tempting people to take out punts. A crowd had gathered for a trip on the river. Anni looked yearningly at them, queuing by the gated entrance to the Anchor pub. They looked cheerful and expectant. The sun was spreading light on the water, which shifted and split as waves spread out from moving boats. It looked so inviting and Anni found herself wishing she and Edward might take a slow punt up river followed by a lazy lunch and drinks in one of the nearby pubs. Edward however, was caught up in his own agenda. Hardly noticing Anni's attention had been drawn to the boats, he took her hand and drew her along a narrow lane, which he said led to Trumpington Street. The tiny street was empty. He pointed to a chapel on their right.

'That's Little St Mary's, the poor relation of Great St Mary's opposite King's College, where I've already taken you. Beyond it is Peterhouse, which is the oldest college in Cambridge. It dates back to the 11th century. I must take you to see the Peterhouse chapel sometime, the stained-glass windows are wonderful.'

Anni would have like to spend time looking at the old buildings, but Edward turned his back on the college and pointed across the street. He seemed determined to fit in as much as possible, and she felt a bit like a student on a school outing.

'That is the Master's Lodge,' he said.

He was slipping into the role of professional guide. She would clearly have to work to keep up with him. 'Does Peterhouse run both sides of the street?' she asked, making an effort.

'No, the buildings lower down belong to Pembroke College. I don't know why the Peterhouse Master's Lodge is the other side of the road instead of in the college grounds; maybe the college once owned both sides of the road. We'll come back another day to see the college properly and perhaps we'll learn the reason then.'

They ran across the busy street, dodging the predictable

cyclists.

'And now I'll show you another, very different, master's lodge.'

He led her through the main entrance to Pembroke College, and out towards the back of the college. Anni trailed after him, admiring the huge covered entrance and the way it opened suddenly onto a perfectly kept quadrangle.

'Stop!' she called. 'This is wonderful. Won't you tell me a bit about these buildings?'

'I'd have to read up to give you the detail, Anni, and I haven't had time to do that. All I know is that the college is about 600 years old, I think it dates from the 14th century.'

Anni lingered, captivated by the utter contrast of old and new she'd experienced stepping from the busy car-filled street into the muffled grounds of Pembroke College. She wanted to see more, but she was very conscious of Edward's impatience to be moving. Looking around once more, she sighed, then took his hand and followed as he led her through a tantalising passage into another larger quadrangle. He stopped by an untidy piece of ground, which Anni recalled seeing before.

'Didn't we come here after the party?'

'Yes,' smiled Edward, 'well remembered. This is the Dean's garden. It's a wild space among the beautifully kept grounds. It's cut just twice a year to allow the wildflowers to grow and insects to flourish.' He pointed to the far wing of a new building. 'That is the new Pembroke Master's Lodge. This section of the college was finished quite recently and I've been told it's built to survive two hundred years without needing maintenance.'

'I'm very impressed.' Anni grinned at him, but she was laughing softly inside at the thought that he was so impressed by a bank of plain stone buildings when the splendour of the older section was so close by.

'Oh well,' he said, catching her grin and smiling back, 'time will tell. There are many new architecturally innovative buildings around Cambridge. We won't live to see if they stand the passage of time as these older buildings have.'

Edward led her through the back gate of the college, onto Tennis Court Road and then Downing Street, which she also recognised.

'Next stop is Emmanuel College,' he announced. 'There is a wonderful little chapel there, designed by Wren.'

'Oh,' said Anni, 'I think I may have seen it, but I didn't have time to go inside.'

'I expect it will be closed, and if so we can save it for another time. Wren's uncle was a Master of Peterhouse, by the way, and the chapel there was given the nickname of *Wren's nest* while he was alive.'

Anni noticed that the porters were in their lodge. 'Why do they wear bowler hats?' she whispered.

'They used to be policemen back in the 19th century, and were called bulldogs. They were hired to keep rowdy students in check. I think they wore top hats originally, perhaps to protect their heads from injury. The police evolved into porters, still with peace-keeping duties and still with a need to protect their heads! I guess the bowler replaced the top hat.'

'Gosh, what an interesting tale. If they're akin to policemen, I will have to watch myself around them.'

They walked through the archway into Emmanuel College, where Anni had lingered previously, and around the quadrangle towards the chapel. They stopped in the cloister and found the chapel was closed.

'Let's walk around the quad and then go down for a quick stroll in the Fellows' Garden. There's a pond there where ducks raise their families and I've seen moorhens and even coots in it.'

Anni really did enjoy looking at the old buildings and her enthusiasm pleased Edward. He led her through the archway into the garden. The ducks came to meet them long before they'd reached the pond, waddling up with the heads to one side as though checking what provisions this couple might have brought.

'That is a fat duck,' said Edward, wagging a finger at the feathered beggar. 'Most of these ducks are so well fed, they find it hard to fly. I suspect the population would fade away completely if they didn't suffer short rations over Christmas when the students are away.'

'What do you mean? Surely it's better for them to be fed than not.'

'I mean that they get a chance to slim down a bit in time for Spring and then they have the energy to chase after each other and get on with the job of making ducklings.'

Anni chuckled at the picture he'd conjured up. 'We've never talked about having children, Edward.' She said, tentatively.

'It's not something I've thought about. Perhaps we could discuss it sometime in the future. I'd like to have you all to myself for a bit longer. I think I need a reasonable amount of time to adjust to married life before becoming a father.'

Anni sighed silently. It was a reasonable reply. She could hardly blame him, wanting to take his time, but lately she'd been feeling more and more attracted to the idea of having children. *Must be my body clock*, she thought. 'Has Richard never married?' she asked.

'No. He's had several relationships, but nothing serious.'

'Did Robert encourage either of you to marry?'

'No.'

'Do you think he minds not having grandchildren?'

'He's never mentioned it.'

Edward's replies were becoming shorter and shorter. Anni was growing conscious of an emerging pattern whereby he would withdraw and become monosyllabic whenever she asked him personal or family-associated questions. The behaviour puzzled and frustrated her. She was tempted to draw him out further, despite the danger of a row, but pushed the thought from her mind, not wishing to detract from their day together. She spotted an amazing tree in a corner of the garden. It looked more like an octopus than a tree, with branches creeping out along the ground at some distance from the trunk, some of which were propped up with planks of wood. She was glad of the distraction. Her lips were becoming sore from all the times she was having to bite them lately.

They left the college and Edward took her along the busy St Andrew's Street, where instead of carrying on to the Lion Yard and shopping precinct, he steered her into Hobson Street. 'Have you heard of the term Hobson's choice?' he asked.

'Yes, it means having no choice. Why do you ask?'

'This is where it originates from. Hobson was a 17th

century carrier, running a mail service between Cambridge and London, and also a horse and cart hire business. The best and fastest horses were the most popular, naturally, and bore the brunt of the hire business, because demand for them outstripped demand for the other horses. That was what led him to set up a rotation system and when someone came to hire a horse he gave a choice of the next horse due to go out, or none.'

'Wasn't that strong-minded behaviour for the 17th century? What if he'd been boycotted? I'm surprised the business prospered.'

'He might have been the only hire firm around, though I don't think that's likely. If so, then that was doubly Hobson's choice for the locals! He seems to have been quite an entrepreneur and did some good for the city. Did you notice the channels running down both sides of Trumpington Street?'

'Oh, that drain in front of Pembroke College, you mean? Yes, I had to jump over it.'

'That's called Hobson's Conduit. It had something to do with bringing clean water into the medieval city, and he contributed to its construction.'

'Ah, how interesting. Trumpington reminds me that I was going to ask you about the name, and where Trumpington Gate is.'

'It's just an old name - I think it appears in The Domesday Book - but the village called Trumpington is now part of Cambridge. That's certainly where Trumpington Gate came from – it's just an entrance into the city, or rather it was in medieval times. You know, like south gate, or west gate.'

'I see. I have lots to learn about Cambridge.

They turned into Sidney Street, laughing and relaxed again. The tricky moment had passed. Edward stopped by Sidney Sussex College.

'Sherlock Holmes studied here,' he said, pointing upwards. 'See the window there? That was his room.'

'Oh Edward, you're an appalling liar.'

He grinned. 'OK, it isn't true. It's a good story though. It was Dorothy L Sayers who first proposed that the famous detective must have been at Cambridge, and she decided he'd been at Sidney Sussex. A Cambridge professor, R J Chorley, wrote an amusing tale supporting the claim. I have a copy at home. I must dig it out for you.'

They carried on down Sidney Street, turning into All Saint's Passage, a little beyond the battered corner of a building. Anni asked if the oriole window was falling down.

'It's not that it's crumbling. Huge lorries reversing down the alley to stock shops from a loading bay at the rear are causing the damage. It's a crazy arrangement. Imagine allowing articulated lorries to manoeuvre in such a small place, not to mention right next to a listed building. But, such is the power of commerce these days!'

Oh dear. This was one of Edward's bugbears. Anni stayed silent. She'd learnt that the way to get him back down from his soapbox was not to engage. Unchallenged, he reverted to the role of guide.

'These buildings are part of Trinity College, and this section is Whelwell's Court. The main college is at the far end of the lane. Housman, the poet and Latin scholar had his rooms here.'

'You're a mine of information,' said Anni.

Edward blushed. 'Am I being too much of a tour guide?

I've lived in Cambridge a long time, it's only natural that I would have picked up titbits here and there.'

'That was a compliment!'

'Good. I wondered if you were getting tired.'

'I am a bit tired but really enjoying the tour.'

'Would you like an early lunch or to carry on to King's College Chapel?'

'Is it nearby?'

'Yes.'

'Let's keep going then. Chapel first, lunch later.'

They walked up Trinity Street, passing the main entrance to Trinity College, which was set back behind a huge arch and pair of impressive doors. Further along the street Edward point out Gonville and Caius College. Anni felt overwhelmed by the unfamiliar names and the sheer number of colleges. She didn't fully understand the role they played in the University. Edward steered her into a cobbled lane just by the Senate House, and Anni hesitated.

'Didn't you say we were going to see King's College Chapel?'

'We are.'

'But I can see it straight ahead. Why are we turning down here? Are we going somewhere else first?'

'The main entrance to the College is ahead, but visitors to the Chapel have to enter through the North Gate. It's a way of managing the flow of human traffic through the college. The walk around is interesting, so no one misses out despite the additional exercise.'

'Spoken like a true runner!' laughed Anni.

Edward grinned. He was really lightening up He made a dramatic sweep with his hand.

'Let me point out a few more architectural delights! On the left, we have the entrance to the Senate House.'

'What goes on there?'

'Graduate ceremonies mostly, but it's a focus point when students want to protest or complain. They gather in large numbers on the green at the far side. The building is wonderful inside to match this fabulous 18th century exterior. The only odd thing I can remember about it is that a group of engineering students put an Austin 7 on the roof in the 1950s.'

'An Austin 7? Isn't that a car?'

Edward laughed. It was a long ringing laugh and Anni saw his face clear of worry for the first time that day. 'Yes, darling, it's a car, or small van, and a group of students put it up on that roof.'

'You have to be joking! How did they manage to get a van up there? Weren't they seen? Why weren't they stopped?'

'They did it overnight while the May balls were going on, and when most people coming along this passage were drunk. They removed the engine and axel to make it lighter, and they got it up using pulleys and ropes which they'd set up on the roof of Gonville & Caius College, just behind you. There should be a picture of it somewhere. We must look it up.'

Anni stared awestruck at the roof of the Senate House. How clever of them to have managed such a feat, or how crazy!

'Now look up to your right,' said Edward, 'that sundial is

part of Gonville and Caius, and around the corner I'll show you the Old Schools, which was once part of King's College,' and he began to draw her after him, grinning mischievously.

'Slow down,' she begged, 'I can't take it all in!'

'It would take weeks to see Cambridge properly.'

They walked on past the entrance to the Old Schools, which looked just like another college to Anni, and past another building with an imposing entrance. A path flanked by flowerbeds led to it and she was reminded of a French chateau.

'Clare College,' said Edward, noticing her gaze.

Finally, they reached the North Gate of King's College Chapel. The promise of the exterior was amply filled by the amazing interior. Anni gazed up at the fan-vaulted ceiling, following the line of the columns between the huge stained-glass windows as they rose up towards the roof of the chapel, opening out like the most delicate of ivory fans. It was breathtaking. She spent so much time with her head bent backwards that she began to feel dizzy. Edward caught her as she swayed and drew her through the screen into the Choir, where there was seating.

'Are you okay?'

'Fine, fine,' said Anni. 'I think I got disorientated. I was turning round and around. Isn't that ceiling magnificent?'

'Yes. Let's sit here for a while,' he said, leading her to a pew, 'and you can look at the windows. That should give your neck a rest. This chapel was begun by Henry VI in the middle of the fifteenth century, and completed by Henry VIII almost a hundred years later. The glass is considered magnificent, and an outstanding example of its time. There are some amusing stories about the glass and the screen, which I'll show you when you feel like standing again. Are you okay, sweetheart?'

He looked intently at her, but Anni was amused that he didn't wait for a reply.

'Henry VIII,' he continued, 'had bits of it modified. See if you can spot a phoenix anywhere. That was the badge of his third wife, Jane Seymour. I gather it was altered from the falcons which were drawn for wife number two, Anne Boleyn.'

Anni was intrigued. 'I can't spot any from here, but I'm ready to stand now so please show me.'

Edward led the way back through the great oak screen, which divides the chapel in two. He pointed out Henry VIII's initials and together they searched for the sets of his and Anne Boleyn's, which were entwined.

'If he had the glass changed, why didn't he remove these initials?' asked Anni.

'I don't know. Maybe he'd forgotten about them, and they're less obvious than the glass, or would be if we could spot a falcon or a phoenix!'

They returned to the Choir where Anni had leisure to admire the carved wooden seats, or pews. They ran lengthways in rows almost to the far end of the chapel, where a painting by Rubens, the *Adoration of the Magi*, hung. Anni had read about that, and she was keen to get a closer look, but she noticed a woman kneeling, head bowed, seemingly oblivious to the hushed but continuous noise of visitors to the chapel.

'It must be difficult for the people who come here to practise their religion,' she whispered to Edward.

'It certainly must be during the summer. Most of the tourists talk aloud. I wouldn't be able to concentrate or pray properly, if it was me. Music is easier to pray to. We've had centuries of practice in that. Choral services are held here during term. Would you like to attend one?'

'That would be wonderful, Edward. I can just imagine a choir filling the chapel with beautiful sounds.'

'We must arrive early. You have to queue to get into the Choir. It can be difficult to hear properly when you're sitting the far side of the screen. And now, let's walk through the exhibition.'

They read short history bites about the Chapel, and explanations of the exhibits. It reminded Anni of their first meeting in Bouillon. When they re-entered the chapel, Anni insisted on having another good look at the ceiling, saying she wanted to put what she'd read into perspective. Eventually, a hungry Edward managed to haul her out and they walked over to the Market Square in search of lunch.

Edward noticed that Anni was finding the afternoon less rewarding. He shouldn't have tried to fit so much in. She had been disappointed to discover the so-called Castle was simply a mound. Kettle's Yard, however, was much more interesting. The gallery was made up of two houses knocked together, with exhibits of early 20th century art in smaller and larger rooms. It was more like walking around somebody's house than being in an art gallery. The laid-back, hippy-like feel of the place appealed to her, and Edward said that small concerts were often held there.

Feeling tired and footsore in the late afternoon, they strolled slowly back along Magdalene Street, with Anni stopping frequently to look into shop windows. Edward stood patiently by. Though less interested in shopping than Anni, his eye was caught by an African carving in one window. It showed a series of human figures wound round and round the stem of what appeared to be a lamp base, each standing on the back of the other as they in turn provided a platform for the next figure. At the top was a carving of a sad-faced individual. The face captivated him and he stared intensely at it. As he stared, the reflection of another head appeared beside it. He transferred his gaze to that and felt his body freeze with shock. A slow sinister smile spread across the reflected face. Edward felt the colour drain from his face. He tried to move, to turn, to look behind him, but his legs seemed made of lead.

Hearing him gasp, Anni looked up at him. 'What is it, Edward? What's wrong?'

He didn't answer. He didn't hear. Having finally managed to haul himself around, he was looking intently across the road, searching for the face he'd seen.

Anni followed his gaze. All she could see was a bunch of rugby players congregated by the entrance to yet another college. They were dressed in shorts and t-shirts and they moved on and off the narrow footpath, chatting and laughing. She could see nothing in them that might cause such distress to her husband. When she looked back at him, Edward was staring up and down the road, eyes narrowed as he scanned back and forth. He was hyperventilating and seemed unconscious of Anni's gaze. She watched anxiously as he slowly regained composure and became aware of her hand upon his arm.

'What did you see that gave you such a fright?'

'I, I thought I saw someone I knew.'

'You look as though you've seen a ghost.'

Edward didn't respond. He still looked shaken. Anni took a firm hold of his arm and they walked on without talking. When she felt he was calmer, she flagged a taxi and they returned to the flat.

Edward was quiet and withdrawn all evening. He sat in the living room pretending to read a book. Left to her own devices, Anni turned the event over and over in her mind. Who had he seen or thought he had seen? Why had it frightened him so? She remembered the postcard. Leaving Edward in the living room, she went firstly to the hall and then to his study to search for it. He hadn't hidden the card well. It was pushed into a filing tray, but a corner was visible. She pulled it out and examined it. Apart from the address, it just held the word *Minnie*. Who was Minnie? Why did he want to hide her? The card was postmarked London. Anni turned it over and looked at the view of a church. It could just be a holiday postcard, but if it was, why hadn't the sender added a message? Something brief such as *lovely old church* or *terrible weather*. Anni twisted the card over and over, but she could interpret nothing from it. She heard Edward moving about. Quickly pushing the postcard back, she crept out of the study and slipped into the kitchen, where she filled the kettle noisily and put it on to boil. She thought about forcing him to talk to her, but when she went back to the living room, Edward was walking up and down the room in an agitated way. He didn't notice her in the doorway. Anni's resolve evaporated. Once again, she let things drift, and settled instead for making him a cup of tea. She softened enough towards him to add three spoons of sugar to it.

Chapter 15 | *Visit to the Fitzwilliam*

It was raining heavily the following morning as Anni ran up the steps of the Fitzwilliam Museum. She was meeting Maud, and the timing was perfect. She needed to speak to someone about Edward, and who better than his cousin? Maud was waiting in the entrance hall, giving a sour look to a group of students who were being shepherded up towards the galleries. She greeted Anni affectionately, and then glared again at the students.

'Blast. I thought the gallery would be virtually empty at this time of day. That's a group of foreign language students, and they're heading in the direction we'll be taking.'

Anni's spirit sank a little. What could a group of students do to them, apart from put Maud into a bad mood? Damn. She needed her to be relaxed and receptive. Anni smiled and shrugged her shoulders. She put her soaking umbrella in with a pile of others and looked around. She was awed by the magnificence of the entrance vestibule. The balustrades and sides of the stairs were cut from pink and beige marble, and the columns holding up the mezzanine, of dark green. The mezzanine walls had columned niches in which stood white marble figures. There was a wealth of detail over the doorways leading to the gallery rooms.

'Gosh Maud, I'd no idea it would be so wonderful inside. I've been looking over at the glass dome each morning and...' Anni broke off to gasp as she looked up at the splendour of the central dome. 'I don't think I need to go further,' she giggled, 'there's far too much to see out here!'

Nonetheless, she followed Maud into the first gallery, stopping to admire the detail of the ivory-coloured plasterwork ceiling. Its simplicity was a huge contrast to the ornateness of the vestibule and she stood gazing at it while Maud began to look at the paintings.

'It's stunning,' said Anni, when she caught up with Maud.

'Well now that you've had your fill of it,' said Maud, who was smiling again, 'come along into these back rooms. I always like starting there because it houses the early 20th century paintings, and the walk through the rest of the gallery gives me a feeling of going backwards in time. I'm probably nuts. Most people would prefer to work forwards.'

Anni was content to be led along. The rooms were wonderful, but their architecture and decoration had none of the magnificence of the vestibule or the first gallery, and so it was possible to devote her complete attention to the paintings. She and Maud moved along fairly quickly, because Maud was on a break from work, admiring works by Picasso, Matisse and Rouault. At Maud's request, they went back on their tracks to look again at an Alma-Tadema, which had impressed them. The description told them that the painting of heads had been retrieved from the doors of a boat.

They were admiring the Pre-Raphaelites when one of the foreign language students approached. Anni heard Maud groan and she looked around.

'Hello good morning day Misses.' The student, who had a large plastic name card hanging from her neck, nodded her head several times.

Anni peered at the clipboard carried by the girl and saw a series of questions listed on the sheet. She smiled at Maud. Now she understood that they were to be unofficial teachers of English to the student.

'I like asking painting question please? You are coming here?'

'We are here!' growled Maud.

The girl's eyes grew larger and she blinked. 'Yes yes, you are coming for paintings?'

'Yes,' Anni answered quickly, seeing Maud's irritation growing. 'They're very good. What have you come here for?'

'English.'

'Oh, English. Not the paintings?'

'You like paintings?'

'Yes.'

The girl began scribbling on her sheet of paper.

Anni turned to Maud.

'How will they improve their English if the questions they ask can be answered in one syllable?'

'I've never figured that one out.'

'Please?' said the student.

'Do you like the paintings?'

'Yes yes. Learn English.'

'God's sake,' muttered Maud, turning to point at the two nearest paintings. 'I like this picture. My friend likes that picture. Okay?'

'Thank you thank you.'

The student began to scribble and Maud pushed Anni quickly into the next gallery. Anni felt guilty as she saw the student look from her list to their retreating figures.

'Oh Maud, that was cruel. Only half her questionnaire was filled in.'

'Tough. Every time I come in here, I'm collared by some student or other, foreign or indigenous, asking idiotically mundane questions. It interferes with looking at the paintings. You'll have just as little patience in a year or two, Anni. Now let's go down to the rooms at the far end of the gallery. I see their teacher in the corner, so they won't stray too far from these rooms. We can jump a few centuries, can't we?'

Off they went, flying past early religious paintings, through the Italian Room and on into the 16th century Dutch paintings. They reminded Anni of Flemish works and she felt more at home. She was drawn to a large still-life painting. The flowers and leaves were beautifully portrayed. The insects, especially the butterflies, were equally richly done and the drops of water - spotted like tears on the petals of the flowers - looked ready to move, they were so real. She was going to call Maud's attention to the painting, but she noticed that Maud was staring at the portrait of a woman. Anni joined her, drawn to the woman's face. She wasn't good-looking but there was something compelling about her. Anni leaned forward to read the artist's name, Jan de Bray. She stood back to look again at the picture, and as she did, had the impression that she herself was being examined. Turning around, she saw the flash of a head in the doorway of a side room to the gallery. She thought of going to investigate, but Maud spoke, looking at her watch.

'Rats. I have to get back to work. I'm really sorry that we don't have time for lunch, but it's busy in the Library at the moment, and I need to relieve George. Why don't you stay on?'

'It's okay. I can come another time. I'll walk back with you. I need to buy a sandwich. Besides I have to be at the Press Office for 2.30pm.'

'Come back and eat your sandwich with me. You still haven't seen those old photographs I mentioned. This is a good opportunity.'

Anni agreed. She was very keen to look at the photos, and this would give her a chance to ask a few questions about Edward.

'Has the burglar been identified?'

'No,' Maud shook her head.

'He wasn't really a burglar, was he - if it was a he,' said Anni. 'Strictly speaking, he didn't take anything, it's more a case that he left something behind.'

'I wish he hadn't,' said Maud. 'It makes me shudder when I think about it.'

'Have you any ideas about who left the heart, or why they left it?'

'I don't know. I've been thinking it over. Clearly, it was deliberate, and there must be a message there, if only I could grasp it.' Maud shivered. 'Even thinking of it makes me feel odd. I had an unpleasant conversation with Dennis Cardigan yesterday. He accused me of being heartless.'

'That was a bit unkind.'

'There's an unpleasant history there.'

Maud said no more. They bought a sandwich for Anni

and carried on to the Department.

'I'm back George,' called Maud to the man who was at the Library front desk. 'Have you met Anni Holroyd?'

'Not properly,' said George, a neat small man in his fifties. 'How do you do, Anni? Sorry to hear of your involvement in that dreadful incident. Not a nice introduction to Cambridge, even if the Department isn't one of its more attractive sights.' He winked at her.

'George!' said Maud, but she giggled.

'Ok ok, I'm going. By the way, Dr Black was looking for you.'

'What does he want?'

'The usual demand, produce the books on his list immediately if not sooner. He says he'll complain to Arthur if you don't.'

'What a cheek! It would cost most of my budget to buy what he wants. Does he realise I have lots of requests? Let him to go Arthur by all means, I doubt he'll get much sympathy. If he comes back, George, just send him in to me. I'd better sort him out once and for all.'

'Ok. Bye.'

George left for his lunchbreak, and Anni waited at the desk for Maud who quickly returned and shook a pile of curly-edged black and white photos from an old envelope. Anni was intrigued to see pictures of her husband in family line-ups looking at various times shy, gawky and mischievous. She listened to Maud's recollections and descriptions, enjoying building a picture of Edward's childhood.

'He really was the jolliest young chap,' Maud said, smiling

at the photos. 'I was the oldest of the three of us, and I well remember him trailing around after me. Richard too. We were terrible together: the three of us got into more scrapes than you could ever imagine. It's amazing that the adults didn't murder us at times.'

'It sounds like Edward wasn't always as reserved as he is now?'

'No, not when we were young. It was later, after...' Maud stopped talking. She was holding a photo in each hand. One was quite old, a black and white picture of a plain unsmiling girl. The other was a colour photo of Edward who looked to be in his 20s. He was smiling at the camera and his arm was round a lovely young woman dressed in red.

Anni pointed to the photo of the young woman. 'Who is this with Edward?'

Maud sighed. 'That was Lucy.' She held up the black and white photo. 'And this was Minnie.'

'Minnie!' repeated Anni. She thought of the postcard that Edward had tried to hide. That had been signed 'Minnie'.

Just then, George came back. Anni looked up at the clock. 'Oh my goodness, it's almost 2.30. I'll be late for the press conference. I'll have to run!'

She didn't want to leave. She had so many questions to ask Maud. Who was Lucy? Who was Minnie? Why had Edward become so gloomy?

'Hey, we'll have other opportunities,' said Maud.

'I guess so.'

Anni left. She would have to make another arrangement to speak to Maud.

Chapter 16 | *Pansy pulls the plug*

The staffroom buzzed at teatime. A rumour was going around that MI5 had called to see Arthur.

'How do we know they're MI5?' asked Anthony, looking sceptical.

Becky was full of the story. 'Bob, one of the site security guards, came over to the Department a while ago and asked if the FBI were still in the building.'

'The FBI?'

'It was just another way of saying MI5. You know the way Bob is.'

'No, I don't,' said Anthony, grimly. 'So, we've just got *Bob's* word for it that they're from MI5.'

'It isn't just that. Security has been stepped up because of Gorbachev's visit and we've had extra treatment because of the burglary, especially as Dr Black is supposed to meet him.'

'He is?' Anthony gawped at Becky. 'How can that be? He's just a researcher!'

'It's a Green Cross project, because I saw a letter from them to Dr Black saying they would arrange the meeting.'

'How did you get to see that?'

Becky went a bit red. 'Em, well, I had to go into his office to check his phone.'

'Check his phone? You're not a technician.'

'Pansy told me to check it.'

'What for?'

Pansy walked into the staffroom and Becky melted away to the far side of the room, looking guilty. Anthony growled, but said no more. Pansy went over to the coffee machine, produced a key, opened the door, poked about inside and pulled out the sachet dispensing coffee. She held it up to the window, looking puzzled. John, the technician, walked past and she called out loudly to him. 'John!'

The staffroom grew silent.

'How many times have we filled this machine?'

'Once,' he said.

'Just once?'

'That's right. They must have a lot in them.'

'Each bag contains enough to produce 100 cups,' said Pansy, waving the sachet at him. 'The average usage is three cups per person per day for forty members of staff. It doesn't add up. It ought to have run out by now.'

'You should move to Economics,' said Dennis Cardigan, who'd sidled close to John.

Pansy stared at him over the tops of her spectacles. 'Do shut up, Dennis.'

'Maybe people are drinking more tea?' ventured John.

Pansy checked the tea sachet. 'This is full too.'

'Fruit teas?' volunteered Harold.

Melanie giggled.

Pansy frowned. 'There's something fishy going on here.' She replaced the sachets and checked the level of the water container. 'It's full!' she cried, 'but you've all got cups of coffee and tea! Where are you getting it from?'

She eyeballed everyone in the staffroom, some of whom blushed under the scrutiny. If Arthur Scott hadn't popped his head around the door at that moment and called to Pansy, asking her to come back to his office, she might have proceeded to interrogate them all. Instead, she closed up the machine with obvious reluctance and left, muttering under her breath.

'There's something fishy going on in the staffroom,' she said, once they were in Arthur's office.

'Fishy?'

'Where are people getting tea and coffee from if the machine is full?'

'Forget the blessed coffee machine, Pansy! What progress have you made over this enormous phone bill?'

Pansy was peeved that she couldn't rant about her favourite subject but everyone knew it was better not to push Arthur when he was in a bad mood.

'Well we've checked through everyone's call list and there is no evidence of major abuse.'

'Major abuse? Major abuse!' Arthur's face grew redder. 'Do you mean to tell me that people are abusing the phone system?'

'I do my best, you know,' she said, defensively. 'I make sure that all the researchers' phones are barred from making long-distance calls. That is standard practice, but there isn't very much I can do about the lecturers' phones. They all insist on having access to long-distance call-making. They, of course, are the worst offenders. For example, Chris White made ten phone calls to Katmandu on Monday last. Ten, if you don't mind, and all in one day!

Why can't he just write to them?'

Arthur sighed. 'I know. I do wish it wasn't necessary, but he is arranging to go on a field trip.'

Pansy snorted.

'You must have discovered some hint of where the extra calls are being made from?' said Arthur, dropping his head wearily into his hands.

'Well actually I have.'

'You have,' said Arthur, raising his head and brightening up immediately. 'So, who's making the calls?'

'Dr Black.'

'Dr Black?'

'That's right. Dr Black.'

'But he's a researcher, his phone should be barred.'

'It is.' Pansy paused for effect, enjoying the way Arthur's face screwed up as he tried to puzzle out what she was saying. 'He's been using the obsolete fax line behind the filing cabinets in his office.'

'Are you telling me that Dr Black has run up £10,000 worth of extra calls in the short space of three months?'

'Yes.'

'How?'

'I don't know that yet, but he's the one who's responsible. No wonder he freaked about the burglar in his office. He must have been terrified that his guilty secret had been discovered.'

'Has Harold given you a report on his computer yet?'

'No, he hasn't.'

'Well get him onto it, Pansy! Report back to me, and make it snappy,' he growled.

Pansy rose to leave, but Arthur called her back. 'How well did you check Dr Black's references and credentials?'

'I haven't checked them. It's up to the Old Schools to do that.'

'Well check if they've checked, and get back to me today,' he barked. Arthur turned his back on her and moved to the computer at the back of his office.

Pansy left his office feeling dismissed and displeased. He hadn't even given her a word of praise or thanks for all her discoveries. Really, it was bad enough that the general staff undervalued her but Arthur! Of all people Arthur should know how hard she worked. Didn't he realise the efforts she put in simply to ensure as little money as possible was spent in the Department? It was so unfair.

Pansy left Arthur's office, muttering under her breath. She walked back to the staffroom in a most unhappy state. Everybody was gone. The cups and mugs were empty and neatly placed in the dishwasher. Pansy poked about the room and quickly discovered the kettle behind the plant display. That cheered her up a bit. Winding the flex around the kettle, she confiscated it and marched back out of the staffroom, grinning broadly.

Chris White had been waiting for Pansy to leave Arthur's office. He watched her tramp down the corridor and when she was out of sight, he knocked timidly at the office door, opening it softly when he heard a grumpy *Come in.*'

'What is it, Chris?' asked Arthur turning towards him.

'Someone has broken into my office. Well, actually, they didn't break in, they just went in.'

'What? When did this happen?'

'Well, em, eh, while I was at lunch, I think.'

'Do you mean to tell me that you went to lunch without locking your door? Are you crazy? What will it take to make you security conscious? I told everybody to lock their doors!'

Chris looked very sheepish. 'Sorry. The trip to Katmandu is on my mind. I went into town to buy a few things and just forgot about the door.'

'Have you locked the door now?'

Chris nodded.

'I'll call the police. Don't go back in until they've checked it for fingerprints. We need to know who the hell is doing this. What is going on in the Department? I've never known such a spate of criminal activity. Have you noticed if anything is missing?'

'I don't think anything is gone. Whoever it was just seemed to go through the filing tray, almost as though they were looking for something specific.'

'Tell Pansy, and say that I'm phoning the police.'

'Will you tell Pansy, Arthur? I, I, eh, Pansy is a bit, eh...'

'For God's sake, Chris, just go to Katmandu. I'll tell her.'

Chapter 17 | *College dinner*

Anni and Maud arranged to meet again, but not for a few days. Anni had received a commission to write a piece on the Norfolk Broads. This was cheering as it held the promise of further work. She was glad of a chance to begin building an interest that would leave her less dependent on Edward. He had been pleasant but uncommunicative when Anni got back from the press conference, so she simply rattled on about who she had seen and other unimportant matters, and they got through the evening. Edward was still distracted and jumpy, but he wouldn't confide in her, and Anni was slightly irritated with him.

On the plus side, she was beginning to feel more integrated into Cambridge. Her growing friendship with Maud was making a big difference. It softened her sadness at no longer having her sister nearby. She missed Cécile very much. They spoke often on the phone but it wasn't the same as seeing her face-to-face. She supposed she would get used to it, but in the meantime, there were distractions. Anni was looking forward to her first formal dinner at Edward's college that very evening. She welcomed the drive up to Norfolk, as it would prevent her worrying about what to wear and how to behave. She still felt unsettled and a little gauche in the formal world of Cambridge University.

The day went well but she was late leaving Norfolk, and she phoned Edward who said he'd go on ahead to the college and leave word at the porters' lodge that she was expected.

Because her meeting had overrun, Anni missed out on a planned shopping spree in Norwich. She busied herself, while sitting in a long slow-moving line of traffic through Elveden Forest, with making a mental check of her wardrobe. She felt unsure about how she should dress. Would it be very posh? Remembering the informality at Edward's Department, Anni decided to dress down rather than up.

When she arrived back in Cambridge, she ran up the flat, and went straight to the bedroom. She opened the wardrobe and pulled out what she'd decided to wear. But when she went to lay it out, she saw that a large box had been placed in the centre of the bed. It was ornate and looked like it held something special. Edward hadn't mentioned that he'd bought her a present. Intrigued, she opened the box.

Beautifully wrapped in gold-flecked tissue paper, was a dress, a bright red dress. Anni held it against her and stood in front of the mirror. Red wasn't a colour she normally wore. She tried the dress on. It was a perfect fit. Charmed and delighted at Edward's thoughtfulness, she finished dressing, called a taxi, brushed her hair, mended her make-up and was ready to leave when she heard the summoning sound of the taxi's horn.

The porters' lodge at the college was warm and inviting. Anni smiled to see one of the porters standing with his back to a real fire as she approached the desk. He wore a black jacket, and dark pinstriped trousers. She noticed a row of bowler hats hanging on the side wall. It all seemed so archaic, and yet so delightful. She was growing used to this feature of Cambridge. Anni gave her name, saying she was joining her husband for dinner, and the porter, whose backside must have been well toasted, unhooked a bowler and walked her over to the dining hall.

He left her at the end of the grand room, and Anni felt awed and daunted by the splendour before her. The room was huge, as big as a medieval banqueting hall. Blazing light from chandeliers and candles brightened up the time-darkened wood panelling. Portraits of impressive looking men from times gone by hung between wall lights. There were four very long tables, each running the length of the Hall. At the far end, another table was set on a raised dais. Anni looked anxiously at this top table. The people who sat there were very much on view. She was relieved when she failed to spot Edward among them. As she looked around, she saw him sitting halfway along a table, which backed onto the left-hand wall. There was an empty space opposite him. Pleased to find that she would only have to endure walking past half the diners, she made her way to his table. Edward noticed her, waved and stood up to greet her, smiling.

Anni removed her coat, and hung it on a rack at the end of the wall. She smiled shyly back at Edward as she anticipated his pleasure in seeing her wearing his gift. What she saw instead was the colour drain from his face. He was staring at the dress, and he looked shocked.

Anni walked quickly towards him. 'What is it, Edward,' she asked Anni, disturbed and distressed by his reaction. 'Are you okay?'

His mouth moved soundlessly. She stood by the vacant space on the bench, waiting for an answer and staring uncomprehendingly at him. They began drawing the attention of nearby diners. The man seated next to Anni's rose and gave her his hand, to help her onto the bench. She felt even more on show, and wished there were chairs instead of this stupid bench. It was like being back at school. She sat, feeling close to tears. Edward continued to stand and stare at her. She heard a voice from the top table call for quiet and begin to speak of she knew not what. She watched Edward slowly sink into his seat and drop his eyes to his plate.

The evening was a long ordeal. She forced herself to pick at her food. Edward barely raised his head. His food lay neglected. He spoke to no one. He refused, or was unable, to catch her eye. Anni's kindly neighbour made attempts to engage her in conversation. She responded distractedly, wishing the evening would end, wishing she understood what was wrong. Finally, diners at the top table began to leave and this signalled the end of the meal. Their departure unleashed a sudden exodus from the Hall. Edward remained sitting as those nearby rose to leave. Anni began to feel exposed. Her kindly companion wished her good evening and left. The people sitting close to Edward were sliding along the bench either side of him, as they left, leaving him silent and withdrawn. Anni leaned across.

'We need to leave, Edward,' she said.

He didn't reply. What was wrong with him? Realising she wouldn't get any sense out of him, Anni made a decision.

'I'll go to the porters' lodge and order a taxi, Edward. Follow when you're ready.'

Edward nodded. Anni retrieved her coat and left the dining hall.

Neither spoke in the taxi that took them home. Anni

finally broke the silence when they were inside the flat. 'What is wrong, Edward?' she asked. She realised there was a sharp edge of anger, and frustration in her voice.

Still Edward wouldn't speak. All he did was look at her coat and then away from her. Mercifully, the phone rang. Anni picked it up. It was Edward's father. She passed the phone to her husband and went into the bedroom, closing the door firmly behind her. Tears flowed as she tore off the dress and went to replace it in the box. The box was no longer on the bed. Anni looked around the room, under the bed, in the wardrobe, but there was no sign of it. She was certain she'd left it on the bed. Surely Eileen hadn't come to flat to clean so late in the evening? But what else would explain its disappearance? Feeling too drained to search, she hung the offending dress in the wardrobe, pulled on jeans and a jumper, and went to sit in the un-lit living room. She stared out of the window, looking into the darkness as she brooded over the disastrous evening. She could hear the muffled hum of Edward's voice as he spoke softly to his father, but couldn't distinguish what he was saying. He replaced the receiver and soon afterwards came into the living room. He didn't turn on the light.

'Anni,' he said. His voice shook. 'I have to go off early in the morning to join Dad on some family business. I should be back tomorrow evening.'

'Where are you going?' she asked, still half distracted.

'It's just a bit of family stuff. Nothing to worry about.'

He turned away before she could ask him what the family business was. It made her mad. Too angry now even to go after him, she remained in the living room until she heard him go to bed. Anni then walked around the flat, looking closely at every room, trying to spot if Eileen had been. But she could find none of the usual tell-tale signs: no bins on chairs, no cleaning materials left in the kitchen or the bathroom. What she did see was that Edward had made himself a cup of tea or coffee and he had spilled sugar on the worktop. His hand must have been shaking.

Now she felt mean. He was very upset about something. She cleared up the sugar spill. When she went to empty the mopped-up grains into the bin, she spotted a plastic wrapper on the floor. If Eileen had seen that, she would have cleared it up. Anni shook her head. It might not have been Eileen who had moved the box. Could she have misremembered where she herself had left it? It was unlike her, but she had been distracted lately, a little depressed and more tired than usual. She sighed, turned out the kitchen light and prepared for bed.

Chapter 18 | *More misunderstanding*

Late the following evening, a distracted Anni was cooking in anticipation of Edward's return when his brother, Richard, phoned.

'He's with your father,' she told him, wearily.

'With Dad? Is Dad in Cambridge?'

'No. I presume Edward went to London.'

'You presume? London? Oh, eh, right. Well would you tell him that I phoned.'

It was unusual for chatty Richard to ring off so quickly, thought Anni as she replaced the receiver.

Edward turned up shortly afterwards. Anni mentioned the call and asked how the trip had gone. Edward sidestepped her questions, and gave a brief answer to her enquiry about his father.

'He's fine. I'd better go and phone Rich.'

Anni found it hard not to feel angry and suspicious, and Edward's behaviour during the rest of the evening did nothing to dispel her unease. He was quiet and withdrawn, and it reminded her of the first time she'd encountered him in this mood.

Edward had turned up in Brussels, out of the blue, about a year after they'd first met. Anni had already arranged to dine with friends and she asked him to join them. He pleaded tiredness, saying he'd rather stay quietly in the flat. It wasn't an engagement she could cancel, so Anni went alone. She kept thinking of him, however. He seemed tired and strained, his face had been pale. Usually, when he came to Brussels, they chatted for hours as they caught up but Edward had said little beyond a quiet greeting, though they hadn't seen each other for a couple of months. When the long evening ended, Anni hurried home, only to find that Edward was gone. He'd left a note saying he was returning to England, as he needed to see his father before Robert set out on a trip to Ireland. Anni was puzzled and concerned. She phoned his Cambridge number the following morning, and several times over the next few days but never got an answer. She became more and more anxious, imagining he'd been involved in an accident or something equally dreadful. It was two weeks before they finally spoke. His manner was quiet, withdrawn and unresponsive. He wouldn't tell her what had happened to distress him and refused her offer to come over and see him. When she hung up, she found she was angry with him. A sense of powerlessness brought home the unsatisfactory nature of a long-distance relationship and she decided not to contact him again, feeling the relationship wouldn't survive the episode.

Edward got in touch several weeks later. Anni cut him short at first, but he continued to phone and eventually, after much persuasion on his part, they resumed their relationship. Neither referred to the incident that had caused the breach. It hung silently between them until pushed aside by time and new experiences.

Now, two years later, Anni saw that Edward's strange behaviour was being repeated. He was distracted and withdrawn, and very obviously distressed. He picked at his food and didn't appear to hear as, trying to lighten the atmosphere, she talked of her visit to the Fitzwilliam

Museum. He jumped up, however, to answer the phone when it rang. Anni heard him greet his father in a tense voice.

'She wasn't there, you say? Okay, I'll drive down immediately and collect you.'

Anni expected him to come into the dining room and tell her what was going on. Instead, she heard him go to their bedroom and open drawers and the wardrobe. She followed him, and watched as he packed a travelling bag.

'What are you doing? Where are you going?'

'I've got to go somewhere with Dad.'

'Where?'

'It's just family business.'

'What family business?'

Edward stopped, and looked up at her, smiling weakly. 'It's nothing that you need concern yourself with, Anni. Really.'

Anni moved into the room and stood by the bed as he continued to pack. She felt a sense of frustration as he ignored her and continued with his packing. She placed a trembling hand on his arm. 'Edward, I'm your wife,' she said, struggling to keep her voice steady. 'Family business is my business now too.' She saw what she thought was a flash of desperation on his face, as though he felt cornered.

'It's historical family business, Anni, and I don't want to trouble you with it. Dad and I will sort it out and everything will be fine.'

'Historical family business!' she repeated, her voice rising. 'Do you ever intend to share family business with me? Even the basics, the things that I should have known before you brought me here, like telling me that Maud was your cousin? What's the matter with you? Why keep that a secret? I don't understand.'

'I meant to tell you, it's just that...'

'Just what? We were bound to meet as she lives in Cambridge. What else haven't you told me? Can't you see how this troubles me? How it makes me doubt you?'

'I would have told you about Maud, but I hadn't told her about you and wanted to talk to her first.'

'Why didn't you tell her about me? Did you tell anyone about me? And if not, why not? Is there something wrong with me? You've been shutting me out of what concerns you most deeply for years. While we were living in separate cities, I could fool myself by saying that I wasn't part of your everyday life, but that's no longer true. We're husband and wife and we live together! There are parts of you, Edward that I simply don't understand. You shouldn't shut me out. It's really hurtful.'

Anni turned away as tears began to flow down her face. She wanted to say more, to ask about the postcard from Minnie, to ask who Lucy was, but she couldn't speak. Edward stood silently beside her. She saw him reflected in the mirror. He reached out to touch her but appeared to change his mind. His hand fell back to his side.

'Trust me, Anni,' he said. His voice shook.

'Why, Edward?' she spun back to face him. 'Why should I trust you when you aren't honest and open with me?'

'Let's talk when I get back, Anni. Let me go. There's something I must do. Maybe I'll be able to talk when I get back.'

'Maybe? That isn't good enough, Edward.' She walked

out of the bedroom without replying, and went to stand by the living room window. Soon afterwards, she heard the door of the flat close softly. Edward walked below the window as he headed to the garage. His movements were heavy and slow. He paused and looked up. Anni heard him sigh. She turned away from the window.

Chapter 19 | *Back to the Library*

The sound of a helicopter overhead woke Anni the following morning. In the hazy world of retreating sleep, she wondered what it was doing flying about at such an early hour. Returning consciousness reminded her of Edward's absence and their argument. She lay there miserably recalling the evening. The helicopter came in close again and she realised it was probably a security measure connected with Gorbachev's visit. She rose reluctantly: the press conference was due to start at midday.

A clump of letters lying on the mat as she passed on her way to the bathroom was a reminder of the postcard from Minnie. She picked the letters up, glad that she would be working that morning, as it would help take her mind off things. She sighed, wishing she weren't so far from Cécile. She thought briefly of going back to Belgium, but to do so, when she'd hardly been in Cambridge a month would seem like defeat.

Rummaging through the post, she found a letter from her sister and the longing to talk to her grew. Cécile wrote that she hoped Anni was settling down well, saying it felt odd not to have her close at hand. She wondered if Edward would mind her coming to Cambridge for a visit. She missed her little sister.

Anni showered in a more cheerful frame of mind. She wasn't alone. It would be wonderful to see Cécile, and there was Maud as well. She would introduce them. Maybe she was over-dramatising the problems with Edward. Apart from the episodes of reserve and withdrawal, he was great. They shared lots of interests, laughed a great deal, and she was certain he loved her, although he wasn't always demonstrative. She wanted so badly to help him. If only he didn't shut her out. When that happened, she felt as though the relationship was disintegrating and that all points of contact between them became suspended. Anni's buoyant mood swung to doubt again. Perhaps she shouldn't trouble Maud with too many questions when she saw her. Would Maud wonder if she was jealous about Edward's life before they met? She didn't think she could tell her about their row or that Edward had left without saying where he was going, or when he'd be back. His lack of openness made her doubt their marriage would succeed. That was an unbearable thought. Best not to say anything to Maud. She needed to keep the problem close, until matters were resolved. It would be better to confine herself to talking it over with Cécile.

She dressed lethargically. The telephone rang.

'Hello,' said Anni tentatively, wondering if it was Edward.

'Anni, it's Maud. Listen, I must see you. There's something I feel you should be aware of about Edward. It's a family matter really, but I do think you should know. I know we arranged to go to the cinema tomorrow evening, but could you pop into the Department today?'

Surprised at the synchronicity, Anni arranged to call into Maud after the press conference. A feeling of relief tinged with trepidation spread through her. She was keenly aware of how much she wanted to believe in Edward, despite her anxieties.

It was close to lunchtime when Anni climbed the steps to the Department. She walked into a Library teeming with students and saw George and a young woman at the issue desk. Both were looking harassed as they dealt with the students' demands. Catching his eye, Anni smiled at George. He returned her greeting and motioned with his head towards Maud's office, which was some distance from the checking desk. Anni pushed her way gently through the crowd.

She knocked on Maud's door, but got no reply. She knocked again. Still no answer. Anni opened the door and went in, thinking noise of the students might have covered the sound of Maud's answer.

'Hello,' she called.

Maud was sitting in her chair, facing the window. She seemed to be watching a squirrel on the adjacent flat roof as it chewed on a chunk of bread. She didn't move as Anni closed the door softly.

'Maud?' said Anni again, wondering at the silence. She walked over to the desk.

Maud's head had fallen to one side. Her eyes were open, but they weren't following the movement of the squirrel. Anni touched her tentatively on the shoulder. Maud tumbled forwards and fell in a heap before the window. Her left side was saturated in blood, and a pool had gathered by the foot of her chair. Shock turned Anni rigid. She stood and stared at the lifeless body.

The squirrel, which had run off at the sudden movement, returned and resumed work on the bread. The creature moved in a jerking manner, stopping and freezing between each step. Anni looked from the squirrel, to Maud, and back again. It was the smell of the blood that galvanised her finally. There was so much blood. It had spread like a sinister blanket beneath Maud.

Anni leaned down and reached out to touch Maud's hand. It was cold. She stood up slowly and walked out of the office. There was a buzzing in her ears as she made her way to the library desk. It seemed to take her hours to get there. Anni felt she was in a dream, a nightmarish dream where her legs wouldn't respond to a desperate need to run. She noticed George staring. He came towards her.

'What is it Anni?' he asked.

She couldn't speak. The words to describe what she had seen wouldn't form. Then she noticed that the girl George had been talking to was heading down to Maud's office. 'No!' she managed to say. 'No!'

The girl stopped and stared at her. Anni gripped George's arm. 'Call police... call the police. It's Maud.'

'What do you mean? Has Maud had an accident?'

Holding even more tightly to his arm, Anni leaned close to George and spoke very softly. 'You need to call the police. Maud is dead. I, I think she's been murdered.'

The look of horror on George's face made her shiver even more.

He turned to the girl. 'Ask Arthur to come down to Maud's office, Melanie. Tell him it's an emergency.'

He began shepherding Anni back to Maud's office. 'I have to see,' he said.

Anni didn't want to go back, but she thought, suddenly, that maybe she'd been wrong. Maybe Maud had just hurt herself. She followed George into the room.

Anni stood with her back to the door. From that position, she could just see Maud's hand and the edge of her head. George walked to the other side of the room There was no sign of the blood from where Anni was standing, and her heart lifted momentarily. A bird screamed outside, scaring the squirrel who ran off in that stop-start manner. George made a noise that seemed like a mixture of a gulp and a swallow. He was standing near the pool of blood and he was shaking. Neither spoke. Someone tapped at the door and called Maud's name. Anni went to the door and cracked it open. Arthur Scott was outside, and Melanie stood behind him.

'Hello Anni,' he said, looking puzzled. 'What are you doing here? Melanie said George wants me for an emergency. Where's Maud?'

Anni drew him in and closed the door quickly.

Arthur immediately saw Maud's head on the floor. 'Maud. Maud. Have you hurt yourself?' he called, moving towards her. He stopped and stood still as he took in the full scene. George had begun to weep. Arthur looked despairingly from George to Anni. His face was ashen. 'It looks like she's been stabbed,' he said, and his voice shook.

'Yes,' replied Anni.

Arthur collected himself quickly. He went to pick up Maud's phone, stopping himself before his hand touched the receiver, and before Anni could frame the word *don't*.

'I'll phone the police from my office. Will you both stay here, please, and don't let anyone in until I return.'

Anni nodded wearily. George continued to sob.

Becky was staring out of the window, trying to catch a glimpse of the helicopter flying back and forth overhead, as she chattered to Sue, who was working diligently.

'Pansy found the kettle yesterday. She was fuming.'

'Hmm,' murmured Sue.

'Yes. She's going to refer us all to Arthur.'

Sue didn't respond. She was busy with a pile of papers. Becky looked back out of the window.

'I wonder what that man is doing, standing by the bicycle sheds. Do you think he might be about to steal a bike?'

Becky's phone rang. She ignored it. Sue looked up and saw her colleague was straining to get a better look at the man outside. The phone stopped ringing, then started again.

'Someone's not giving up,' said Sue.

Becky sighed, returned to her desk and picked up the phone.

'Becky, it's Arthur. I want to see everybody in the staffroom in five minutes. Don't go near the Library, though. Enlist what help you need, but make sure that every single person in the building turns up. Okay?'

'But Arthur, it's almost lunchtime. People will be going out!'

'Lock the front door. Do it now. Put a note on it - whatever, but make sure that you get everyone to the staffroom in the next five minutes. Do you understand?' He hung up without waiting for an answer.

'Did you hear that?' said Becky to Sue.

'Em, just your side of the conversation.'

'Arthur wants everyone in the staffroom in five minutes. Everyone in the building, he said.'

'Really? Did he say why?'

'No.'

'Do we all have to go? I'm trying to sort out a lecture timetable. Could you ask him why?'

'I don't think so,' said Becky. 'He sounded incredibly firm. I'd be afraid to ask. It was his serious *Head of Department* voice. He said I was to lock the front door.'

'Lock the front door?' repeated Sue. 'Gosh, I've never known him to say that before. It must be serious.' She stood up and looked at the clock. 'We've now got four minutes. I'll start at the top and you start at the bottom.'

Everybody wanted to know why they were being summoned to the staffroom, and it was difficult to persuade their colleagues to go downstairs. Several people ignored them.

Arthur was waiting by the door looking at his watch, when they reached the staffroom.

'Is everybody here?' he asked.

'Em, well, eh, no,' said Becky, looking nervous. 'Dennis said he was too busy and Victoria said I was to push off and...'

'Becky, I said everyone and I meant everyone. Now go back and get them!'

Becky's lower lip began to tremble. 'But they refused and said that...' She started to sniff and a small tear oozed from the corner of one eye. Arthur covered his own eyes.

Chris and Anthony, who'd been looking on, exchanged glances. They walked up to him. 'We'll produce the missing persons, Arthur,' they said.

While they were gone, Arthur stood by the door. Pansy approached him.

'Is this meeting about the kettle, Arthur?'

'No Pansy, this meeting is not about the blasted kettle!'

It was obvious to all that he was close to tears, Pansy stayed uncharacteristically silent, and drifted slowly backwards into the gathered group.

Shortly afterwards, a sheepish Dennis, a cross-looking Victoria and two cowed researchers edged in past Arthur's distracted glare. The room was silent, despite the throng of people. The sound of a police siren in the distance joined the noise of the helicopter overhead, and impressed those gathered with a greater sense of unease. Finally, Arthur spoke.

'I am sorry to haul you away from your various pursuits. Sorrier than you can imagine.' He stopped to clear his throat and blink away tears. 'I have some very bad news about Maud. I can't think of a way to break this news gently, and you need to know because the police will arrive shortly and they want to speak to everyone in the building.' Arthur cleared his throat. 'Maud is dead.' He paused. 'Actually, it's worse than that. It looks like she's been murdered.'

A hush fell over the room. If Arthur had been looking at his staff instead of the floor, he would have seen the looks of horror and astonishment and the unspoken questions on their faces. *Maud dead*? *Murdered*?

Arthur spoke again as the sound of the police siren grew

louder. 'Would you all stay here please until I've spoken to the police?'

The siren stopped, but the car's blue light kept flashing. It was just beyond the windows and it lit the staffroom in bursts of blue, framing the people who were standing still, as though they were on the set of an old silent movie. They had gathered close together.

In a corner of the staffroom, Becky began sniffing and sobbing. Pansy walked up and down the length of the room, like a caged and frustrated animal. Every now and then, she shot irritated glances at Becky. Harold was rapping, as usual, on the window sill nearest the coffee machine. That everyday sound was curiously soothing. Pansy ignored him and everyone else stayed silent. Potty sat patiently in the centre of the room Chris perched quietly on one side of him and Victoria on the other. Now and again, she shook her head. Becky let out a louder sob and Pansy stopped pacing.

'For God's sake, Becky, stop snivelling! We're all upset.'

Becky tried to snivel more quietly. Several people glared at Pansy. Sue went over and put her arm about the girl.

Arthur returned with Inspector Grant and Detective Sergeant Meredith. The Inspector told them that no one was allowed to leave, as they would be interviewing everyone who had been in the building at the time the body was discovered. His words echoed around the room. The body. Not Maud, but the body.

The police rounded up the students who'd been in the Library. Anni, George, and Melanie who was semi-hysterical, were taken to Arthur's office, accompanied by a constable. Grief seemed to have robbed George of the ability to do more than cry quietly. Anni hugged the distressed Melanie tightly - comforting herself as well as her companion.

In the staffroom, people were called out individually, interviewed and asked to leave the Department. Coats, keys and bags were collected under police supervision. Bags and pockets were searched before people were finally allowed to leave. Dennis looked at his watch as numbers in the staffroom slowly dwindled.

'How long more are we going to be left here? I have a seminar at three o'clock.'

'Not anymore you don't,' said Sue. 'Can you imagine the police directing the undergrads past the body on their way to the seminar room?'

'Oh. I suppose not. Blast it, I'll have to make that seminar up later.'

'Dennis!' remonstrated the mild and gentle Sue. 'Surely your seminar is a small thing under the circumstances.'

'Huh.'

Another long silence fell, broken finally by Victoria. 'What sort of place is this, where innocent people can be murdered at their desks?' Victoria launched herself off her seat and began striding around the room.

Becky was heard sobbing again and the heartless Pansy began to approach her threateningly. She was prevented from chastising her by the entrance of a policeman.

'Miss Mallard?' he called. Pansy jumped. 'We'd like to speak to you.'

Chapter 20 | *The Backs*

Having questioned them briefly, Inspector Grant left Anni, George and Melanie alone. Melanie was the first to be questioned more thoroughly, and she was still weeping as she left Arthur's office in the company of a kindly WPC. Her statement must have been quite short as it wasn't long before a detective returned for George.

Anni looked out the window. She'd come in to see Maud just before one and the sky was now beginning to darken. She looked at her watch and found it was nearly four o'clock. Three hours. Maud had been dead for almost three hours. Shock and a sense of unreality had made the time skip past almost without her noticing. She tried to persuade herself that it was a dream, a nightmare, but failed. All that her mind's eye could see was Maud: Maud sitting, Maud falling, Maud bleeding, Maud lying dead on the floor. In her abstraction, she hardly noticed the detective return. He took her back to Arthur's office.

'I'm sorry that we've kept you so long, Mrs Holroyd,' said Inspector Grant. 'It was necessary to establish who was the last person to see Miss Cadogan alive. Melanie Jones was talking with her about fifteen minutes before you entered her office. We are questioning all the students, but so far no one noticed anyone else entering her office before your arrival.'

Anni had a moment of panic. *They suspected me!* she thought.

The Inspector raised his hand, seeming to guess what was going through Anni's mind.

'We don't suspect you. The reason you've been here so long is that we have been establishing your innocence. It's fortunate that you have a watertight alibi, Mrs Holroyd. As it is, you must have walked rather quickly from the press conference to arrive here when you did. We have established you were there until 12:45pm, and George has confirmed that he saw you come into the Library at about 12:55pm. We will need to finish fingerprinting the office before we can exclude you completely, but that is simply routine. It's most unfortunate that the Library security camera had no film in it.'

Anni looked down at her fingers, which were stained black around the nails. The police had taken her prints.

'Inspector, Maud was my husband's cousin. Far from wanting her dead, I wish very much that she was still alive.'

The Inspector pulled at his moustache. 'You husband isn't in the Department today, Mrs Holroyd. Can you tell me where he is?'

'I'm afraid I can't, Inspector. He's away on family business.'

'Family business?' repeated the detective. 'Where has he gone?'

'I don't know,' said Anni, without thinking, and feeling a surge of the sorrow she had felt the previous night. And now there was cause for greater sorrow. She looked up at the Inspector. He was staring keenly at her, and Anni felt like she was being peeled and her inner secrets and vulnerabilities being exposed.

'I gather you haven't been married very long,' he said,

'but do you know how relations were between your husband and his cousin?'

'Fine, I believe,' said Anni, conscious that her voice was wobbly. 'I've never noticed any reserve or ill-feeling between them.'

'Why don't you know where your husband is?'

Anni looked down at her hands. Her palms were sweating. Could he see that? 'He left suddenly last night after a phone call from his father. He said it was urgent. His father lives in London.'

The detective asked for Robert's number, which Anni didn't have. She watched him raise his eyebrows. It all sounded so lame. She felt a tightness in her chest.

'Are you and your husband getting on well together?'

'We get on fine,' said Anni, painfully aware of the tremor in her voice.

'But he went away last night and didn't tell you where he was going.'

'No.'

Inspector Grant stood and pulled a card from his breast pocket.

'Mrs Holroyd, we would like to speak to your husband as soon as he returns. Will you give him my card and ask him to phone me, please?'

Anni extended a shaking hand to take the card, puzzled at the detective's insistence about speaking to Edward. She heard him ask the WPC to take her home.

'I can manage,' she said, 'I can manage.' She had to turn aside to hide the tears that were leaking into her eyes.

'It's no problem, Mrs Holroyd,' said the WPC, and she put her hand on Anni's arm. 'Where do you live?' Anni felt too miserable to argue or resist further.

As they were leaving the building, an ambulance drew up to the main door. The driver and his companion moved quickly to the rear doors and unloaded a trolley. They wheeled it past Anni and the WPC as they were descending the steps of the building. Fortunately, this action drew the attention of the small crowd who'd gathered to see what might be seen. Anni and her escort managed to sneak away quietly. When they reached the edge of Coe Fen, Anni insisted on making her own way to the flat. Mercifully, she was allowed to do so.

Once inside, Anni walked through the growing darkness and sat by the window. The manner of Maud's death seemed to hit her like a collapsing wall. She sank to the floor and wept. Though their acquaintance had been brief, Anni felt the loss keenly. Maud, who had been bright, amusing and communicative, was dead. She stayed on the floor in the dark, wondering if Edward would return. An hour passed. Then another.

No longer able to cope with inaction, she got up, washed her face, pulled on a coat and went for a walk. Sounds of merriment and laughter came from the Mill Pond as she passed on her way towards the centre of town. She walked more briskly to leave it behind, wondering where to go and feeling the strangeness of the city by night. The road ahead led to The Backs. The long stretch was deserted, and the backs of the colleges well hidden by dark, shielding trees. She walked along aimlessly, feeling alone despite passing pedestrians, motorists and cyclists. She stopped at the top of the road, crossed over and gazed in on Westminster

College from behind its row of railings. She saw nothing, however, her gazed was turned inwards. The memory of finding Maud's body was going round and round in her mind. She thought she could still smell the blood. There had been so much of it. Tears poured down her cheeks as she leaned her face against the cold railings.

The sound of thumping house music from a passing car drew her back to the present and she noticed a couple of pedestrians staring curiously at her. Craving solitude, she retraced her steps, moving away from the busier area of Northampton Street. She made out the vague shape of King's College Chapel in the distance, as she walked back along Queen's Road. It reminded her of the visit there with Edward, and she slowed down, thinking she would stop and look, when she was nearer. She might draw comfort from a pleasant memory. Unaccountably, she began to feel she was being watched. Turning around, she saw a shape a few feet from her, bending over the low rail which ran along The Backs. The person's head was turned away and she couldn't say if it was a man or a woman. Feeling shaky and disconcerted, Anni moved off. She heard the sound of footsteps behind her, and cast a surreptitious glance backwards. Was the person who'd been loitering was following her? Anni began to walk a little faster. The footsteps gathered speed. Her heart began to thump.

She spotted a group of people about to cross to her side of the road. She began to run and came up level with them as they headed down a path that led to the river. Feeling safer, she again looked behind her. The follower had stopped as she came up with the crowd. It was the same person. Why would anyone follow her? Anni turned back and walked quickly to stay in step with the group, hoping the path would lead to light and public spaces. She crossed a hump-backed bridge and drew closer as they walked up a dark narrow street with tall stone buildings rising either side. At the top, she realised she was in Trinity Street. She clung to the reassuring company of rowdy crowds. Now she feared solitude. Had she imagined malevolent intent in the unknown person? It was possible. Maud's murder, a strange town and a husband who seemed to be hiding a secret had deprived her of her usual equilibrium.

Anni walked round and around the peopled parts of Cambridge city centre, trying to shake off the sense of fear and unease, but being in the middle of people who were doing normal enjoyable things made her feel incredibly lonely and it emphasised her sense of isolation and distress. She walked the long way back to the flat, keeping to main streets all the way. She looked up at the windows from the street, hoping Edward would be home. The windows were dark. Anni felt in her pocket for the key as she walked up the stairs, and had a moment of panic as she realised she had come out without it. Relief washed over her as she remembered the spare key over the lintel. It was quite a stretch to reach it, but finally she managed and, letting herself in, she turned on the lights. She found a note propped by the phone in the hallway.

> *I can hardly believe Maud is dead. And that you should have found her! Oh Anni. The police say it happened in the Department. Who could have done it? I've been in London with Dad and the phone was ringing as I walked in. The police insist on seeing me tonight. But I'm sure I'll be back shortly. We have to talk. Edward.*

Anni picked up the phone and dialled her sister's number.

'Cécile?' she said, feeling a surge of relief at the sound of her sister's voice. 'Oh, I am so glad to find you home. Will you be in Bouillon for a few days? Yes, good. I'm, I'm coming over. Can you pick me up in Brussels?'

'But why, *chérie?* Is something wrong? How is Edward?'

'Yes, there is something wrong. Oh Céc, I really do need to talk to you. I'm all right, and so is Edward, but I'd prefer to tell you my story when I see you. I'm heading to London and I'll let you know what train I've caught.'

Edward returned to a dark and empty flat, and he too found a note propped by the phone.

> *I can't cope, Edward. I have to get away for a few days. I'll be in touch. Anni*

Chapter 21 | *No escape*

Anni gazed out from the tower of Great St Mary's. It was early in the morning and the sun was just a little above the horizon. In good light, the view of Cambridge would be panoramic, but in the weak shafts of rising sun, many of the buildings were still in shadow and even those she knew to be built of warm-coloured stone, looked grey, like cold old men in long drab coats. The roof of King's College Chapel caught the light. It looked so delicate, like handmade lace that had been starched and ironed.

'Isn't it beautiful, Edward?' she said.

There was no reply. Anni turned in time see her husband disappear around the bend of the steps which they'd climbed to reach the tower. Puzzled, she followed him, but he disappeared each time she turned a curve in the winding stairs.

When she reached the ground, Anni discovered the door to the church was locked. Frightened, she called to Edward, but all she could hear was the distant sound of his footsteps going down and down a stairwell she hadn't noticed earlier. Anni followed and finally saw him standing in what seemed to be a crypt beneath the church. Edward walked into a corner and vanished from sight.

Anni gazed around the empty crypt. A bird with brightly coloured tail feathers appeared carrying a flower pod with a lighted candle in its centre. He laid it in the middle of the room, as though it was an offering. The bird hovered, then lifted up the light, and flew with it to the corner where Edward had been. He laid it by the wall, chasing away the darkness. One of his tail feathers fell off and Anni bent to pick it up, but the bird swooped and caught the feather before she could, then quickly flew away.

She looked warily at the coffins lining the walls of the crypt. Where had Edward gone? She could see no exit beyond the stairwell. Then, somewhere behind her, she heard the grinding sound of stone on stone and turning, saw the cover of a sarcophagus begin to slide open. Terror gripped her like a vice.

'Edward!' she screamed, but there was no reply.

Anni stood still, hardly daring to breathe, her heart thumping with terror. Slowly, the crypt blurred and faded from sight. It was pitch dark, but she no longer felt as cold as she had in the crypt. Something beneath her felt soft. The bed. She was in bed. She sat bolt upright. The relief of finding she had only been dreaming was swamped by feelings of panic as she looked around wondering where she was. Slowly, through the darkness, she recognised her surroundings. The 'sarcophagus' was a linen chest, just a piece of harmless bedroom furniture. She was in her room at her sister's house, in Bouillon.

'Anni?' Her sister's anxious voice cut through the darkness. 'Are you all right?'

The door opened and a comforting light shone through.

'I've just had a bad dream,' she replied, shakily.

Cécile came in and sat on the edge of the bed. She stroked Anni's hair. 'What was it about?'

Cécile took Anni for a walk in the nearby forest the

following morning, certain the exercise and change of scenery would do her good. Anni knew her sister was watching her surreptitiously. She took long deep breaths, stopping often to smell the heavy pine-perfumed air. It was pushing that awful smell of blood away. Even now, two days later, it lingered in her nostrils.

'Are you okay, *chérie* Are you having trouble breathing?'

'No. It's so lovely to be back, and the air is wonderful. I can't get enough of it.' Anni looked around at the beautiful scenery, though she'd known it all her life. 'How different the landscape is from Cambridge,' she sighed.

'But you said Cambridge was lovely too.'

'Oh, Cambridge is beautiful, but not like this. It doesn't have the power to heal and uplift as these forests and hills do. Buildings don't soothe you in the way that natural scenery does.' She stood awhile, quietly taking in the view, while Cécile waited patiently by. Anni sighed again. 'I guess I feel quite disturbed about the murder, and it has coloured how I feel about Cambridge.'

The sisters were standing on the side of a mountain looking down onto the valley below and gazing at a peninsula in a bend of the river *Semois*, known as *Le Géant.* Most of the island was covered in trees. The sense of peace and solitude was intense.

'Hmm,' said Cécile, 'Cambridge isn't getting a very good press.'

They walked on, stopping eventually in a little mountain village. Cécile drew Anni into a little café, and watched as Anni stirred her coffee distractedly. 'You haven't talked much about why you're here.'

Anni looked up. 'I don't know where to begin.'

'Well if I say that it's not very nice to leave your husband after such a short space of time, especially without telling him where you were going, will that prompt an answer?'

Anni stared at Cécile. 'How do you know I didn't tell him where I was going?'

'Because he phoned looking for you.'

Anni had a sudden feeling of nausea. 'What did you tell him?' she asked.

'Simply that you were on your way to Bouillon to stay a couple of days with me. Reserved as ever, he asked no more. I couldn't miss the distress in his voice, however.'

Cécile paused, and Anni knew she was waiting for a reply. Well this was why she'd come to see her sister. She had to talk to someone or she'd go mad.

'No,' she sighed. 'It wasn't very nice to walk off without a proper explanation. But I really wasn't thinking straight. Besides, he's not been great with explanations either.' She, in turn, paused, and this time Cécile kept quiet. Anni tried to pull her thoughts together. It shouldn't be difficult, but lately she often felt tired and drained. She looked out through the glass of the window. The peaceful view calmed her. 'Sometimes,' she said, 'I don't know whether I feel worse about Edward or about Maud. I still can't quite believe she's dead, though I saw her myself. I keep wishing that it was just a bad dream. Why would anyone kill her? She was friendly. She was fun. She seemed to be well liked. And to think she was murdered in a Cambridge University department, with lots of other people around. It's almost unbelievable.'

'Yes. It even made the news here, probably because it happened in the University of Cambridge.' said Cécile.

'Did it? Oh Cécile, Maud was so good to me. She made me feel at home and she made me laugh and she told me heaps of things about Edward and his family that I never knew before. And in the short time that I knew her, I had already begun to value both her companionship and the sense of her being a relation. And with Edward behaving so oddly, I think I connected more quickly and more deeply with her than I usually do with people. In a sort of a way, I relied upon her to, well to be another link with Edward. Hoping, I suppose that she could give me some explanation for his odd behaviour. You would have liked her too. She was down to earth, amusing, capable and intelligent.'

'Poor Anni, I can see you've lost a friend. One wouldn't wish such a death on an enemy, let alone someone who was valued. And I think finding the murdered body of a friend must be one of the worst things imaginable.'

'Yes.' Anni stopped talking. A whiff of the smell came back. She lifted up the cup of coffee and breathed in the smell. That helped. 'Yes, murder is a desperate thing. I've always thought that, but always at a remove. This dreadful crime has been a double blow, because I knew Maud and because I found her body. I feel connected with the murder, and I can't shake that feeling off.'

Anni began to cry. Cécile pulled her chair closer to her sister and hugged her. 'Come on, let's go back outside. There's a bench at the end of the village.

Anni looked up. The woman behind the counter was staring at her. She hadn't realised because she'd been sitting with her back to the counter. Cécile was right. They needed more privacy to talk about these things.

The sisters walked through the small village, and found the bench. They sat quietly for a while. Tears would keep oozing from Anni's eyes. 'I do know that, given time,' she said, wiping her eyes, 'I will deal with Maud's loss and the manner of it. But I do need that time.'

'Yes. But it is not just Maud, is it, Anni? What are you not telling me?'

Anni looked at Cécile. Her sister knew her too well. She never could hide things from her. 'It's just that, well, the murder coming, as it has, on top of my worry about Edward, it's almost unbearable. I'm haunted by that worry. I can't get away from the fact that he is behaving strangely.'

'What do you mean, *behaving strangely?*'

'He's different, Cécile. I've always thought he was a strong character, but it's, well it's like something or someone has sucked out some of his character. He's different to the man I knew in Brussels.'

'That could be because, like you, he's getting used to being married. It is a big change for both of you.'

'I think it's more than that. There are important things I don't know about him

'Such as?'

'To begin with, why is he so, so clammed up? No normal person hides their family, unless they're ashamed of them. His father seems fine, and so does Richard, and Edward is clearly very fond of both of them. Maud was funny and generous and he seemed to be fond of her too. So why, Cécile? Why is he hiding something from me? Why didn't he tell me about his family?'

'You're sure that he is hiding something?'

'Yes, yes I am. Add that to the way he's behaving. He seems tired a lot of the time, he's having nightmares though he pretends he isn't, sometimes he's distracted. He's not the man I thought I married. He's lost his oomph, his drive. And I know that something is eating away at him. But why won't he tell me what it is?' Anni felt herself getting angry.

'I don't know,' said Cécile. 'I don't really understand Edward...'

'And there is another thing,' said Anni, butting in. 'Though I don't know whether it's related to me feeling so unsure about Edward.'

'What's that?'

'I've begun to feel I'm being watched. I felt it first shortly after arriving in Cambridge, at the Fitzwilliam Museum, where I met Maud, and again the evening poor Maud was murdered. I was walking along The Backs, on Queen's Road, and I'm sure someone was following me. I couldn't make out who it was but, well you know the way you sometimes get a cold feeling - hairs on the back of your neck - that sort of thing?'

'Anni! Are you just being a bit fanciful? You've suffered a dreadful experience and I think you simply feel vulnerable. After all, why would anyone follow you?'

Anni shrugged. 'I can't think why. Perhaps I'm imagining things. I've certainly been overwrought, which explains that nightmare last night. But it doesn't fit with the feeling of being watched in the Fitzwilliam. That happened before the murder.'

'You went there with Maud. Has it occurred to you that perhaps you weren't the person being watched, that attention was really being focussed on Maud? Perhaps you just got a passing glance because you were with her.' Cécile shivered. 'Have you told the police about that?'

'No, I didn't think of it. Oh Cécile, what if that was the murderer?'

'You must tell the police. The museum may have CCTV footage. This could be important, Anni.'

'Why didn't I think of that? But what about the episode on The Backs though? Oh, I don't know. I can't figure any of it out.'

'*You* don't have to figure it out, Anni. That is the job of the police.'

Anni felt close to tears again. 'And I just can't understand why anyone would want to murder Maud,' she said.

'You didn't know her very well, Anni' said Cécile, taking her sister's hand and stroking it gently. 'There may have been something about Maud, something neither you nor her work colleagues were aware of, something that was sufficient to drive someone to kill her. I don't mean that unkindly, but I think we must assume that the killer meant to murder her, and that it wasn't a case of mistaken identity.' Cécile tightened her arms around her sister. 'Promise me one thing, Anni, that you won't go near the Department until the police find out who killed Maud. I want to hear they're behind bars, and only then will I be certain that you're safe.'

Anni hugged her back. That was an easy promise to give. She shuddered at the mere thought of going anywhere near the Department ever again. It would always remind her of Maud and finding Maud's body.

They spent the rest of the day peacefully, walking and shopping for dinner. Cécile cooked, leaving Anni to rest and sip a drink, think her own thoughts and gaze out from the balcony onto the lights of the town below. When they had eaten, Cécile cleared away and sat back down at the table. Her expression was serious.

'Can we talk about Edward now? You have to go back, you know, and you have to talk to him.'

'Oh, I don't know what to do,' replied Anni, standing and beginning to pace up and down the balcony. 'It just isn't right! To go off and not even to tell me where he was going. *Family business* he said. I am his wife! Is that not family?'

'You don't need to convince me. I admit it is an odd thing for a newly-married man to do, but he has behaved this way in the past.'

'I know, but we weren't married then!'

'I don't think people change, just because they get married. A disposition to disappear will be as much a feature of a husband as of a boyfriend.'

'I know, I know,' said Anni, continuing her pacing.

Cécile took a long look at her younger sister. 'You're thinner, Anni. Your hair has lost some of its bounce and shine. Have you been ill?'

'No, though I have been more than usually tired.'

'Sit down, Anni.' When her sister sat, Cécile reached across and took Anni's hands in her own. 'You always knew Edward was reserved,' she said, softly. 'I used to think that you enjoyed the mysterious side of him.'

Anni glanced at her, surprised that her sister could know such a thing. It was true. 'Perhaps I did in the beginning,' she acknowledged. 'But the more I began to care for him, the harder it was to deal with the idea that he was conducting another life elsewhere, one that I couldn't share in. I have to be able to trust him, Cécile, and I can't if he keeps important matters from me. It's not just that he went off without telling me where he was going or when he'd return. There was something else.'

'What?'

'It probably sounds a bit silly now that I look back on it.'

'Tell me.' Cécile pressed Anni's hands.

'A postcard turned up a few mornings ago, addressed to Edward. There was no message, just a simple signature. Someone called Minnie. He hid it away. He never even referred to it.'

'Why didn't you ask him about it? That would have been the obvious thing to do.'

'Well, I... I didn't ask him because I didn't believe he would tell me who it was from.'

Cécile made a clucking sound. 'Don't you see that you're not trusting him? There may be a simple explanation to the postcard.'

Anni felt miserable. 'I see what you're saying, but I'm so used to him clamming up. He stops dead in the middle of a conversation, like a horse that refuses to jump a fence. I thought it would make a difference, our being married. Strange and terrible things are happening and I need to be able to talk to him and understand. He makes me feel like a stranger.'

'Anni, I am very concerned about you. That was a disturbing dream you had last night. It's clear to me that you mistrust Edward and I think that accounts for his disappearance in the dream. He leaves you by yourself to face the unknown. I guess it's hardly surprising that you should dream of coffins given Maud's murder.'

'I'm afraid of Edward's secret, of whatever it is that he has buried, and why it is hidden. Part of me doesn't want to unearth it. What am I going to do, Cécile?'

'Why are you asking for my advice? You asked for that a long time ago when he disappeared off the scene and I told you then that, in your shoes, I wouldn't consider having a relationship with a man who was capable of walking out on me for months on end, without even checking to see if I was alive or dead. You chose to resume your relationship with him, and you did it for your own reasons. I wouldn't have done it. I don't know why you did.'

Anni sat pale and quiet. Cécile leaned over and took her hand.

'I'm sorry. That was harsh. It isn't that I don't like Edward. You know I care very much for him, and, so far as I have had anything to do with him, he has always had both my respect and regard. But I don't like the way he seems to be keeping secrets from you. You are correct. Something is very wrong and you simply must try and sort it out - if you want to stay with him, that is. I presume you do want to stay with him?'

Anni had been staring down at the table. Now she looked up at her sister. 'Maybe several years down the line I will feel calm about him, not worry if he goes off and blocks me out, if indeed the marriage lasts that long. Right now, though I can't manage to do that. The intensity of my feelings for him, oh how can I describe them?' Anni struggled to explain herself. 'It's as though he is the axis upon which my world swings. If he weren't there I would stop swinging, stop living. I simply can't contemplate life without him. And I swear that, outside of the times he behaves like a stranger, I'm sure he feels the very same way about me.'

'Well if you feel that strongly about him, there is only one answer. You have to go back and sort this mess out. But for your own peace of mind, Anni, insist upon him being open and honest with you. If you don't do that, the marriage is doomed. That may sound unkind, but I believe you know it to be so.'

'Yes,' Anni's reply was more an intake of breath than a word.

'On a more hopeful note,' said Cécile, 'the bird carrying the lighted flower pod is, I think, an encouraging sign. It seems to symbolise a relationship, which is bright and alive, even in the surroundings of a crypt. So maybe it will be worth the effort after all.'

Chapter 22 | *A visitor*

Anni returned to Cambridge, feeling less tense and distressed. Cécile had offered to travel back with her, but Anni said she wanted to confront her fears and Edward alone. The short break and the chance to speak openly about her fears had done her good. She also felt somewhat recovered from the initial shock of finding Maud dead. She picked up a newspaper at King's Cross, only to see that the national press was making a big story of the murder. They'd found out about the burglary, and the heart that had been left on Maud's desk. There was quite a lot of coverage and the usual speculation but, from what she could gather from the reports, the police had yet to establish a motive for the murder, let alone identify the killer.

For the first time since dashing off to Belgium, Anni realised it might have been wrong of her to leave the country without referring to the police. She felt a ripple of guilt as she thought about Edward coping with the consequences of her impetuous flight. The feeling was quickly followed by one of anger at him. That was exactly the position he'd left her in the evening before Maud was killed. *God. It's all so complicated,* she thought. *Will we ever sort it out?*

Anni caught the train to Cambridge and took a taxi home from the station. It was early evening when she reached the flat. She let herself in quietly. Looking down the long hall, she saw Edward sitting in the dark living room looking out the window. Anni pushed the hall door closed. It clicked loudly in the silence. Edward looked up. He rose to meet her.

Later, as she was cooking, he came up behind her, placing his arms around her, kissing her head and hair, speaking softly to her. 'Why didn't you leave me a proper note, Anni? I was crazy with worry until I phoned Cécile and found you were on your way to see her.'

She turned around to reply, hugging him back to soften what she was going to say. 'I couldn't forgive you for going away and leaving me to deal with Maud's death. You should have been there, or at least I should have known where to contact you.'

'Anni, Anni, forgive me. It will be all right. Really it will.'

'We have to deal with this Edward. To talk about it.'

'I know. I've had quite a bit of time to think about things. I haven't been to work, Anni. The Department is closed. Mostly as a mark of respect to Maud, but I guess Arthur realised that we would find it difficult to carry on as normal after the murder. It will be hard enough when we return, but at least we'll have had an opportunity to get some distance from what has happened. The only people I've seen in the past few days are the police, and Paul. Otherwise, I've been here, waiting for you to phone, wishing you would, and realising more than ever the depth of my feelings for you.' He buried his face in her hair. 'Tomorrow, Anni, in the daylight, I will tell you a sorrowful tale. Let's have this evening just to ourselves, like the evenings we used to spend alone in Brussels.'

Before Anni could reply, they heard a ring at the door. Edward pulled a face.

'It's probably Paul,' he said. 'He might have noticed you returning and he's probably baked a cake or something. He was worried you'd left me for good.'

Anni smiled a little guiltily as Edward went to the hall and peered through the spy hole. He called back to her.

'It's Richard!'

He opened the door and soon the brothers joined her in the kitchen.

Richard left his bag by the door. 'I thought I'd come over for a few days, chaps,' he said, hugging both of them. 'I've been to see the old man who is feeling low because of Maud's death, and I'm sure the pair of you aren't much better.'

Anni felt frustrated with the interruption, but it was hard to be cross with Richard. His smiling face and Edward's obvious pleasure in seeing him, prompted her to return his hug warmly, say they were delighted to see him and tell him that his timing was just right, as supper was almost ready. Richard grinned at her, moved his bag to the spare room, and was back in a flash, rubbing his hands together, and sniffing as he walked over to the stove.

'That smells wonderful, Anni,' he said, lifting the lid of a big pot. 'Edward is a lucky man!'

Chapter 23 | *Back to work*

It was shortly after 8.00am and the staffroom was full. Arthur had asked his staff to come in early for a brief chat before getting back to work. They were gathered in small groups, with one or two people sitting or standing alone. Dr Black was one of the loners. He spotted Melanie, who was also on her own. Pursing his lips, he marched up to her. 'Have you been in my office?' he asked, aggressively.

Melanie looked startled and clearly found it difficult to reply to the unexpected onslaught. She stayed silent, looking lost for words.

'You have, haven't you? You nosy interfering little b...'

Harold grabbed Dr Black by the shoulders and turned him away from Melanie. 'Like man, cool it This is no time for picking on people.'

Dr Black cowered a bit under Harold's angry gaze and muttered. 'Someone has been in my office, moving my papers and I don't like it.'

Pansy came up to them. 'Don't be silly. Someone has been in everybody's office. The police have been checking the whole department for clues to Maud's murder.'

Dr Black shrugged off Harold's hand and moved to the far end of the staffroom. Harold glared after him.

'By the way,' said Pansy, also glaring after the retreating figure, 'have you checked his computer yet?'

'He's been refusing to let me into his office. I feel so

angry with him now that I swear I'll stay late and get the job done this evening.'

Pansy smirked. 'Good, but I'd better give you a master key so that you can go in while he's out.'

'Only way to get the job done, doll.'

Pansy scrunched up her face, as though she'd suddenly smelt something nasty. 'Must you call me *doll*?'

Harold hardly heard her rebuke, he was still glaring at Dr Black. 'I don't usually like doing things behind people's backs, but did you see the way he behaved to Melanie?' Harold shook his head and his orange locks bounced. 'Out of order, man. Out of order!'

'Fine,' said Pansy. 'I'll let you have a key when the meeting ends.'

Melanie came back up to Harold as Pansy walked over to Becky.

'Babe!' said Harold, greeting her warmly. 'Like how've you been?'

'Oh Harry, it was so brave of you to save me from Dr Black. I'm really scared of him.' She gave a little sniff. 'It's all too much, you know' She sniffed again. 'And I just don't think I can go into the Library again. I've been having nightmares about the murder.'

'Poor Babe. You just leave it to Harry. I'll sort it out for you. Go and get a cup of tea.'

Harold went after Pansy, passing Sue and George who were sitting by the window. George was pale and seemed twitchy. Sue seemed to be trying to soothe him. Potty was looking on benevolently.

Dennis cut into their conversation. 'I need a few things

from the Library urgently, George. Can you look them out for me as soon as this meeting is over?'

'I don't know, Dennis. Can it wait for a bit?'

'No. I have to have them now. I can't have this business getting in the way of my chance of promotion.'

George shook his head sadly. 'Whoever left the heart on Maud's desk made a mistake,' he said. 'They should have left it for you. You're the one with a gap where your heart should be.' He and Sue stood up and moved away.

Dennis looked after them. 'What's biting him?' he asked, addressing the whole room.

Arthur came in at that point, sparing Potty the trouble of replying.

'Thanks everyone,' he said loudly, drawing their attention, 'for coming back early this morning. I know it hasn't been easy and that it won't be for quite some time. We will all miss Maud very much.'

Arthur paused and looked at the faces before him. Many were showing signs of distress. He sighed. He was sad himself but he needed the Department to be up and running as soon as possible. That was his job as Head of Department. Glancing out the window, he saw students arriving in time for the resumption of lectures at 9.00am. One was locking his bike under the windows of the staff room, and Arthur saw him being approached by a man who was obviously a reporter. He turned back to his audience.

'Another thing we will have to handle over the next while is nosey reporters. I can see one at this very moment.'

'It's not just the press and TV, Arthur,' said Anthony, 'the Department has become a tourist spot. When I tried to get in yesterday, I had to face of a coach load of tourists, snapping everything with their pesky cameras. They even had a guide and he was pointing out the Library windows. How are we to live with that?'

'Hmm, it is bad but we've been promised extra security, so I'll try to get them to stop the 'tourists' coming in through the main gate. That at least we can manage. As for the press, I would greatly appreciate it if people didn't talk to them. They'll hang around as long as they think there is something to be gained, but if we present a united and silent front, they will soon give up and find another story. I am very concerned at the impact this will have on the student population. It may mean there'll be a drop in student numbers next year.'

That prospect didn't seem to interest his audience much. Next Michaelmas was a whole year away and Arthur knew it was his problem, and not something they would need to be concern about. He understood that the recent murder loomed far larger for them.

Pansy spoke, 'Have the police made any progress identifying the murderer, Arthur?'

'They have found a set of fingerprints in Maud's office which they think belong to the murderer. It is possible that you will all be re-interviewed.'

'Interviewed again?' exclaimed Dennis. 'Whatever for? What do we know? And why aren't they talking to the students? After all, a crowd of them were in the Library when Maud was killed. It could very well have been one of them!'

'Of course they'll be talking to the students,' growled Arthur. 'And what are the parents and friends of these students going to say about us? A murder committed in the Department, and the first term hardly over? It's appalling, just appalling.'

Sue went across to him and patted his arm sympathetically. He shook his head sorrowfully. 'I know you're very upset about Maud,' she said, tactfully. Arthur was drawing angry glances. It was the loss of Maud that was uppermost in their minds.

'Of course I am!' Arthur sounded weary and dispirited. 'Of course I am,' he repeated, more softly, and took a deep breath. 'Well I guess we should head off to our duties now. Oh, and those of you on the Grant Committee, could we meet in my office this afternoon? Pansy, will you arrange that please?'

Everyone filed out of the room, following instruction to set about the business of getting back to normal.

Pansy received a call from the police as soon as she returned to her office. They were looking for Edward Holroyd. She checked the timetable and said that he wasn't due to teach until the afternoon and would probably be at home. They rang off. She continued with the task she had set herself, which was to search through every file for a note or letter or anything on, from, or about Dr Black, though she still maintained adamantly, to Arthur, that it was the responsibility of the Old Schools to check out his credentials. The task took Pansy's mind off Maud, giving her something pleasurable to do. The prospect of bringing a difficult person down was just the sort of thing to delight her. And the timing was just right. Arthur had insisted she put the kettle back. He said it was hard enough on people to manage the loss of Maud without having to deal with the loss of a cuppa too. Pansy didn't want to give in but Arthur made her.

Potty had followed Arthur back to his office and he closed the door firmly behind them. 'Arthur, I need to speak to you.'

'What is it, Peter?'

'It's Dennis. His behaviour is getting worse, and that's saying something. It's worse than what one would expect even from the ill-disposed person we all know so well.'

'What do you mean?'

'It's the way he's so fired up about Victoria. He really is going too far this time.'

'He's always been a difficult man to handle, Peter.' Arthur sat heavily into his chair, and waved his old friend to a seat.

'It's more than that now, though,' said Potty. 'He seems totally unmoved by Maud's death, yet he's known her for years. And from what I overhead this morning, he behaved quite badly to her the other day.'

'He used to admire Maud,' sighed Arthur. 'He even tried to start a relationship with her some years ago.'

'I didn't know that,' said Potty.

'No one did, except myself and Edward.'

'What happened?'

'Maud, in her friendly way, went out with him a few times, for a drink, to the theatre, that sort of thing. He read more into it than friendship and she had to make it plain that she wasn't interested. He took it badly. I don't think he ever forgave her. I have always thought that he remained quite split about the episode - angry with her for rejecting him, but still admiring her on another level.'

'Hmm, that fits with my own opinion of Dennis. You know he still lives with his mother?'

'I certainly do,' said Arthur feelingly. 'The blessed woman phones me to complain whenever he's late home.'

'She has quite a hold over him. He's never married, nor has he managed to move out and set up his own home. We know only too well that he doesn't enjoy teaching. It doesn't sound like much of a life. I think Dennis lashes out at women because he can't forgive his mother for the lack of success in his life. He blames her, but he can neither confront her nor to break away. Instead, I see him getting into situations where he can vent his anger on other women - Victoria, Maud, the younger non-academic staff, the students. I wonder if he's even conscious of how bad his behaviour is.'

'Potty! I'm impressed with your in-depth study of Dennis. Should you have chosen a different profession?'

Potty gave a short laugh. 'I'm an old man, Arthur. It's just a case of having seen it all before and recognising the signs. Speaking of signs, the reason I'm mentioning all this to you is that I think things might be coming to a head with Dennis. I fear he won't be able to hold his anger in anymore and that means the Victoria business may well escalate.'

'Blast the man. I've enough on my plate without having to add him to it. The situation doesn't bode well for the meeting this afternoon.'

'Well I suppose I could try having a word with him though I don't think it will make much difference,' said Potty.

'Please try, Peter. A blow-up between Dennis and Victoria is not what we need. She's no pushover. She'll give as good as she gets. In fact, I'd put my money on her to gain the upper hand. But we don't need this, Peter. We don't need this.'

'I know, Arthur, I know. We all miss Maud, and we're all shell-shocked. I'll do what I can.'

Chapter 24 | *The Grant Committee*

The meeting of the Grant Committee was short and to the point. Arthur had called them together to discuss one matter only, that of funding for the new chair.

'What I have to say is that a bequest has recently been made to the University and the Vice-Chancellor has decided to award it to this Department. There is sufficient money to fund a chair and two researchers. It is also possible that we will attract more in the way of grants from the Research Councils, and maybe the EU, depending on who gets the chair. I am explaining it in this way because I want you to see very clearly that the person appointed will need to be conducting successful research at the present moment and they must have a viable proposal for extending that research into the foreseeable future. We will be advertising in all the usual places and the national papers, but I am expecting a strong submission from this Department.'

Arthur then brought the meeting to a close, without the usual question and answer session. 'Put any questions you have into a letter or an email,' he said, looking around the circle of surprised faces, 'and I will reply individually to each.' He knew there would be fall-out from the announcement and he had decided it would be politic not to be present when that occurred. He picked up a pile of notes and departed to a convenient lecture, leaving his colleagues behind to discuss the news among themselves.

Dennis's face looked as dark as a thunder-filled sky. 'Well I know just what all that means,' he spat the words out, and the people sitting either side of him sat back into the chairs to avoid the blast. 'It really makes me furious that every time I put in for a research grant, a reason is found to refuse me the funds.'

'Try taking a closer look at your research proposals, Dennis,' said Victoria, who was sitting well away from Dennis.

'My research is perfectly viable,' shouted Dennis, 'and I'm convinced that I don't get half the recognition I am due. All because Arthur is following the government's lead on slotting women into positions of power.'

Victoria snorted and her dark eyes flashed angrily. 'Anything I get, I get on merit,' she said. 'And if I get this chair, it will be purely because of the quality of my work.'

'And you will have my complete support, Victoria, if you get the chair.'

The look on Victoria's face made it clear to her colleagues that she understood support from Dennis was the very last thing she might expect. Several of them wriggled uncomfortably in their chairs.

'You are a nasty, anally-retentive, spiteful under-achiever, Dennis,' she said, standing up and leaving.

The other academics afterwards swore they saw steam emerging from Victoria's ears as she swept out of the room. Dennis carried on abusing her in her absence, ignoring the stream of people getting up and leaving in disgust.

Eventually, Potty was the only one who remained. He tapped Dennis on the shoulder. 'Get a grip on yourself, man. She's the best candidate in the Department and you will have to swallow humble pie if she does get the position. What is the point in building up so much bad blood?'

'The woman irritates me!'

'You need to separate her manner from her work, Dennis, if for no other reason than out of respect for Maud's memory. It's not very nice to be creating a lot of unnecessary unpleasantness when most of us are upset at losing her. You will make enemies not friends if you continue like this.'

'Don't you think Arthur is promoting her because she's a woman?'

Dennis seemed not to have heard a word of the advice Potty had given. 'I do not.'

'Well I'm sure he is and I won't take this lying down.'

Potty shrugged his shoulders. He sat a while, looking at Dennis. For his part, Dennis didn't even seem aware that he was in the room. Potty sighed, rose slowly, and went to the door. He looked back at Dennis, but there was no response. He left the room.

Dennis looked at the door as it closed behind him. Even though he'd worked himself up into a passion, a tiny voice inside told him he was foolish to lose the support of the one person who was always polite to him. He had an urge to follow Potty and ask for help, but a welling up of anger drowned that good intention, and he sat on in the room, alone and fuming.

Chapter 25 | *A window on the past*

'That's great coffee, Anni,' said Richard, leaning forwards for a refill. Anni saw that Edward was grinning at her. 'More toast Richard?' she asked.

'Em, well, I might just have another piece to go with the coffee. And the apricot jam is smashing.'

Anni laughed. 'I'll begin to think that you're never fed in Ireland, Richard. You had two helpings of supper last night, and here you are this morning, hungry as ever.'

'I never bother cooking for myself. It's not worth the trouble when you live on your own.'

'Don't be tempted to feel sorry for him, Anni,' said Edward, giving Richard a playful dig. 'He plays that 'poor me' card so successfully in Dublin, he manages to be fed by others six days out of seven.'

'It's not fair to be giving Anni such a bad notion of me, Edward. I thought I might manage to pass myself off before her with some credit, seeing as she doesn't know me so well yet.'

'Edward is only teasing. You're welcome to coffee, toast, suppers and anything else we can offer when you come to stay,' said Anni. This was the most relaxed she'd seen Edward since he had brought her to Cambridge. The atmosphere in the flat was warm and cosy.

Richard munched away happily, finished his coffee and, taking her at her word, refilled his mug. The phone rang and

Edward went to answer it. He came back to the kitchen quickly. Anni noticed the happy look had gone from his face.

'That was the police. They want me to go over to Maud's house with them.'

All three fell silent. Richard laid down his piece of toast and stood up to join Edward in the doorway.

'Would you like me to come with you?' he asked.

Edward looked as though he was going to accept the offer, but Anni watched his eyes settle on her. She knew she looked sad and she made an effort to lighten her expression.

'It's okay Rich,' said Edward. 'I think it might be kinder if you stayed with Anni for a while before going back to Dad's place in London.' He kissed Anni and left, saying he hoped he wouldn't be long. Richard sat back down.

'Poor Anni,' he said.

'Oh Richard, she was your cousin. You must feel so much worse than me.'

'Yes, I do feel bad, but I didn't find her body. That must have been a dreadful experience.'

Anni suddenly began to weep. Richard leaned forward and squeezed her hand. 'We have all been very attached to Maud. It's almost impossible to take on board that she is gone, let alone take in that she was murdered. But, Anni, I think you and Edward will feel her loss more than I will. Living in Ireland, I saw very little of her but she's been a good friend to Edward for many years and I can see that you became fond of her quite quickly.'

'Yes,' replied Anni, dabbing at her eyes.

'We can't change what happened, Anni. I comfort myself with thinking that Maud did have quite a good life, for all that it was a terrible way to die.'

Anni tried to smile, but she knew she wasn't making a very good job of it. Each time she finished mopping up her tears, her eyes filled up and over-spilled again.

They sat for a while without speaking. Richard broke the silence. 'Would it cheer you up at all to hear some of the tales from when life was good and lots of fun for Maud, myself and Edward?'

It was a straw to grasp. 'Oh yes,' said Anni. 'I think it would help if I had nice thoughts of her to overlay the sadness. The odd thing is that Edward has no family photos here. If I didn't know better, I would swear he was an orphan. I did ask if there were any but he said everything was at your father's house. I have seen a few photos because Maud had them in her office. Maybe the police will let me have some as a reminder of her.'

'Well I'll tell you what, Anni, we don't need photographs because I will draw things for you. I'm a dab hand with a pencil, though I say so myself. Have you got a drawing pad, or some plain paper?'

Bemused but interested, Anni went to fetch a large writing pad. They cleared the table and sat down again.

'The first thing I will draw is the house at Druchsheen where the three of us used to spend all our holidays and get up to the most enjoyable devilment that you could ever imagine. Maud lived there with our grandparents.'

Richard checked the point on the pencil. 'First there was a long drive which went around a corner before you could see the house.' He drew quickly as he spoke, and a curving gravel drive came to life, with potholes, trees, grass and flowers at the sides, and even a rabbit.

'I always remember the feeling of excitement as we drove up the driveway. Parts of the house would become visible, bit by bit.' Here he began to draw chimneys and the roof. Anni laughed to see him begin where most people would end.

'Now you have to see it the way we did,' said Richard. 'There was the roof; we could spot that over the trees. Then Ed and I would crane our heads through the windows of the car and it was a competition as to who would spot the house proper first. That made us even more excited, but Dad and Mum never minded. They laughed at us. And the first thing to be seen was the side wall and the window of what was always our bedroom. See, there it is. Then, underneath, we'd spot the long windows of the dining room and then, almost too quickly,' and his hand flew across the drawing as he tried to keep pace with himself, 'the middle top floor windows and the main door below. First the fanlight and then the door itself, or part of it really, because it was always open and Maud was always waiting at the top of the steps, looking out for us. There she is, her little face pale with excitement and she stretching up on her toes to see the car through the trees. A big grin would spread across it when she spotted our two heads hanging out of the car. And we would call out to her, saying, *we're back Maud, we're back! did you miss us?*' Richard drew the car with little heads and arms poking out from the passenger side.

'And then she'd get all shy and so would Edward and it had to be me who would leap out of the car, run up the steps and say it was great to see her and weren't we all going to have lots of fun again this summer and how were the dogs, though I could have seen that for myself because they were barking and jumping up and down around us. And then she would laugh and say it was grand to see us and, losing her shyness, would come clattering down the steps to help get the suitcases out of the car. And Gran and Grandad would appear in the door smiling, and Ed and I would race back up to give them a hug too.' The grandparents smiling faces appeared on the page above Maud's, and Anni felt almost as if she was there watching everything happen.

'And once the bags were unloaded, we'd all go off inside to the dining room and have tea, with brown and white soda breads and the most marvellous rock cakes that ever I've had in my life. Ah, Gran was a wonderful cook. And the three of us would sit together eating and drinking tea and laughing at everything and nothing, while the adults sat smiling tolerantly, doubtless hoping for a bit of relative quiet in which to catch up with all their own news.'

Richard pulled the drawing from the pad and started on another page.

'You paint such a different picture of Edward,' said Anni, scrutinising the finished drawing. 'I see this smiling happy youngster, full of fun and not at all reserved. Do we all change so radically in our lifetimes?'

Anni looked up suddenly, and saw the sadness on Richard's face, mixed with a searching look at her. He said nothing, though, but licked the tip of his pencil and continued drawing.

'As soon as we had eaten all the rock cakes, we ran off into the orchard at the back of the house. Here it is, with fruit trees of all ages growing in a higgledy-piggledy way.

Dad used to hang ropes from the sturdier trees to make swings for us, but you had to have a few cushions or the coarse rope would cut mercilessly into the sides of your thighs.' Richard drew Maud swinging up into the branches, while the boys stood nearby.

'We'd spend hours together out in the orchard. That is where we would catch up with our own news - out of sight and earshot of the *ould wans* as we called them - and where we would cast massive aspersions on other members of the family, depending on who we felt cross with at the time. And, invariably, we would be cross at Saint Him and Saint Her.'

'At whom?' asked Anni, intrigued but puzzled. Was this an Irish way to describe people?

Richard stopped drawing and looked at her. 'Do you mean to tell me that Edward hasn't told you about Saint Him and Saint Her?'

Anni had to laugh at his expression. 'He has not,' she replied.

'How much has he told you about the family?'

'Hardly anything, Richard, I didn't know Maud was his cousin until she told me so herself.'

'He must be in a worse state than I realised,' said Richard, and he looked worried.

'What do you mean?'

'Oh, nothing much,' he said, shaking himself. 'He's become more and more reserved over the years, but I take no notice of it myself. It will be all those dry dusty Cambridge University colleagues of his. Never mind, Anni. A few years with you will change him back to his old self.'

Anni smiled but shook her head. It was hard to feel confident about that.

'And in the meantime, I'll tell you this story far better than he might.' Richard removed the orchard picture from the pad and began drawing a face.

'This is Great-Uncle Gussie, or more formally, Father Augustus Cadogan. He was known as Father Cad in the parish, behind his back of course, and 'Saint Him' to Edward, Maud and myself. He was Grandad's elder brother and lived the life of a gentleman at Druchsheen until claiming to have a miraculous vision which had such a powerful effect that he immediately went off to train for the priesthood. As he got the calling late in life, he never progressed beyond parish priest, but it would be difficult to meet a more pious, hypocritical old git if you walked the length and breadth of Ireland forty times.'

'That bad?'

'Worse. Look at those beady eyes full of arrogance and disdain. He considered himself above everyone in a strongly-held belief of his own outstanding holiness.'

Anni watched, fascinated, as Richard finished drawing a wizened face with scraps of hair hanging onto the sides of the head, the beady eyes prominent despite being small dots in tiny slits, and the whole face sitting upon a scrawny neck set into a commanding dog collar.

'Who was Saint Her?' she asked.

'She was his sister, Miss Concepta Cadogan. She used to live with Gran and Grandad, but as soon as Saint Him was given a parish, she raced off to act as his housekeeper.' A female version of the wizened face came alive under Richard's speeding hand. The main differences were the greater quantity of hair, and the collar to her dress. It was high and stiff.

Anni could see that she must have been a very prudish old maid. She was amazed at the way Richard brought the stories to life with the drawings. 'Why didn't you work as an artist, Richard?'

'It would have been too lonely. I enjoy company and I certainly get plenty of that working as a genealogist. People always want to tell me their stories and I always want to listen. I couldn't have chosen a better field.' He gave a last flourish to his drawing. 'There she is, the mean-minded old crone.'

'What did they do to annoy you so much?'

'Well she annoyed us because she treated him as if he were on the brink of canonisation, puffing him up by referring to him as *Your Reverence* to his face, *His Reverence* to our faces, and making out that we weren't fit to be in his company and that we should be grateful to *His Reverence* and to God, not to mention herself, for the opportunity to spend time with such a holy man. We wouldn't have minded enduring all the holiness, and we might even have borne with the arrogance and the sermons, but it was on the question of food that we hit a sticking point.'

'Food?'

'Indeed. Food. Whenever our parents and grandparents went to the theatre or a concert, we were marched off to the presbytery for a religious dinner. Saint Him would recite the longest grace in history before allowing us to sit down and then, we would be given a lone anorexic sausage while Saint Her placed a steak the size of Africa in front of him. And for dessert, he would have what amounted to a bowl of sherry trifle, while we would be given a ramekin of rice pudding. She gave him wine and port to drink, and gave us tepid tap water. The injustice of it used to make us seethe.'

'Oh Richard,' said Anni, laughing, 'you must be exaggerating.'

'I am not! Edward will back me up. We revolted in the end and refused point blank to be sent there again for meals. After that, on their night out, Gran would make us a cold pie and we used to set everything up in the dining room just as it was in the presbytery and take turns pretending we were Saint Him and piling a huge serving onto one plate and laughing so much that we could hardly eat at all. And I know it was desperately irreverent of us, but whoever was acting as Saint Him would be allowed to trade his giant portion for the highest offering of Hail Mary's, Our Father's or whatever prayers we could think of.'

While he was talking, Richard had been filling in the drawing, putting the plate with the huge steak in front of Saint Him, tucking a napkin into his dog-collar, drawing Saint Her standing to his right, beaming down on his bald head, and putting the children at the far end of the table, staring at their sausages and water with disbelieving horror. Anni was spellbound.

'Of course we had all of this fun in the days before Minnie. It never was the same after she came on the scene.'

'Minnie was there?'

Richard glanced up sharply at Anni. He looked a bit guilty, and she thought he'd mentioned Minnie before thinking, so caught up had he been in the drawings and the past. 'Ah,' he said, 'you know about Minnie.'

'Well, em,' mumbled Anni, wondering how to reply.

The phone rang and Anni rose to answer it, glad to have

a little time to frame an answer. It was Robert, looking for Richard. Anni passed the phone over and went back to the kitchen, where she began making a pot of hot chocolate. Richard followed her after having a short conversation with his father. He came and stood by her at the hob. He sniffed the bubbling pot.

'He's very shocked about Maud. I've said I'd go up to London straightaway. He's going to meet me at King's Cross station. Do you mind me heading off?'

'No, no, of course not. Well I do in a way, because I've really enjoyed the stories and especially the drawings. But there will be other opportunities and of course you must go up to Robert. But have a cup of hot chocolate before you go. It's bitterly cold out there this morning.'

'That would be lovely, Anni.'

She poured a cup. 'Would you like it sweetened?'

Richard laughed. Anni smiled. He was just like his brother. She didn't ask how many spoons, just piled sugar in and stirred. Richard cupped his hands around the steaming drink.

'Well I'll be staying until the funeral,' he said as he sipped, 'so I'll see you again in a few days.'

He patted his pockets. 'Do you have a train timetable?' he asked.

Anni went to the hall and picked up the one she kept by the phone.

'Oh good,' said Richard, consulting it. 'There's a train in half an hour. I'll catch that easily. It's only a fifteen-minute walk from here.

'Let me drive you to the station,' pressed Anni.

'Not a bit of it, I'll be fine.'

'But Richard, it's so cold today.'

'I'll walk quickly. That will warm me up, as well as the delicious hot chocolate.'

'Let me give you one of Edward's coats,' she said, as Richard was about to walk out of the flat in just a jacket. 'I'll feel happier thinking you are warmly wrapped up at least.'

'You're a darling,' said Richard, 'and Edward is a lucky man. I'll borrow the coat, since I'm only off to London and I'll be able to return it soon.'

Anni helped him into the coat and waved him goodbye from the door. She went back inside, smiling to herself as she tidied up in the kitchen and placed the drawings safely in the sitting room. When she had finished, she decided to go for a walk herself.

It really was bitterly cold outside and she had to walk briskly to keep warm. She decided to go only as far as the nearby shops in Newnham, then made her way quickly back to the flat, feeling it was brave of Richard to walk all the way to the station in the freezing temperature.

Edward returned a little while later. He told her of the sad visit to Maud's house, identifying her personal possessions for the police. 'They're going through everything minutely,' he said, 'all her personal papers and letters. Maud would have hated such intrusion.'

'It's a horrible thought, but they need to find out who had a motive for killing her.'

Edward sat silent, thinking over what had happened, then sat up and looked around. 'Where's Rich?' he asked, suddenly remembering his brother.

'He's gone to London to see your father. He phoned and seemed depressed, so Richard went to cheer him up.'

'Did he say when he'd return?'

'No, but I think he doesn't mean it to be too long. I loaned him one of your coats. Imagine coming out in the depths of winter without a warm coat!'

Edward smiled and shrugged his shoulders.

Anni told him what she'd heard of Richard's conversation with Robert. 'Was your father very fond of Maud?'

'Yes. She used to visit him regularly. They started up quite a friendship when she moved to London. I guess he was lonely after Mum's death.'

Anni looked intently at Edward, and for once he didn't turn away. 'There are things I should tell you about the family. Perhaps I should have mentioned them before.' He stopped speaking, and Anni held her breath, intent on hearing what he might say. 'You know my mother has been dead for many years?'

'Yes, you told me that.'

'What I haven't told you is that she was murdered.'

'Murdered!' repeated Anni, shocked. 'Oh Edward, that's terrible. What a dreadful thing to happen.'

Anni thought of Maud. 'Has Maud's violent death reminded you of that?'

'Yes. In a way, it has made it a double shock.'

He stopped talking, put his head into his hands and began to weep. Anni was shocked. She sat next to him, stroking his arm, and letting him cry undisturbed. Eventually, he raised a wet face. 'It's funny,' he said, and his voice shook, 'how one can manage to forget all the horrendous feelings associated with a terrible event. They disappear and you think they are gone forever, but when I heard about Maud, all the pain of Mum's passing welled up inside me, as though it had lain dormant in some corner, like a clawing beast waiting for its name to be called aloud, so it could come out screaming and roaring.'

Anni was struck by the strength of the image Edward had conjured up. He was shaking. She wondered what it had cost him to keep those emotions hidden. She was stricken with guilt at having left him after Maud's murder. 'I'm so sorry I left you alone to bear it,' she said, and her own tears began to spill.

Edward hugged her. 'I know I haven't been straight with you, Anni. I know I have caused you anxiety. I understand that you were hurt and angry and needed to speak to someone you believed you could trust. I'm not angry with you for going to see Cécile.'

He wiped the tears gently from her eyes. 'Sweetheart, it's okay, or perhaps it will be. Maud's murder opened up a part of me that has been locked away for years. Maybe it was as well that I was on my own. Without you to console me, without work to divert me, and forced as Maud's closest relative to deal with the police, I found myself facing up to the very events which made me withdraw all those years ago.'

'Do you feel you can talk about it now?'

'Yes, I think I can.' Anni felt her heart begin to pound. Edward stretched his hands across the table to hold hers. The sound of a police siren cut through the moment, heightening its intensity. The patrol car's flashing light was just below the windows of the flat. As they registered that something unusual was happening, their doorbell pealed.

Chapter 26 | *Tackling Dennis*

Ignoring Potty's advice, Dennis Cardigan again began to canvass his colleagues in an attempt to secure support for his research. He gave them copies of his most recent publication, a piece from three years earlier, co-written with a team from the Centre for Soil Research. His name was last on the list of contributors, indicating how little he'd put into it, but Dennis had skin as thick as rhinoceros hide, and rarely felt the need to blush. He outlined his research plans vigorously, suggesting to his colleagues that they might like to work with him, even going so far as to offer a 'coalition' arrangement to Anthony Macmillan. Of all the people he approached, this was his most serious mistake. Anthony was known for being cutting and sarcastic. Fortunately for Dennis, he'd approached Anthony in his office and the dressing-down he received was private rather than public. Nonetheless, the sound of raised voices from the ferocious argument that followed drew attention. People stopped as they passed Anthony's office. They couldn't hear clearly what was being said, but they could identify Dennis's voice and the tones were sufficiently vitriolic to prompt them to express fears that a second murder might be committed in the Department.

The police were still conducting interviews in the building. Somebody mentioned the argument to them and they decided to re-interview Dennis and Anthony. When Arthur heard about this, he called all the academics to the boardroom for an urgent meeting.

Arthur started the meeting by saying that the police had suggested to him that he needed to sort out an internal problem which they felt was interfering with their ability to do their job properly. Arthur was furious, but trying desperately to contain himself. The tension in the room was tangible, and he feared a major screaming match would erupt if he said one wrong word.

'Who was involved in this argument?' he asked.

'I was,' said Anthony, sheepishly.

Dennis, clearly still cross and obviously smarting from the cutting edge of Anthony's tongue, was not at all remorseful. 'He started the argument. The blame lies entirely with him.'

Coughs and murmurs spilled from those around the table. Arthur ignored them. He realised he would finally have to take the bull by the horns. Offering up a silent prayer, he turned to face Dennis. 'What was the argument about?'

'Funding and research,' said Dennis somewhat arrogantly.

'Don't you mean *funding and research ... and who gets the new chair*?' said Arthur.

'Well of course it has to do with that,' shouted Dennis. 'I want to see that the selection process is above board and that I get a fair chance at the professorship. After all, I am the longest serving member of staff here.'

'Not quite,' said Potty.

'I'm the longest servicing member of staff without a professorship,' Dennis raised his voice even further, almost howling in Potty's ear. Potty drew back in surprise at the attack. 'And if I'm not satisfied with the person who's appointed,' continued Dennis in a slightly lower tone, 'I will lodge a complaint that you have ignored my long service and expertise in the interests of awarding the job to a woman just because she is female!'

'I just can't believe the prejudice of this guy,' said Victoria glaring at Dennis.

Arthur turned to her. 'Victoria, would you be so kind as to leave the room? Temporarily, of course,' he added, seeing the look of confusion on her face. 'I suspect Dennis has more to say. It will doubtless be non-flattering and I would like to spare you further distress.'

Victoria stood up. She was clearly reluctant to leave, but no one could miss the look of determination on Arthur's face. When the door closed behind her, Arthur lowered his voice and looked solemnly at Dennis.

'Once and for all, Dennis, let me tell you that the award of a professorship will be made purely on merit. You insult your colleagues and me, not least Victoria, by suggesting that other reasons will influence a decision on who should be appointed. You've been told before that you're upsetting your colleagues at a time when we can ill afford the additional distress. You should not make any further attempt to canvass support. You should apologise publicly to Victoria for causing her distress.' Everyone held their breath. 'Finally,' said Arthur, 'I will suspend you if you don't comply with these requests.'

No one dared speak and the atmosphere in the room was electric. Dennis began drawing breath noisily through his nostrils. No one had ever heard Arthur speak so seriously. Victoria, who put her head around the door, broke the suspense.

'Is it safe to come back in yet? I feel a right prawn out here.'

'You may as well come back in, Victoria,' said Arthur. 'Dennis, do you have anything to say to Victoria?'

'I do not.'

'In that case, please leave the room, lock your office, and leave the building. I will be in touch.'

Dennis rose slowly, casting malevolent glances at Arthur, his colleagues and especially Victoria. He left the room, slamming the door behind him with such ferocity that they felt the vibration through the table. When the door had stopped shaking, Arthur, still standing, turned to Victoria.

'Victoria, I would like to apologise, on behalf of Dennis, for the distress that his clumsy canvassing for support has caused. Everyone present will join me in assuring you that he has acted independently. He is alone in his paranoiac speculations and all of us wish you - and anyone else who considers applying - success and may the best man, or woman, win the post.'

The chorus of *hear hear* was unanimous. The cheer dissipated the tension and smiles began to appear on the previously troubled faces. Dennis had his ear pressed firmly to the door, so heard it all. He stomped off down the corridor.

The meeting was breaking up a few minutes later when Pansy burst into the office.

'Have you got a minute, Arthur?' she asked, breathlessly. 'I need to speak to you alone.'

Full of bonhomie after vanquishing Dennis, Arthur

answered flippantly. 'There will be no more secrets in the Department, Pansy. What is that you have to say?'

Pansy bit her finger, and looked very different from her normal assured self.

'Come along, spit it out,' encouraged Arthur. 'Whatever it is, we're all ready to hear it.'

'It's the police,' she said. 'They arrested Dennis as he was leaving the building!'

The buzz of approval in the room was thunderous. Somebody rapped on the table, and others joined in, stamping their feet on the floor. Arthur looked shocked.

Pansy kept chewing on her finger. 'It's worse than that,' she said.

The occupants of the room fell silent. Pansy had their undivided attention.

'What is it, Pansy? What is the matter?' asked Arthur, impatiently.

'The police actually came looking for Edward. They only took Dennis away because they couldn't find Edward.'

'But what do they want Edward for?'

'They say, they said... they said that Edward's brother has been murdered.'

Chapter 27 | *An arrest*

Inspector Grant burst into the hallway as soon as Edward opened the door. He was accompanied by Detective Sergeant Meredith and two uniformed constables.

'Dr Holroyd,' he said, hesitating, Anni thought, when he saw she had come into the hallway to stand by her husband. He was silent for as long as it took to fill his lungs with air. The Inspector looked away from Anni and began again.

'Dr Holroyd, your brother, Richard Holroyd, has been found seriously injured with stab wounds at the railway station. We're treating the incident as attempted murder.'

Anni felt the pit of her stomach fall away. She put a hand on the wall to support herself. Edward stood like a statue. The policemen stared at them.

'Injured? Injured, not dead?' gasped Edward, managing to speak.

Anni put her arms around him and they clung to each other for support.

'He is very seriously injured,' said Inspector Grant, 'but not dead. We've taken him to Addenbrooke's Hospital.'

Tears welled up in Edward's eyes. He sank his head into Anni's hair and she felt him shaking.

'When did you last see your brother, Dr Holroyd?' asked Inspector Grant, in a hard and aggressive tone.

'This morning,' said Edward, lifting his head and wiping

his eyes. 'At breakfast, just before I met you at Maud's house.'

'Did you drive your brother to the railway station?'

'He walked,' broke in Anni. 'I offered to drive him there but he said he wanted to walk.'

'What time did he leave?'

'Could we defer answering these questions, Inspector?' pleaded Edward. 'I want to go to Addenbrooke's to see Richard.'

The Inspector ignored him and repeated his question to Anni.

'It was shortly before lunchtime,' she replied, puzzling over why he wanted to know the time.

The Inspector Grant took a step towards Edward. 'You left Miss Cadogan's house just before midday, Dr Holroyd. Where did you go if you didn't come back here? We already know you haven't been in the Department this morning.'

Now it was Edward's turn to look puzzled. 'I went for a walk, Inspector. I got back here around 2.00 or 2.30pm.'

'Why did you go for a walk on such a cold day?'

Anni understood that Edward was finding it difficult to reply. Anni spoke for him. 'My husband had just been helping you go through his cousin's belongings. That was upsetting for him.'

'Dr Holroyd,' said the Inspector, solemnly, 'I'd like you to accompany us to the station as we think you can help us with our enquiries into the murder of Maud Cadogan, and the attempted murder of Richard Holroyd.'

'Can I help you more there than here?' asked Edward.

'You will be helping us with our enquiries if you accompany us to the station. There are questions we would like to ask about the death of your cousin. The situation is more imperative now that your brother has also been attacked.'

Anni's face was pale as a bleached sheet. She could hardly take on board that Richard, with whom she'd been laughing a little over two hours ago, was critically ill. He might even be dead. Edward was speechless.

Edward must realise he was suspected of being involved in the crimes. The uniformed policemen stepped forwards at a sign from the Inspector, and they began to draw him away from Anni.

'I'm sure this won't take very long, Mrs Holroyd,' said Inspector Grant, as he watched Anni's hang onto Edward. But she failed to stop them separating her from her husband.

'Wait!' she shouted, pulling a coat from the hooks in the hallway. She passed it to Edward but Inspector Grant intervened and took it from her.

'Is this the coat you were wearing earlier, Dr Holroyd?'

'Yes.'

The Inspector gave it to his colleague. 'We'll need to keep that for forensic checks.'

Edward seemed too stunned to react. Anni was furious. 'I'm coming to the station as well,' she said, emphatically. 'You are very wrong to suspect my husband of harming his brother or cousin. You will quickly find he is not involved, and that this additional distress could have been avoided.'

She drew another jacket from the coat rack and handed it to Edward, then put on her own coat.

Chapter 28 | *Waiting*

Anni sat in the dull public area of the police station. She could hear the chattering of people working in a room behind the front desk. Every now and then a constable would come in from the back room and flick through a large register, or open cabinet doors or drawers. Anni knew she was being observed but she was too anxious to care. The wait went on and on. She rose and paced up and down, looking at notices on the walls - about keeping your house secure, setting up a neighbourhood watch scheme, and spotting the signs of drug taking. Nothing held her attention for long. She kept thinking of Edward and Richard. Why would anyone want to stab Richard? Was it drug-related? Was Cambridge such a violent city? Why were they questioning Edward? It was extraordinary that two members of his family had been attacked in such a short space of time. What could it mean?

The constable came back to the desk. She went up to him. 'Do you know if my husband will be much longer?' she asked.

'There's no saying how long they might be,' he replied, though not unkindly.

Reluctant to leave, Anni sat back down. Hardly had she done so when a couple of policemen entered the station with Dr Black. She recognised him, though she'd only seen him once. He recognised her but looked away quickly. 'This way, sir,' said the policemen, leading him to the door through which they'd taken Edward earlier. It comforted Anni to think Dr Black was also being questioned.

Now she began thinking of Richard, and worrying about him. She thought back to the morning and his laughing face, how it had glowed as he told his stories. It was hard to overlay the image with one of him being critically ill. She looked out of the window. It was getting dark. The whole afternoon seemed to have worn on and still she was sitting, waiting. What if Richard died? and Edward didn't get to see him? She must do something. Anni went up to the desk. 'Have you heard anything from the hospital. Is Richard Holroyd recovering?'

'We haven't heard anything yet. That usually means there is nothing to report.'

'Can you tell me where Addenbrooke's Hospital is? I really think I should go and see how he is.'

'Best to get a taxi, Miss,' then added, 'I'll call one for you.'

'Thanks. Could you also let me have some paper? I'd like to leave a note for my husband.'

He brought her paper and Anni scribbled a note to Edward. She folded it over and wrote his name on the front. As she handed it across the desk, a man entered the station calling *taxi!* 'Yes,' she answered, 'that's for me.'

Anni left.

Chapter 29 | *Interview*

Edward had been shown into a small dingy interview room where he was left under the supervision of a constable. He paced and sat, paced and sat, until Inspector Grant came back, accompanied by DS Meredith, who carried a large brown envelope.

'Have you told my father about Richard?' asked Edward, rising. 'I think he was meeting my brother at King's Cross.'

'We haven't been able to contact your father.'

Inspector Grant turned to the constable who was standing by the door. 'Phone through to the incident room at King's Cross,' he said, 'and ask them to put a call out for him.'

'For God's sake tell him Richard is okay,' called Edward as the constable was leaving the room.

'Oh dear, oh dear,' he sighed, sitting and laying his head in his hands. 'He will be anxious and probably trying to phone me at the flat. It's most inconvenient you bringing me here. The family have been so upset by Maud's death, especially my father who was very close to her. And now there is additional distress because of the attack on Richard.'

'That is why we want to talk to you, Dr Holroyd. Miss Cadogan was murdered and an attempt has been made to murder your brother. It's all very curious. Two members of your family attacked in such a short space of time. The questions is, *Why*?'

Edward knew he was right, and that he had to help the

Inspector to find the murderer. His head felt fuzzy, and a headache was developing. He tried to pull himself together. 'You think there is a connection between Maud's murder and the attack on Richard, Inspector?'

'Yes, I do. We're no further forwards with Miss Cadogan's case. The attack on your brother is too much of a coincidence. There must be a connection. I ask you again, what did you do after leaving Miss Cadogan's flat this morning?'

The same question was repeated over and over for several minutes, and Edward became tired of answering. He'd repeated details of all his movements since leaving the flat, hoping that a helpful attitude would secure him an early release and enable him to leave and go to see Richard. The Inspector didn't appear to believe him. Wretched with anxiety, and a headache that had increased painfully, Edward pleaded with him. 'Please tell me what happened to my brother.'

Inspector Grant stared down at him. Edward knew it was weak, but his worry and frustration were joining to undermine him. He couldn't stop tears flowing, though he wiped them immediately with the back of his hand. The Inspector relented. 'All we know about the incident at this stage is that he was stabbed on the platform while apparently waiting for the King's Cross train. We have plenty of witnesses who saw him fall, but no one who saw the attacker.'

Edward stood up. He had to do something. 'You have no reason to keep me here, Inspector,' he said, trying to keep his voice steady. 'Why would I attack my brother or my cousin? I have no motive. You're clutching at straws because they're both members of my family. That is not to say that I am responsible.'

'Relax, Dr Holroyd. Your brother is in good hands. He was fortunate that help reached him quickly and he's in one of the best hospitals in the country'

Edward shot him a less than grateful look. 'And while he's critically ill in hospital, I am wasting time here. I insist upon being set free to go to him.'

'Just a few more questions, and then we can wind up. Is it possible that someone has a vendetta against members of your family?'

Edward was feeling exasperated. 'No,' he said, almost shouting. 'Maud was good to just about everyone, and Richard rarely came to Cambridge. We weren't even expecting him, so how could anyone have planned to murder him? You must be wrong, Inspector. There can't be a connection.'

'Most murders involve a member of the victim's family.'

'Then spread your net wider than me, Inspector. Please let me go and see my brother. What if he dies?' Edward's voice shook. 'How will you feel about having kept an innocent man from his brother if that happens?'

'Does any other member of your family live in, or near, Cambridge?' asked Inspector Grant, as though he hadn't heard.

'No!' shouted Edward. 'There is no other member of the family nearby.' Even as he spoke, Edward slowed down. He drew his eyebrows together and looked perplexed. He shook his head.

'Are you sure?' asked the Inspector, as though picking up on the change. 'You might as well tell me. I'll find out anyway.'

'The nearest family member is my father, and you know he lives in London. Don't even suggest that he might have stabbed his son. Could it have been robbery?'

'We don't think so. Your brother still had his wallet on him.'

The Inspector put out a hand to the sergeant who was holding the brown envelope. He tipped the contents onto the table, picking up a glasses case and small notebook.

'Is this your brother's spectacles case?' he asked.

'Richard didn't wear glasses,' replied Edward.

'They were in his coat pocket.'

'I think those are my glasses.'

'Why would your brother be wearing your glasses?'

'I don't know. It makes no sense. But wait!' Edward leaned across and took the case from the Inspector's hand. 'These *are* mine,' he said. 'Oh my goodness, I think I know what happened. He was wearing my coat! My wife gave him a coat to wear because he'd come over from Ireland without a warm one.'

'Can your wife corroborate this?'

Edward nodded and Inspector Grant signalled to DS Meredith who left the room. He took the glasses case back and laid it on the table.

DS Meredith came rapidly back, saying that Anni had gone to Addenbrooke's. Edward looked a mixture of pleased and relieved. He stopped pacing and pointed to the notebook. 'That's Richard's notebook. He always carried something to scribble in - bits of drawings, ideas, notes, all sorts.'

Inspector Grant opened the book and held it up. 'Is this your brother's writing and sketching?'

'Yes, it is.'

The Inspector flipped through the pages. Watching him, Edward noticed a corner of one page had been turned over. 'The last page contains writing,' said Inspector Grant, stopping at that page. 'It looks like notes. One of them reads: *did Maud plan to tell Anni?* Do you know what that might refer to?'

'I don't know.'

'I'm curious about this entry because it connects with the dead woman. What would Maud Cadogan have been planning to tell your wife, and why did your brother feel it was sufficiently important to note down?'

Edward stayed silent. He thought he knew what Maud might have told Anni, if she'd lived.

'Dr Holroyd, if you know anything you must tell us.'

Possibilities were flying through Edward's mind. If only he'd had more time with Anni before the police had taken him to the station! He didn't know what she and Richard had discussed, but, but, if he had told Anni about... surely she wouldn't have been so relaxed when he got back to the flat.

'There is one more entry,' The Inspector broke into his thoughts. 'It reads: *check Minnie*. Does that ring a bell?'

Edward sat bolt upright. 'Oh my God,' he said.

Inspector Grant's attention was diverted from Edward's reaction by the rising sounds of a commotion outside the room. The desk sergeant burst in. He glanced at his superior, and then addressed Edward. 'Is Robert Holroyd your father, sir?'

'Yes,' said Edward, standing.

'Then you'd better come outside, sir, quickly.'

Chapter 30 | *Edward's father*

'Officer?'

The desk sergeant raised his eyes and saw a tall elderly man. He was frowning and looking anxious.

'Officer,' repeated the man, 'I'm not sure if you can help me: I am anxious to contact my son but can't locate him at his home or place of work. It really is important that I get in touch with him as soon as possible.'

The man looked weary as well as anxious. He rested an arm on the counter, as though in need of support. A phone rang and the sergeant stretched out an arm to pick it up.

'I'll be with you in just a moment, sir. Take a seat over there. You look tired.'

The man looked over at the seats but remained where he was.

'Parkside Police Station. Hello Peter. Are you still at Addenbrooke's? Yes. Yes. Out of danger. Good. Yes, I'll pass that news on to the Inspector.'

He replaced the receiver and turned back to the counter. 'Now, sir, you're having trouble contacting your son. I'd better take a few details from you. What is your son's name?'

'Edward Holroyd. Dr Edward Holroyd. He's a lecturer at the Department of Environmental Sciences.

'Holroyd? You did say Holroyd?' checked the sergeant, looking surprised. 'Who are you, sir?'

'I'm Robert Holroyd. Why is our name familiar? Is my son alright?'

'I think we can help you locate your son, sir. Dr Holroyd is here at the moment helping with enquiries into a serious attack.'

'Edward helping with enquiries? Why?'

'It's just routine questioning following the attempted murder of a gentleman at the railway station.'

Robert Holroyd's frame seemed to shrink and the knuckles of his hands turned white as he held more tightly to the edge of the desk. 'The railway station?'

The sergeant looked unsure what to say. While he hesitated, Robert spoke again.

'I remark on the mention of the railway station because my younger son, Richard, was getting a train to London from Cambridge. I arranged to meet him at King's Cross, but he never arrived. I've been phoning and phoning my son Edward's flat, but there is no answer. I presume neither he nor his wife are at home. I can't get Edward at his workplace, nor on his mobile, and that is why I've come here looking for help. Please tell me if it is one of my sons who has been hurt?'

'The injured man was taken to Addenbrooke's hospital. His name is Richard Holroyd, sir.'

'Richard in hospital?' Robert's face went ashen and he started to shake and sway.

Alarmed, the sergeant called out to a colleague. They went out into the public area and helped Robert to a chair.

'What has happened to my son?'

'There was an attempt on his life, but he is... sir, SIR!'

Robert seemed unable to sustain the shock and he began to fall from the seat. The sergeant put an arm out to steady him. Robert was trying to talk. 'Anni. Where is Anni?' he gasped.

'Johnson!' called the sergeant to his colleague. 'Get Dr Holroyd out here. On the double!'

Edward and Inspector Grant came quickly. Edward was shocked to see his father looking so ill. He sat beside him, propping him up as he was handed a glass of water. Edward held the glass while his father sipped, and listened to the sergeant as he told them what had led up to Robert's collapse. Edward sat with his arm around his father, watching anxiously for signs of recovery.

Before long, Robert began to revive and he looked up at his son. 'I'll be all right in a while, Edward. What has happened to Richard?'

Inspector Grant, who'd been speaking aside to the sergeant, approached. 'Your son is unconscious but out of danger, Mr Holroyd. The doctors say he'll make a full recovery.'

Edward hugged his father gently.

'I went to meet him at King's Cross, but he never turned up,' said Robert. 'I waited and waited. He said he would be on the two-fifteen from Cambridge. I checked to see if the trains were running to time. He wasn't on that train, nor on the next one. I phoned your flat but there was no answer and you weren't at work. I decided to take a train up here myself. I had to come up. Edward, is it Minnie?'

'I'm beginning to think it's possible. But why would she try to kill Richard?'

'Who is Minnie?' asked Inspector Grant.

'My adopted daughter,' said Robert. He appeared to shrink into Edward as he spoke. 'We found out a little while ago that she was released on parole from the institution where she's been held since being convicted of murdering my wife.'

Robert turned to Edward. 'We should have known sooner. We should have been told!' He looked up at Inspector Grant. 'She's been reported missing from her placement in Surrey.' Robert gripped his son's arm. 'She must be in Cambridge, Edward. Where is Anni? Did she go back to the flat? I've been trying to phone you there but I couldn't get a reply.'

The sergeant told them Anni had gone to Addenbrooke's to see Richard. He picked up a piece of paper and handed it to Edward. 'She left this for you, Dr Holroyd.'

Edward unravelled the note as the Inspector snapped at the sergeant. 'Get onto the hospital quickly. Check if she's still there.'

'Oh God,' gasped Edward. 'She says she'll just see how Richard is and then she'll wait for me at the flat.' He stepped away from his father. He had begun to shake. 'Minnie knows our address, Dad,' he whispered. 'She sent me a postcard.'

The sergeant interrupted to say Anni had left the hospital.

Edward crossed to the desk and without asking, picked up the receiver and phoned his flat. The phone rang and rang. There was no answer. He dropped the phone and doubled over as though in pain. He saw that his father's face had lost most of the colour he'd regained. Edward straightened up and ran from the police station, closely followed by the Inspector who shouted at him to get into a nearby police car, then back at the sergeant, asking him to keep phoning the flat.

Chapter 31 | *Stranger from the past*

Anni heard the *Introitus* from Mozart's *Requiem* blasting from Paul's flat as she mounted the stairs to the flat. She smiled. Keener than ever to encourage a taste for better music in Paul, Roger was encouraging him to join a choir. Paul had his heart set on King's College Choir, and this was a piece they sang. Edward told him it wouldn't be possible to join, but Roger disagreed and had successfully managed to turn Paul's head to the degree that he'd already invited Anni and Edward to his debut performance at Christmas. The music was very loud, but it was a piece that Anni liked.

The door to the flat opened as she prepared to insert her key. Thinking Edward must have returned, Anni walked in calling his name and closing the door behind her. She was startled to see a strange woman emerge from their bedroom.

'Who are you?' she asked, stopping in the hallway.

The woman was in her forties, and taller than Anni. She was almost as tall as Edward and the coat she wore gave the impression of a broad build. It was a shapeless mass, which seemed square rather than long. The arms were too short and it looked as though she'd grown out of it in her teens. Her hair was grey with lank curls dripping the length of a long face. It was the face that held Anni's attention. The eyes were extremely bright, almost glasslike. The lips were spread in a smile that was more sinister than friendly. The woman gazed intently at her and Anni felt a shiver of fear.

'Who are you?' she repeated, edging slowly back to the door.

'Minnie. I'm Minnie.'

The woman turned her head slightly as she spoke, almost as though she was listening to herself and checking the truth of what she was saying. She looked back at Anni and her eyes opened wider as she began examining her from head to toe. Anni remembered the photograph she'd seen in Maud's office and thought there was a resemblance between the young girl standing with Edward and Richard at Druchsheen and this woman. Making the link did not ease her mounting fear.

'What are you doing here? Why were you in our bedroom? Is Edward home? Did he let you in? Edward, Edward?' she shouted.

'Slut!'

Anni gasped as the word was flung at her. Minnie's eyes flashed with anger and her smile turned into a grim angry line.

'Edward's room,' she said, menacingly, standing in the doorway of the bedroom, as though she would block Anni from entering.

The hall was narrow and Minnie walked closer towards her, so close that Anni began to panic. She turned and moved towards the door, calling 'Edward, Edward!' She had hardly completed the turn when she felt her head being tugged back in a vicious grip. Minnie was grabbing her hair. Anni began to fall but Minnie raised her up by the head and hauled her round so that their faces were inches apart.

'EDWARD'S ROOM!' screamed Minnie.

Anni felt hot breath upon her face. Her legs turned to

jelly.

'SLUT!' screamed Minnie again and her face bulged with rage.

She flung Anni across the hallway. Her head hit the wall and Anni heard the crack of the impact as she lost consciousness.

Anni regained consciousness slowly, aware at first of nothing beyond her pounding head. It felt as though her brain was pulsing and banging itself repeatedly off the inside of her skull. Waves of pain ebbed and flowed. She tried raising her hands to cradle her head but found she couldn't move them. Turning her head carefully, she stared uncomprehendingly at her wrists, which came slowly into focus. They were tied firmly to the arms of one of the kitchen chairs. Anni tried to stand, and became aware that she was also bound to the chair by her waist and ankles.

She lifted her throbbing head and looked around. She was in the living room, and the chair had been placed near the external wall of the room. She could hear the sound of Paul's music but it was very faint. Minnie was sitting on the sofa and Anni saw a triumphant smile on her face. She had what looked like a knitting bag on her lap, and she was clutching the handles. She might have been any benevolent older woman, just to look at her. The image shattered as she opened the bag and slowly withdrew a long knife. Anni watched in mounting horror as Minnie raised it to the light. The last few inches of the blade were blood-stained.

Minnie seem to notice the direction of her gaze. Anni watched her glance down at the knife. She drew her fingers through the stains and Anni thought she could hear her murmur Edward's name. She seemed entirely consumed by the action, almost as though she'd forgotten Anni was in the room. Minnie kissed the blade of the knife and the blood became smeared on her lips, like badly applied lipstick.

'No time to clean it. No time,' she said, in a low, singsong tone.

The phone rang. Minnie looked away from the knife, startled. It rang and rang but she made no move to answer it. The ringing stopped. She cackled, dropped the bag and knife, and heaved herself off the sofa towards the phone table. She stopped as she saw a framed photograph, which stood beside the receiver. It was Edward and Anni on their wedding day, Edward was looking laughingly at Anni who stood smiling, one hand raised to ward off a shower of confetti.

'NO!' screamed Minnie and Anni heard the anguish in her voice.

Anni's heart began to thump harder.

'Mine. Mine. MINE!' screamed Minnie.

She turned and flung the photograph at Anni. It shattered against the wall above her head and she felt sharp stings as shards of glass struck her head and neck. When she looked up, Minnie was rocking backwards and forwards on her heels, muttering.

'I told him he was mine. MINE!'

There was hysteria in her rising voice and Anni felt terrified.

'Edward was always mine. Why didn't he listen?' Minnie dropped to her knees and began to weep.

Anni strained to hear what she was saying.

'Love me,' it sounded like. 'Why didn't he love me?'

After a while she fell quiet and Anni thought she'd fallen asleep, but she raised her face eventually. It was a frightening face to gaze on: her hair was wild, her eyes bloodshot, and the stain of red above and below her lips looked like a gash.

'Watched Maud,' she said, looking at Anni. 'Watched her. She was helping you. Helping you. Not me! How could she? Heartless. Bad heartless Maud.'

Minnie's sobs grew louder and louder and she lay upon the floor weeping as though her heart was breaking. The phone rang again. Anni wondered if she could stand. Could she make it to the table? She could knock the receiver off with her mouth. Maybe the caller would hear her cry for help. Before she could propel herself forwards, the phone stopped ringing and she heard Minnie's sobs subside. As she grew quieter, she began to mutter Maud's name over and over. Suddenly, she sat up and turned towards Anni. The expression on her face was one of furious anger. She leapt toward the fallen knife with surprising agility and grasping it, lunged down the room to Anni, who screamed with terror.

Minnie stopped and put her head on one side, as she had done earlier in the hall. She seemed surprised at the sound, disconcerted even. Anni watched the knife fall from her grasp.

'Maud didn't scream,' she said, shaking her head. 'No scream, no sound.'

Anni held her breath.

'Why did you marry him? He wasn't yours to marry.'

'I didn't know about you,' whispered Anni.

Minnie grabbed her hair again and tugged as though she'd pull it out by the roots. She screamed and let it drop suddenly. Anni saw blood running from the palm of Minnie's right hand. She'd cut herself on shards of glass from the photo frame. Minnie roared and grabbed Anni's neck. She shook and squeezed. Anni blacked out.

Chapter 32 | *Listening in*

When Roger returned from work, he discovered Paul listening through the wall adjoining Edward's flat. He sneered. 'Eavesdropping again?'

'Something's happening in there, Rog. There's a lot of banging on walls, and I'm certain I heard screaming. I'm thinking I had better knock on the door, you know, check they're okay?'

'Give it a break, Paul. You're obsessed with Edward. It makes me wonder what's going on under my nose.'

Paul stared at Roger. 'Don't be such a fool. There's nothing going on between Edward and me.'

'In that case, let's forget him and focus on us. I'm putting a lot of work into educating you. The least you can do is pay me proper attention.' Roger drew a CD from his jacket pocket and waved it at Paul, who withdrew the glass from the wall.

Paul pursed his lips. 'Well okay, but I'm definitely going to investigate if I hear any more suspicious noises.'

Chapter 33 | *Suttee*

Anni was pulled back to consciousness by a feeling of something tugging at her head. She opened her eyes painfully and tried to focus. Her clothes were piled in heaps around her. Directly in front, she saw the red dress she'd worn to the college dinner. Anni struggled to grasp what was happening. As she watched, curls of hair floated down to the ground and Anni realised that it was her own hair falling onto the pile of clothes. She became aware of her head being pulled and of curious sounds of laughter. Her head began to clear and she realised it was Minnie, cutting her hair and laughing as she let each strip drop. To Anni's ears, it sounded like a cross between the braying of a donkey and the chatter of a monkey. The extraordinary sound added to the sense of unreality.

Now and then, Minnie would mutter a few words in a singsong tone. 'No one else, no one else. Just Minnie. Just me.'

Anni stayed still, trying to make sense of what was happening.

Finally, Minnie seemed satisfied and, flinging the scissors from her, stood in front of Anni to survey her handiwork. 'Not pretty now, no, no no.' Still chuckling, she left the room.

Anni looked around the room. Nothing else had been touched. The mess was just around her. She saw that most of her clothes had been torn or ripped. Her head dropped onto her chest. She felt hopelessness and despair.

In the stillness, she heard Paul's doorbell and then a burst of Stravinsky's *Rite of Spring* as the door to his flat opened. How macabre, she thought. Even if she could make a sound, it wouldn't be heard over the loud passages of the piece. She wished Edward were there. Her heart leapt momentarily as she thought she could see his outline in her peripheral vision. She turned her head to look. He wasn't there. The wish must have given birth to a picture in her mind's eye. There was no other comfort, so she let her head fall again and slowly the impression of him re-appeared, standing by the window. It was more of a shadow figure than a substantial one, but she felt less alone.

Minnie returned to the room. She had a bottle of brandy in her hand. Anni watched, horror-struck as it was poured over her and her clothes.

'Suttee!' Minnie cut an incongruous figure as she danced lumpily around the living room. 'Suttee,' she repeated, gleefully.

Desperate, Anni grasped at the only straw she could think of.

'Edward isn't dead, Minnie. You didn't kill him. This can't be suttee.'

Minnie stopped dancing and looked confused. Then she came and placed her bulky figure in front of Anni. 'Dead, dead. Edward is DEAD!' Once again, she held her head on one side, listening to what she'd said. She began to shake. 'I killed him. I killed Edward. I stuck a knife into his bad treacherous heart. I killed Edward.' She began to sob. Tears rolled down her cheeks and she sank to the floor moaning loudly.

Despite her fear, despite her loathing for this woman who clearly meant to kill her, Anni felt a touch of pity. She shook the thought aside. It wouldn't help her. She watched and waited until Minnie calmed, then spoke loudly and clearly. 'It was Richard,' she said.

Minnie looked up at her, puzzled.

'You stabbed Richard. You didn't stab Edward. It was Richard.'

'It was Edward.'

'No, it was Richard' said Anni, emphatically.

'EDWARD!'

Anni wondered fleetingly if it was wise to continue, then grunted at herself for hesitating. Death was as close as Minnie's hot angry breath upon her face. 'Richard,' she said again, more loudly, more clearly. 'It was Richard. He was going to London to see Robert. I loaned him Edward's coat because it was cold.'

Minnie drew back a little. 'Richard?' she said.

'Richard in Edward's coat. I gave him Edward's coat.'

'Yes, Edward's coat. I followed Edward in Edward's coat.'

'It was Richard. I gave him Edward's coat.'

'I killed Edward.'

'You stabbed Richard. Edward is alive.'

'NO!'

While Minnie screamed, Anni turned her head aside, and she noticed Richard's drawings on the coffee table. 'Look, look!' she screamed. 'Look at the pictures on the coffee table. Richard was here drawing pictures. Do you remember him drawing pictures? Look!'

Minnie loped towards the table and grabbed the sheets of paper. Anni watched her mouth open as she looked intently at the drawings, then back at Anni. 'Richard was here?'

'Yes, Richard was here. He drew those pictures of Druchsheen. He was here and he's the one you stabbed, not Edward. Edward is alive.'

Minnie threw the drawings from her. She raised her face to the ceiling and bellowed. The sound was so loud that Anni held her breath. Surely someone would hear. Surely Paul would come to investigate? She heard his door open. The doorbell rang. Minnie turned towards the door. Anni shouted *Paul*, but the sound wasn't loud enough. Minnie ran across and put her hand roughly over Anni's mouth. Anni felt her heart thumping so loudly she was sure it would burst. Minnie's hand clamped more tightly on her mouth. The doorbell rang again. Minnie's other hand was pressing against the back of Anni's head, just above her neck. She felt close to suffocation. She could hardly breathe, let alone scream. She heard Paul's door close. He'd given up. Tears welled up in her eyes and she tried hard not to cry.

Hearing the door close, Minnie removed her hands and stood before Anni. She was panting. Her eyes had narrowed and the irises looked like dots of faded blue on a bloodshot background. 'Where is he?' she said, through gritted teeth.

'I don't know.'

'You lie.' Minnie lumbered across to the sofa and picked up the knife. This time she came towards Anni slowly. She pointed the blade at Anni's ribs. 'You lie,' she said again and jabbed the knife.

Anni felt it penetrate.

'Where is he?'

'I don't know,' sobbed Anni. 'I don't know. At the police station, at the hospital, I don't know where he is!' Anni stared at the bloodied point of the knife. Sounds erupted close to her. She thought she could hear Paul saying he'd heard a scream. She thought her name was being called.

'Anni!'

It was Edward. She turned her head towards the door and tried to speak to him. She saw his anguished face as she felt the knife penetrate more deeply.

Edward saw Anni's head drop to her chest. He saw the knife with its blade covered in blood. Minnie turned towards him, her face rampant with rage. She lunged at him, howling. The police grabbed her.

Edward knelt by Anni's slumped body, smelling the brandy. He raised her head, feeling his heart would burst with grief. He sobbed, calling her name, holding her white face in his trembling hands.

Robert was beside him, undoing the ropes. Edward heard Minnie's screams and moans behind him.

'Mine,' she was shouting. 'Mine! You should be mine! You be mine. She's dead. DEAD!'

'Anni, Anni,' he cried.

Minnie screamed more loudly as she struggled with the police. Edward heard the click of handcuffs. Anni's body fell towards him as Robert loosened the rope that had held her waist.

Chapter 34 | *Black news*

Harold and Pansy were sitting in Arthur's office. The morning was dark but Arthur hadn't turned on the main light. Instead, he'd lit the desk lamp and it threw everything beyond the desk into shade, including Arthur each time he sat back into his chair. Harold had the impression of being in a cave.

Pansy was speaking and the triumphant glow on her face was impossible to miss, even in the dim light.

'So, you see, the mystery is solved. Dr Black had connected to the Internet via the fax line in his office, and he left it on all the time. Honestly, you'd think he would have had some idea of the cost of such a connection.'

'But what did he want to do that for?' asked Arthur, shaking his head sorrowfully. 'Everyone is networked through the University service. We all have access to the Internet and email.'

Harold leaned into the light and his orange locks shone. 'Yes, but those connections are monitored,' he said, 'and Dr Black, well I guess he just didn't want anyone to know what he was getting up to. It took some doing but I was able to trace *exactly* what he was doing by checking which files had been processed on the machine. And, like he's either been downloading other people's research with their permission or else he's been hacking into their computer space and copying their files across to his own computer. See here, I've got a list of what he worked on.'

Harold handed a sheet of paper to Arthur who leaned forward to read the list under the lamplight. His eyes almost popped out of his head as he read the filenames.

'Well this is all to do with his own area but now I see where the ideas and research have really come from. In fact,' he said, pointing to a couple of lines, 'this is a research paper he told me he was writing. Good God, these references are almost exactly the same as those on the book list he was plaguing Maud to buy. She gave me a copy of the list before she, before ...' Arthur struggled to continue.

'It's like, well he's not doing the writing or researching, man, is he?' said Harold.

Arthur's face was a picture of mingled grief and disgust. He began to look ill. His mind leapt forward to possible scandal. Those blasted newshounds were always sniffing about, looking to find something, anything, which would discredit Cambridge. He tried to remember if he had agreed to act as referee for any journal articles being submitted by Dr Black. While these thoughts were leap-frogging through his mind, Arthur had leaned back again. Pansy and Harold were sitting quietly and politely in the pool of light. He noticed a smug smile spreading across Pansy's face. His heart sank.

'I have a little more bad news for you,' she said, pausing for effect. 'Dr Black's references were false.'

'False?'

'The man is an impostor.'

'I hope you're sure about that, Pansy. That is a very serious accusation to make against anybody.'

Arthur wasn't sure why he was making any attempt to

protect Dr Black. Maybe he wasn't up to the job of Head of Department. The threat of further scandal began to loom larger and larger in his mind. He groaned. Pansy was still grinning.

'I'm certain, Arthur,' she said. 'I've checked and double-checked, and added to what Harold has discovered, the case against him is pretty black.'

Pansy stopped and sniggered heartily at her own pun.

Harold took advantage of the opportunity. 'And I'd like you to know, Arthur, that Melanie helped me to solve this puzzle. She's been very helpful and, well I was wondering, well, you see, I have so much more to do now, what with emailing getting so busy and everyone wanting speedier internet connections and help with lots more programs like, and it would be great if I could have Melanie as an assistant, you know, train her in computing. You know. She has a real aptitude for it.'

'Okay, okay!' wailed the harassed Arthur. 'I'll think about it, but not just now. The Dr Black business is more than I can cope with at the moment. Pansy, I want to see him in my office as soon as he turns up.'

Arthur's phone rang and he picked it up absently. 'Arthur Scott.' His attitude changed quickly. He sat bolt upright in the chair and put his hand over the mouthpiece. 'It's the police. Can you leave this with me for now?'

Pansy's nose twitched and her eyes began to bulge with curiosity, but Arthur waved her and Harold away imperatively.

Later that morning, Pansy entered the staff room, smiling broadly and carrying a large cake box. She passed the dismantled coffee machine and the smile faded a little. Potty was making himself a cup of tea and he noticed her look. Then, much to his surprise, she brightened up again, laid the cake box on the worktop and began cutting up the contents and placing slices on plates.

'No hard feelings about the coffee machine, Pansy?' he asked, mystified at this unprecedented generosity.

'No, not really.'

Potty pointed to the cake. 'Is it your birthday?'

'No, but there is something to celebrate,' smiled Pansy, and he was reminded briefly, very briefly, of the Mona Lisa.

'I'll be emailing everyone with an invitation to a special coffee morning today. All will be revealed later.'

And off she went, smirking, leaving a puzzled Potty in her wake.

The staff room was full to overflowing at break time. Pansy passed the plates of cake around. She was positively preening and her colleagues couldn't understand why, especially as the coffee machine was lying discarded and ready for removal. When they weren't wondering at Pansy's unaccustomed generosity, the big topic of conversation was Dr Black. He was nowhere to be seen. Melanie was inclined to be a little indiscreet.

'Harold says...' she began, but she shut up quickly when she noticed Anthony glaring at her.

Anthony turned to Chris. 'Terrific,' he growled. 'We're going to be treated to yet another episode of the gospel according to Harold. I just can't bear it.'

Anthony was spared however, by the entrance of Arthur,

who walked purposefully to the top of the room.

'The police have been in touch' he said, when he had everyone's attention, 'and you'll be pleased to hear that Maud's killer has been caught.' He paused to let a buzz of conversation ripple through the room. He let it come to a natural halt. 'It is, I'm sorry to say, a particularly sad story. The murderer is Edward Holroyd's adopted sister. She was caught yesterday evening as she tried to kill Edward's wife.' He paused again, allowing the second announcement time to sink in and expecting another burst of comments, but everyone seemed too shocked to speak. Sue piped up.

'She didn't kill Anni, did she?'

'Happily, no, though Anni is in hospital.'

'Poor Edward,' said Sue.

'What about Edward's brother?' asked Pansy.

'He's recovering. I have two more pieces of information to give and then could we all try and get back to normal please?'

The murmurs subsided.

'Dr Black has resigned. He,' Arthur coughed, 'he, well, he left yesterday.'

The police had phoned Arthur that morning to say that although they'd taken Dr Black and Dennis in for questioning, they had of course let them go when they realised who the real murderer was. Arthur had gone to Dr Black's office after his conversation with the police, only to find that it had been completely cleaned out. No trace of Dr Black remained, apart from the computer. The office looked like it had been given an intensive cleaning. He had run his finger along the top of a bookcase. There wasn't a speck of dust on it. Arthur looked grim. He was furious that

Dr Black, or whoever he was - he might not even be a Dr - had cheated him by doing a bunk. On the other hand, it meant he didn't have to take any further action and that meant one less story for the press to get hold of. Arthur had enough worries.

'Where has he gone?' asked Potty.

'Erm, he didn't say,' said Arthur.

The noise levels in the staffroom rose.

'You said you had TWO pieces of news, Arthur,' said Pansy, loudly enough to catch attention. The room became quiet again.

'Yes, Pansy.' Arthur looked solemnly at everyone. 'The other news is that Dennis Cardigan has been given a year's sabbatical.'

This news was greeted with grins and smiles and even a couple of whoops of delight. Arthur shook his head and looked over at Potty. Potty shrugged his shoulders. It would be silly to pretend to be sad. Arthur shrugged back. People broke into small groups and Pansy went around again with the cake, looking more pleased than anyone ever remembered seeing her before. Arthur left the room quietly.

Becky's eyes were bright with interest as she discussed Dr Black with Sue and Melanie. The man would become far more interesting in his absence than he had been while in the Department. Anthony and Victoria stood together. She was dunking a fruit tea bag in her mug and smiling smugly.

Potty turned to Harold. 'I gather you and Pansy have been working closely together on the Dr Black case, and that you've pulled off quite a coup. You need to be careful, Harold, you're in danger of becoming part of the establishment!'

Harold cringed and blushed rosy red all the way to the roots of his orange hair. 'Oh, er, um.'

Melanie stood by, grinning approvingly, and holding two plates loaded with cake.

Chapter 35 | *Edward opens up*

Edward spent the night at the hospital, sitting by Anni's bedside. He looked haggard and gaunt. By contrast, Anni, though pale, was sleeping peacefully. The stab wounds were slight, as the knife had glanced off her ribs. She'd regained consciousness after minor surgery and had even managed to smile at Edward before dropping off to sleep.

Though exhausted, he was trying to stay awake. He found himself re-living the scene he had witnessed each time he drifted off, watching Anni being stabbed, as he had thought, to death, over and over and over again. Behind that image lurked another, which he felt totally unable to confront. When awake, he kept checking to see if Anni really was still alive, leaning over her to catch the sound of her quiet breathing, and gazing sorrowfully at her hacked hair. As morning dawned, he fell into a light doze.

When Anni awoke, she saw Edward sitting beside her, head lowered onto his chest. She lay quietly, looking at him, noticing his pallor and the grey tinge to his skin. To see him at all was so precious. She was alive, and he was here with her. It was impossible to block out the memory of what had happened, but Anni was very glad to be alive.

Edward woke abruptly at the entrance of a nurse who'd come to check on Anni. Appearing satisfied with her patient's progress, she brought in a breakfast tray for both of them. When her cheerful face was withdrawn, Edward stood up, meaning to help Anni.

'Hey,' she said, 'don't worry about me. My hands are fine.'

She smiled at him, but her cheerfulness appeared to have a negative effect on Edward. He looked gloomier than ever. Anni laid down the slice of toast she'd taken a bite of, and picked up the cup of tea. 'Have a cup of tea,' she said, 'and talk to me.'

Edward sipped some of the lukewarm mixture, to please her, then put the cup back on the tray.

'Rubbish, isn't it?' she said.

He wouldn't even look at her. Anni laid her own cup on the tray, and pushed it away. 'It's time we talked properly, Edward, and no more excuses or evasions. It was Minnie who killed your mother, wasn't it?'

'Yes, that was what I was going to tell you about when the police burst in.'

He spoke so softly that she struggled to hear. She tried to sit up so that she would be closer to him, but the movement hurt her injured side and she gave an involuntary gasp.

Edward leapt up. 'What is it? Shall I call the nurse?'

'It's okay. Just speak more loudly, Edward and then I won't be tempted to sit up.'

He laid his head in her lap, and his shoulders began to heave. 'I'm so sorry, Anni,' he mumbled. 'This is all my fault.'

'Hey, don't take it that way.'

'I wish I'd had the courage to tell you about her before. Maybe this could have been prevented.'

'Tell me now,' said Anni, quietly and patiently.

Edward sat up, pulled his chair closer to the bed, and took Anni's hand. 'It's a long story. Are you strong enough to hear it? Maybe I should wait until you're better.'

'Tell me now,' she repeated, squeezing his hand.

Edward swallowed. Anni waited. Finally, he spoke.

'Minnie was the only child of my mother's oldest friend. Jean and her husband were killed in a car crash when Minnie was twelve years old. I was sixteen at the time, and Richard was fourteen. Mum and Dad took pity on her because there were no relations on either side of the family, and they decided to adopt her. You might think that would be easy, given Mum and Jean had been such good friends, but we'd never met Minnie before. Her father was a strange man, who didn't like company, and they lived in an isolated house on Exmoor. Mum used to visit. I think she was the only person allowed to stay. Jean's husband was a writer and quite wealthy. Jean didn't work. Mum thought she probably wasn't allowed to, because her husband was possessive and controlling. Do you know, I can't even remember his name - I never met him. Anyway, Jean looked after the house and their daughter. Minnie was home-schooled because they lived in such a remote area of the moor. Goodness knows how many people she met in that place. So it wasn't a surprise that, when she came to us, she was taciturn and withdrawn, and apt to take offence easily. It must have been a dreadful change for her, losing her parents, and leaving her home to come and live in noisy lively London. I felt sorry for the kid, we all did. It seemed like she'd been dealt a rotten hand. I worked hard at being kind to her and that turned out to be a mistake.'

'Why? Surely being kind can't have done any harm?'

'She developed a crush on me.'

'Oh,' said Anni, and she shivered.

Edward stopped talking. He had another flash of the scene he'd walked in upon. There would be a connection to what he'd just said to Anni. Edward knew that he would hear about what happened in the flat sooner or later, either because Anni was well enough to tell him, or because the police would insist on getting a statement from her. He suddenly remembered that he'd seen a policeman sitting outside the door of Anni's room. At least Anni was secure here.

He raised her hand and kissed it. She gave him a weak smile. He carried on talking. 'We all thought the crush was harmless, initially. Indeed, Mum said it was a good thing for Minnie, as focusing on a living person might help her to come to terms with her parents' death. Oddly enough, she never mentioned them, and whenever my parents brought up the subject, she would stare coldly at them and refuse to answer.'

'That was a strange way to react. Didn't you wonder that she showed no emotion about them?'

'I was sixteen, going on seventeen, I didn't think about it. My mind was on other things. It was only after she'd been at school for a while that my parents began to realise something was seriously wrong with her. She flew into rages if any of the other children crossed her, but for a long time, that was put down to bereavement distress and the teachers were told to keep an eye on her, and calm her down if necessary. One day, she became so furious with a classmate that she began knocking the girl's head off the wall.'

Anni winced at the reminder of her own injury and touched her head. Edward looked stricken.

'Is that how you got the bruising on your head?'

'Partly. It doesn't feel too bad now though.'

'Oh Anni, and your beautiful hair!' Edward began to weep.

Anni stretched out a hand to stroke his face. 'Don't upset yourself, sweetheart. I'm all right now, really I am.'

Edward looked at her face and the brightness of her eyes. She really was positive. He caught her mood and dried his tears.

'That's better,' said Anni. 'Yes, I thought I was going to die, Edward, but I didn't. Surviving is so amazing and I feel good, despite everything.'

Edward managed a little smile.

'Now tell me what happened to the classmate,' asked Anni.

'Oh, yes, that poor child. It took three teachers to pull Minnie off her and the girl's parents charged her with assault. That was awful. I remember how distressed Mum was, but it had a good outcome. Social Services got involved and they insisted on a psychological assessment. The report concluded that she was suffering from an inability to deal with anger, probably due to her parents' unexpected death. They couldn't carry out a more in-depth assessment because Minnie wouldn't co-operate. My parents felt that it was cruel to force her. The family dropped the charge and Mum and Dad removed her from the school and found a smaller place for her.'

'But surely the problem wouldn't go away just because

she changed schools?'

'We're probably looking at this with the benefit of hindsight, Anni. My mother was sure that Minnie would soften if treated nicely. Richard and I were given instructions on how to deal with her. Arrangements were made for her to receive private tutoring and counselling. She seemed to settle down and did well enough eventually to be accepted onto an expensive secretarial course. There was a lot of money in trust for her, and there are places where they expect students to behave like spoiled brats. Maybe she blended in. I don't know.'

'Do your students behave like spoiled brats?'

'Not really, well maybe one or two, they're mostly very smart and eager to learn. If they give trouble, it's generally the administrators and the colleges who have to deal with them. I just teach, and if they don't want to learn, I don't push them. Lectures and supervisions are time-limited. I don't know how Minnie got on at her secretarial college, but she must have been difficult and the staff must have noticed. She was there all day. But I don't really know. Anyway, she got through it and managed to get a job in a solicitor's office in north London. Richard and I were no longer at home by this time. I'd finished my BA and I was about to start my MA. Richard went off to study in Dublin. He'd always wanted to go and live in Ireland.'

'Yes, he told me about your holidays in Druchsheen. He even drew pictures of the house for me, and of you and Maud.'

'Did he? Poor Rich.'

'Isn't he okay?' asked Anni, and Edward saw the look of panic on her face. 'He was when I came to see him, yesterday, before, before... going back to the flat.'

'He's fine, Anni, he's fine. I looked in on him before I came to sit with you. But oh God, it's awful that she mistook him for me. He might have been killed!'

'Or you might have been.'

'Yes, you're right.' Edward's mood changed. He stood up abruptly and went to the window, making fists of his hands. He took a couple of deep breaths, exhaled, then returned to sit by the bed.

'Minnie!' he said, vehemently. 'She has such a lot to answer for. Sometimes I want to explode with the strength of my anger against her. If Dad hadn't forgiven her, I doubt if I would have agreed to go and see her. I wish I'd been stronger. I wish I'd insisted in pushing her completely out of our lives.'

'Go to see her?' Anni looked astonished. 'When did you do that?'

'Sorry, that was later. Let me tell the story the way it all happened.'

'Okay, but it wouldn't have made a difference, Edward. She was determined to get to you.'

'Yes, and I blame myself for being kind to her.' Edward stood again and paced the small room.

'Hey, come back,' said Anni, patting the bed. 'Tell me the rest.'

Edward looked around the hospital room. There was nowhere to hide. He went back to sit by Anni.

'She never missed Richard when he went away, but she was usually all over me during term breaks. If it wasn't for missing Mum and Dad, I wouldn't have come back. It was becoming a problem and more especially as I had begun a relationship and I wanted to bring Lucy home so that my parents could get to know her.'

'Lucy?'

Edward was about to ask how she knew about Lucy, but Anni forestalled him.

'Maud showed me a photo of the two of you.'

'Oh.' Edward covered his eyes. 'Lucy,' he repeated, then got up and walked again to the window.

'Edward?'

He heard the concern in Anni's voice. He didn't feel able to answer.

A nurse came in, to check on Anni 's dressing, she said. Edward grasped at the opportunity.

'I'll just go down the corridor, Anni. I won't be long. Is that okay?'

'Of course,' she said, looking anxious.

He left the room, nodded to the policeman still sitting outside, and wandered down the corridor.

Chapter 36 | *Sad story*

'How are you today?' asked the nurse.

Anni tried to smile, but failed. She felt like bursting into tears. 'Okay.'

'Was that your husband?'

The nurse looked kindly, so Anni nodded.

'We've all heard about what happened to you. Your husband must be feeling dreadful. She was part of his family, wasn't she, the one who did this? Must be awful hard for him to take, seeing you like this.'

'Yes, I know it is.'

The nurse finished her work and stood back from the bed. 'Takes a long time to get over something like that. Takes a lot of love and patience. For both of you, I mean.' She left the room before Anni could reply.

She lay there, thinking. Where would they end up, she and Edward? Anni felt sure she could get past this, and though she felt angry with Edward for not telling her things she really should have known about him and his family, she understood too how damaged he'd been by what had happened. How damaged he still was. Actually, Edward was the one who needed to work most on getting over it all. Fine for her to say, she realised. How would she feel if there had been a Minnie in her background? If such a person had killed her mother? Shattered and crushed, she decided.

He came back, carrying a cup of coffee. He laid it down and came up close to Anni. 'You've been crying,' he said. His own eyes filled.

'Sorry,' she said. 'I can't help it. Reaction, I think. Sit back down beside me, Edward.'

He sat awkwardly, like a child or a frightened animal who only wants to run away. And maybe it was cruel of her to make him keep talking, but it wasn't just about him. She'd almost been killed because of what he'd been hiding. It would be good for both of them.

'Tell me about Lucy?' she said, reaching over to take his hand. It felt clammy and cold. She thought she could feel his pulse, jumping and hopping under the skin.

Edward moved his eyes only, glancing over at Anni, and then into the distance. 'I met Lucy at University. She was my first serious girlfriend.' He stopped and looked at Anni, perhaps to check that she didn't mind him mentioning a former attachment. Anni squeezed his hand. He gave a tiny smile. 'We'd been seeing each other for a couple of years and the relationship was becoming serious. She came to stay with us for the summer the year I finished my MA. But she'd only been with us a couple of weeks or so when, seemingly out of the blue, she told me that she needed to spend the rest of the summer on her own, and left. I never understood why she did that, and she never explained. I think I understand now.'

'Minnie frightened her off?'

He nodded.' 'That's probably what happened. We, we, we got back together when I was doing my PhD at Warwick, but neither of us ever discussed why she'd changed her mind about spending that summer in London. Eventually, we decided to get married. We were full of happiness, Anni, the way you are when you're young, full of joy and the promise that the future held. We arranged a family party in London, with Lucy's parents and brothers, and my family. But, but she died.'

'Died?' said Anni. She hadn't expected that. 'What happened to her?'

Edward stood up and went again to stare out of the hospital window. There was a long silence, and then he said, 'I'll tell you that story another time, if you don't mind.'

Oh for goodness sake, she thought, but she said, 'sure.'

If Edward had been looking at Anni, he would have seen the frustration and tiredness on her face. Instead, he stayed by the window, and spoke over his shoulder half to himself and half to her.

'Mum was so good to me after Lucy died. She never asked questions about why Lucy had left London without a word. She never condemned her at that time or ever. Mum was like that. She loved people. She had loved Lucy. I didn't have to say anything to her, never had to ask her to behave in a particular way. She was wonderful. She knew I needed to be left alone to deal with my loss. God, I miss Mum!'

Edward turned around. Anni had closed her eyes. She heard him walk softly across the room, and felt his head close to hers. 'Are you asleep,' he whispered. 'At least you're breathing. Oh Anni, I couldn't bear it if I lost you too.' Tears fell on her face, and she became more alert. Edward eyes had begun to droop.

'What did you do after that?' she asked, startling him. His eyes opened suddenly. Edward probably wanted to stop. She felt cruel, but she pushed on. 'What about Minnie?' she asked.

Edward sighed and continued his tale. 'I went back to University the following October, and arrived home as usual, at Christmas. There was no-where else to go. Minnie was being extra friendly, suggesting we go to see films, and thinking she was trying to be kind to me, I went. After a while, she suggested going to a dance. Reluctantly, I agreed. It was so obvious at the dance that her crush on me was as strong as ever. I talked to Mum about it and she suggested I returned to university and leave her to deal with Minnie. Poor Mum, she took on all the hard work of managing Minnie, who could have afforded to move into a place of her own. I think she felt responsible. Anyway, she tried talking to her, tried to get her to see that I wasn't interested. The talk went very badly. Minnie shouted that she loved me and said she was sure I was in love with her. She was furious at Mum for saying that she didn't believe I felt that way about Minnie. She got it into her head that Mum was to blame for separating us, and gradually became more and more difficult. I stayed away the following Easter and summer, on Mum's advice. She came up to Warwick to see me instead. I felt badly about leaving her to deal with Minnie, but she insisted that she and Dad could manage. I was struggling to come to terms with the loss of Lucy and make progress with my career. It was easier to go along with Mum's advice.'

'You mustn't blame yourself, Edward. Mums are like that.'

'I do, though, I do! Mum phoned one evening to say that Minnie had flown into a ferocious rage, going on and on about Mum separating us and accusing her of destroying Minnie's life. I kept in touch after that, phoning during the day when Minnie wasn't around. Mum told me that Minnie would sit in the evenings and eye her in what she described as an 'evil' manner. She was concerned and becoming frightened. Minnie had grown up into a substantial young woman, only too capable of venting her anger physically.' Edward stopped, realising what he'd said.

Anni shivered. She kept getting flashbacks, and it was all too easy to see the looming shape of Minnie standing before her. Edward must feel the same way. 'Please go on,' she said. 'Don't stop now. Did your mother try to get help? Why didn't she ask Minnie to leave? What an awful way to live.'

'She decided to consult a psychologist on the best way to handle her. She'd made an appointment, but never got to see him. There was a lot we didn't know, but we later heard that Minnie had been running into difficulties at work. She'd been growing more aggressive with her colleagues. The problem was that she took offence so easily. The tea-lady forgot to give her a cup of tea one morning and she flew into a rage and smashed a lot of crockery. She was sacked immediately. She made her way home in that mood and we can only imagine that her anger boiled over at Mum.'

'Oh Edward, that's awful.'

'I'd received a letter from Mum that very morning, and she wrote that Minnie's fixation on me was dangerous. Minnie had found a photograph of Lucy and me in Mum's room, where she shouldn't have been, of course. She tore it to pieces and left it on the dressing table. Mum was going to ask her to leave the house. Maybe that was what pushed Minnie into killing her.'

Edward stopped talking. Anni didn't know what to say, what to do to comfort him.

'Dad found them,' he said. His head was bent over, and there was a terrible flatness to his voice. 'Minnie was sitting by the body, still holding the knife and talking away to Mum as though she was still alive. She kept saying Mum shouldn't have done it.'

'Done what? Didn't she say why she'd killed your mother?'

'We never found out. Killing Mum seemed to push her into a state of insanity. She was tried and found guilty of murder while of unsound mind. That was the term the judge used. They sent her to a secure mental institution. Dad was the only one she spoke to, aside from the psychiatrists. I doubt she gave much away to them. She's the most obdurate person I've ever met. If she didn't want to talk, nothing and no one would persuade her to.'

'Did your father see her after she was sent to prison? How extraordinary. How could he bear it?'

'Dad is an amazing person. A welfare worker at the prison told him she wanted to be reconciled with the family. He took pity on her, and began visiting a couple of times a year. He says it helped him, in a way. He also said he felt responsible for her.'

Anni began to see a pattern, a similarity between Edward and his father. That poor man. She would make a point of being kind to him in the future. She squeezed Edward's hand again. He needed lots of kindness too. 'Did she ever say why she did it?'

'No, she never mentioned Mum, but she often asked after me. It took a long time, but Dad finally persuaded me to go and see her. Richard would have nothing to do with her.'

'I wouldn't have gone,' said Anni. 'I don't think I'd trust myself close to someone who'd killed my mother, even if she was declared insane. That itself would be reason enough to stay away.'

'Maybe. I went because I felt it was unfair that Dad was shouldering the burden of visiting. I offered to take turns with him, and it was only once or twice a year. You do get used to things, even strange things, and she seemed normal most of the time. But it was hard work and I used to drift off into my own world because I couldn't think what I might say to her, and there were times when I caught her looking at me as though she was sizing me up, examining me. It was a very uncomfortable feeling.'

Edward sighed. Anni thought he understood what those stares from Minnie now meant. She must have been trying to gauge if his distractedness had any bearing on a new woman in his life. Anni shuddered. Minnie must have been watching him, and her. How had she discovered where he lived? And how had she managed to get into the flat? She suddenly remembered the spare key. 'Edward,' said Anni, touching his arm, 'where have you gone?'

'Sorry. It's hard to stop the memories flooding in. Where was I?'

'Visiting Minnie in prison.'

'Oh. Yes. Right. Well, time moved on,' he said, picking up the thread of the story again. 'I think going to see her depressed me and kept the memory of those awful events alive. I know I became somewhat withdrawn, and though I had several short-term relationships over the years, I got into the habit of keeping my personal business very much to myself. Then I met you.' He leaned across and kissed her.

'That's why you didn't mention me to anyone?'

'Yes. I soon began to realise that you were becoming

very important to me, and that awakened my old anxieties and distress about Lucy. I'm certain now that Minnie threatened Lucy and frightened her away that summer. She couldn't do that again, after all, she was locked up in an institution, but I developed an irrational fear that she'd manage to get to you anyway, that somehow she would find out how much I cared for you.'

Once again, Edward paused. He rose, poured a glass of water and went back to the window. 'Do you remember the time I came unexpectedly to Brussels?' he said, turning back. 'Two or three years ago.'

Anni nodded.

'I'd made one of my visits to Minnie and I must have been distracted. I was probably thinking of you instead of concentrating on her. She was always very sharp. She shot a question at me, asking if I was seeing someone. I said no, but I was a bit slow. I was taken aback by a look of venomous anger on her face. She must have picked up something in my behaviour that led her to think I was involved again. I was very disturbed and made my way to Brussels. You, I remember, were going out to dinner. When you left, I sat alone in your flat, imagining what Minnie might do if ever she found out about you. I kept picturing Mum's body and couldn't bear thinking that you could be hurt. I wasn't rational. Even though she was in an institution, I feared Minnie. I decided that the only thing to do was to stop seeing you. Then you would be safe. So I left and returned to England. Forgive me, Anni, for the distress I must have caused you. I couldn't tell you why I was staying away. I couldn't even bring myself to lie to you and say it was all over. I knew you would see though me.'

Anni stretched out her hand to him. He came away from

the window, took her hand and sat beside her.

'I stopped going to see Minnie after that, and it did me good. You know the rest of the story - I couldn't stay away from you.' He gave a tiny laugh. 'Over time, I persuaded myself that it would all be fine, that Minnie wasn't a threat to anyone while she was locked away, but I couldn't tell you about Mum, or Lucy. I really did bury my head in the sand, Anni, and I will have to live with the thought that my behaviour could have led to your death, and to Richard's. It was probably the trigger for Maud's.'

'But we didn't die, sweetheart, and please don't blame yourself for Maud's death,' said Anni. 'Minnie said something about Maud. Yes, I remember. She said she'd been watching her and that she thought Maud was 'fixing me up' for you. I think she really did have her own reasons for killing Maud. Do we know for certain that Minnie killed her?'

'Yes, I gather the police matched her fingerprints with a set found in Maud's office.'

'Why didn't they match them before? Surely her fingerprints were on some sort of national database?'

'You would think so, but they said the prints hadn't been filed. Perhaps because her crime had been committed so long ago. I don't know. But she really did do it. What a sad waste of a life.' Edward shook his head. 'Minnie always disliked Maud, mostly because Maud made no attempt to include her in our excursions on her visits to London. There was the age difference, of course. Minnie was far too young to come out to a pub or a dance in the early days, but Maud used to get really impatient with her. She disliked the way Minnie hung onto me. She was uneasy about her living in the same house when it was obvious she had a crush on me. How right she was. Maud did her best to draw me out after Lucy's death. She tried to get me interested in somebody else, anybody else. Cheering me up was Maud's agenda. Minnie hated her for it. Yes, I think it is entirely possible that Minnie decided Maud was responsible for my involvement with you. I can't think why else she would have killed her. She knew that Maud worked in the same Department and so it would have been easy to trace her.'

Edward sighed and covered his eyes with his hands. He did look exhausted, but he carried on talking. 'Minnie never let go of grudges. I didn't visit her during the summers I spent with you in Brussels. She once asked if Maud was taking me to see people. I denied it, but I didn't answer her questions about my long absences. She must have been blaming Maud. I didn't go to see her for quite a while before you and I got married. I was avoiding it, but she sent a postcard shortly after you came to Cambridge. I decided then that it would be prudent to go and see her, if for no other reason than to put her off the scent.'

'Ah,' said Anni, 'the postcard.'

'You saw it?'

'Yes.'

'Ah, I was hoping to spare you.'

'That was her reflection in the shop window in Magdalene Street, wasn't it? the day we went sightseeing?'

'Yes,' replied Edward. 'It almost made my heart stop. I phoned Dad that evening and he told me that Minnie had qualified for parole two months earlier and that she'd been released from prison under a Care in the Community order. He and Richard had decided to keep the news from me as long as possible. They didn't want to spoil the beginning of our marriage with bad news.'

'What on earth is Care in the Community?'

'A scheme that was introduced to try and integrate mentally ill patients into hostels, hotels or other places in the community, rather than lock them away in asylums or mental institutions.'

'But why wasn't Minnie considered dangerous? She was a murderer.'

'Yes, but she'd served her sentence. She'd been in prison for twenty years. They believed she was fit to be released. Dad was informed. He was Mum's next of kin, and they had to tell him she was being let out. He saw no reason to object. I don't know what I would have said or done, if I'd known. Anyway, I went to London the following morning, picked up Dad, and we drove to Surrey to talk to the social worker who'd been assigned to Minnie. She insisted everything was fine. Minnie turned up promptly for every appointment and was very co-operative. They were pleased with her progress and were even thinking of putting her into a work placement. Dad and I decided to leave well alone. Minnie was taking, or supposed to be taking, medication, which modified her behaviour, something to damp down her aggressive urges. Unfortunately, there is an idiotic scheme in place which allows even seriously mentally ill patients to self-medicate.'

'You think Minnie wasn't taking her medication?'

'I think that's almost certainly the case.' Edward sounded very angry. 'I wish I hadn't allowed myself to be reassured that everything was fine. What a fool I've been. I guess I wanted to persuade myself that I'd been mistaken in glimpsing her reflection. I desperately wanted to believe I was wrong. That didn't last long. Dad got a call from the social worker that very same evening. She'd been trying to contact Minnie for a job interview and when there was no response, she went to see Minnie at her flat. When there was no reply, she went to the caretaker who said she hadn't seen Minnie for several days. The social worker asked us to come back down and help find her. Naturally, I said I would go, I couldn't leave Dad to deal with that alone. And that was when we had our argument. Now you know what the '*family business*' was about.'

'You must have suspected she was responsible for Maud's murder. Didn't that occur to you when you heard she wasn't in Surrey?'

'I didn't make the connection. I didn't think she would be a danger to Maud. I only thought about you. We were thrown off the scent by her claiming, when she eventually turned up, that she'd gone to stay with an old friend from college. Everyone believed her. I pushed the whole thing out of my mind. When you went off to Belgium, Anni, I nearly went demented. That was all I thought about for days. As far as I was concerned, Minnie had been found. I returned to Cambridge to find Maud dead and you missing. I phoned Cécile eventually and she said you were there. Without your company, I became morbid and spent my time thinking back over the past. I knew I'd have to tell you everything as soon as you came back. I don't think I ever got over Mum's death; a bit of me was in denial because I'd been pushing it away for so long. Oh Anni, how I wish I'd told you about Minnie long ago. I can't forgive myself, you know. What a mess, what an awful, dreadful mess.'

Edward laid his head on the bed. Anni stretched out a hand to stroke him, but her hand soon fell away. She slept.

Chapter 37 | *Surprising news*

When Anni woke, she saw Edward sleeping in the chair beside her. He looked so tired. She pushed herself up slowly and painfully. Her ribs were throbbing and so was her head. The kindly nurse returned.

Edward stirred, and jumped up guiltily. 'Sorry,' he said, 'I fell asleep.'

The nurse laughed. 'You look in need of a lot more sleep. There is a room available, if you'd like to lie down for a while.'

'I can't leave Anni.'

'I'm okay, Edward. Go. You do look terrible.'

'And you look pale,' said the nurse to Anni. 'Is that wound troubling you?'

'Yes,' said Anni. 'and so is my head. Can you give me something to ease the pain?'

'I'll call the doctor and ask her to prescribe something. She wants to speak to you. To both of you, actually.'

Off she went, leaving Anni and Edward feeling puzzled and worried.

Fortunately, she came quickly back, followed by the doctor, who examined Anni and said she was doing well. 'I'm glad to find you awake. I've looked in a couple of times, but you've both been out for the count. I have a bit of news for you.'

Edward and Anni looked at the doctor. She was smiling.

'Did you know you were pregnant?' she said, smiling at Anni.

'Pregnant!' repeated Anni, sitting up and wincing at the pain the sudden movement caused. Edward was speechless.

The doctor wrote on Anni's chart, and asked the nurse to fetch a painkiller. 'Yes,' she said, turning back to Anni and including Edward in her smile. 'You're three months pregnant. Didn't you know? We'll do a scan, but in case you're worrying about the stab wound, try not to. It hasn't gone anywhere near your womb, and it's not very deep.'

Anni began to smile. The room was filling with sunlight and she wasn't sure if it was real sunshine or just how good she felt. She looked at Edward. He was watching her, and she couldn't hide her joy. She saw his eyes welling up, and she knew he was happy for her. The news was a shock, but this was something good to think about, she hoped, something good amid the tragedy.

They hugged each other when the nurse and doctor had left. Edward was trying to frame words to fit the news when they heard sounds of a commotion outside the room.

'I'm Anni's brother,' said a voice in the corridor.

They both stared at the door, recognising Paul's voice. He burst into the room, followed by the policeman. 'Family only,' said the constable.

Anni began to laugh. Paul could never be mistaken for her brother. The policeman looked from her to Paul and back again. 'It's okay, constable,' she said. 'He's not my brother, but he's a friend and please let him stay.'

Paul was staring at her hair. 'Oh that wicked woman,' he

wailed. 'What has she done to your lovely hair. Oh, I can't bear it. If only I hadn't let Roger persuade me not to listen through the glass, and if we hadn't been playing that awful music I would have heard you, I would have tried to help.'

Paul looked serious. This was a side of him Anni hadn't yet seen. 'I've told Roger to go,' he said, lowering his voice. 'It's his fault, trying to change me. I never liked that horrible music. I prefer modern classics, like Elton John or George Michael. I'll never forgive him. *Rites of Spring*, huh. That's what he insisted on playing to stop me trying to hear what was going on in your flat. Huh. *Wrongs of Spring*, is what I say!'

'Yes,' said Anni, full of her own good news, and finding it impossible to blame Paul for anything. 'Much better to listen to what you like. Be yourself. No one should try to change you.'

'Oh Anni,' Paul wailed again, coming closer and inspecting her hair. 'Let me fix it for you. Let me make it up to you in a small way.'

'Is it that bad?' asked Anni, who hadn't seen herself.

'I'll go and get my travelling pack from the car,' said Paul, looking cheerful at the prospect of a bit of action. 'I always carry an emergency kit with me.' Paul went skipping out of the room, full of the chance to make amends to Anni.

The door closed and Edward and Anni looked at each other. Both began to speak at once. They stopped and laughed. The door opened again, and Cécile came in.

'Laughter?' she said, her anxious look at Anni turning to a smile as she saw the grin on her sister's face. 'What is going on? I expected to find you at death's door, not grinning like a Cheshire cat.'

Anni stretched her arms out to her sister. Cécile hugged her carefully. 'I've been imagining all sorts of terrible things. Never has a train journey been so slow. But here you are, laughing like an imp. What have they given you to cheer you up this much?'

'Good news,' said Anni. 'Wonderful, unexpected news!'

'But what is it? Tell me.'

'And tell me,' said Richard, wheeling himself into the room, following by Edward's father. 'I need cheering up too.'

Robert looked searchingly at Anni. He was surprised at the gaiety, but didn't cheer up in the way Richard and Cécile had. Edward and Anni exchanged glances. 'You tell them,' said Edward, squeezing her hand.

Anni turned her head and looked at her sister, father-in-law and brother-in-law. 'The doctor has just told us that I'm pregnant,' she said. 'Three months. She also said Minnie's attack wouldn't have harmed the baby as the knife just glanced off my ribs.'

Cécile shrieked and hugged her sister again. Richard gave a whoop. Robert shook hands with Edward. What else they might have said to each other had to wait because Paul burst through the door again, holding an open sports bag.

'That policeman is a suspicious creature. I told him I was just going to cut your hair, Anni. He's taken my scissors! Edward, talk to the man. Make him see sense. Do I look like a murderer?'

Anni and Edward laughed, but the others fell silent. 'This is Paul', said Anni, 'our next-door neighbour. He's a hairdresser and he's going to fix my hair.'

'Ah,' said Richard, 'that will be good.' He turned his

wheelchair to look at Paul, and give him room to draw closer to the bed. 'I think we've met once or twice. I'm Richard, Ed's brother.'

Edward returned, holding the offending scissors. Cécile moved off the bed as Paul pulled a cape from his bag and, with a magician-like flick, tied it around Anni, and began snipping at her hair. 'Line up if you like,' he said over his shoulder. 'I can give you all a trim.'

Chapter 38 | *An offer*

Edward's delight at finding Anni was pregnant seeped away over the next couple of days as they began to understand the full extent of what Minnie had been up to. Inspector Grant came to the flat and interviewed him again after the hospital discovered Rohypnol in Richard's bloodstream. He said it must have been recently administered or it wouldn't have shown up at all. Edward was mystified. He was sure his brother wouldn't take drugs, besides, he'd been with them in the flat for almost 24 hours before Minnie attacked him.

'We realise that, and it's why we're here,' said Inspector Grant. 'You will understand that we have to question you and your wife about it, because it was most likely administered here.'

'But why would we drug Richard? Please don't distress Anni further, Inspector. She's due to be released from hospital soon. Minnie must have been the source of it.'

'That's likely. We've asked for a copy of her medical record. It's possible the drug was prescribed for her while she was in prison.'

'But why?' asked Edward, puzzled.

'As a sleeping pill.'

The Inspector departed and Edward decided to keep the information to himself. It added a further disturbing dimension to the burden Edward was carrying, though, and he looked increasingly haggard and haunted. The news that Minnie had been transferred to Broadmoor did little to cheer him.

Anni swung between feelings of delight at being pregnant and worry about Edward. Despite them, however, she made rapid progress. She was sitting on the edge of her bed, looking gamin-like in her new short hairstyle, when the door opened and a smiling Richard was wheeled in by Robert. She saw the smile on Edward's face. This family of his were so important. What a shame they were scattered.

'Are you all right Anni?'

'Yes, Richard, I'm fine. So well in fact, that the doctors say I can leave hospital tomorrow.'

'Well so I heard, and I'm to be allowed out myself, having made what can only be described as a remarkable recovery.' Richard's sense of fun hadn't deserted him. 'In fact,' he said, standing up, 'I don't need this thing at all now.'

Robert eyed him sternly. 'I'll be wheeling you back to your room in it, and make no mistake about that.'

'He's worse than a mother hen, Anni.'

'He's not as well as he makes out, yet,' said Robert.

'Well maybe not,' said Richard, sitting on the bed beside Anni. He took her hand. 'Dad and I have a proposition to put to you. I'm banned from being too active and I imagine you'll have to take it easy for a while too, Anni. Poor old Dad doesn't want to go back to London on his own and you, Edward, look like a walking ghost.'

Edward looked pained.

'Dad and I are pretty worried about you, Ed. You shut up like a clam after Mum's death and we think you may be taking this equally badly.'

Edward didn't respond. Anni knew it wasn't that he didn't appreciate his family's concern. She was aware that he felt choked and unable to talk most of the time. Poor thing.

Richard turned to Anni. 'I don't suppose you want to return to the flat, at least not yet?'

'No Richard, I don't,' sighed Anni. She sank into the bed at the very thought of going back there. She and Edward had already decided that was impossible. The police were still in and out of the place, checking this and testing that. Edward didn't want her to put up with that disturbance, and she was relieved he understood. They were considering spending time in Bouillon with Cécile.

'Well,' said Richard, 'I propose that you all come over to Dublin and stay with me for a bit. Cécile too, if she'd like. I have plenty of space if someone volunteers to sleep in the living room.'

Chapter 39 | *Dublin*

Richard and Anni were sitting in the untidy garden of his Dublin house. It was littered with leftover leaves from autumn. A light breeze shuffled the leaves, letting them sink softly back onto the grass and path, as it died away. They had been in Dublin for two weeks. Anni had recovered completely and Richard was improving every day. Edward had travelled back and forth to Cambridge, but he remained withdrawn and Anni was beginning to despair of him coming to terms with what had happened. While she sat in the garden with Richard, Edward stayed up in their bedroom.

'Is he still having the nightmares?' asked Richard.

'He seems to have the same dream every night. I don't know how to handle this, Richard. I thought he would pick up when we got away from Cambridge, but he seems worse than ever. Does he have to keep going back there?'

Richard knew that his brother was helping the police, but he too thought it was time Edward shook himself out of his black moods. He looked down at Anni. She was mostly cheerful, but he'd noticed worry lines on her face when she was looking at his morose brother. It was a shame. Part of him wanted to shake Edward, but he knew more about Edward's past than Anni.

'I bet the bad dreams are about Lucy,' he said, 'because he never had them before she was killed. He found her body, you know. It had a profound effect on him. He was never the same afterwards. He became more and more reserved from that time on. Poor Lucy. She was so lovely.'

'Yes, Maud showed me a photo of her, and she looked beautiful, with her long blond hair contrasting with a bright red dress.'

'Ah yes, red was her favourite colour. She wore it most of the time.'

'So that's why Edward reacted so badly when I removed my coat in College that evening!'

'What do you mean?'

Anni told him about the appearance of the dress on the night they had dinner in his college, and described Edward's reaction when she took off her coat. She said he'd refused to talk about it afterwards. 'When we got to Cambridge, Edward seemed to change. It wasn't very obvious at first, and it took me time to put my finger on the differences, but he was less alert, less lively. He began having headaches. I put it down to stress, and sometimes... oh I don't know. I just couldn't get him to talk about things!' Anni sounded exasperated. 'Your father phoned shortly after we got back to the flat and, well events occurred so rapidly afterwards that we never did get an opportunity to discuss it properly.'

Richard was horrified. 'My God, Anni, Minnie must have put the dress there. It sounds like she was stalking you almost from the beginning.'

Anni looked up at him and Richard saw she was pursing her lips. 'I've had lots of time to think it over, Rich, and I'm certain it was she. She must have discovered the spare key to the flat. Probably because she was watching Edward.' Anni shivered.

'Hey,' said Richard, putting an arm around her, 'are you

cold?'

Anni kept on talking. 'I remember, right at the beginning, the feeling of someone else being in the flat. I used to blame Edward's cleaner, Eileen, for stuff that would be moved from place to place. I've been wondering if that was Minnie, and not poor maligned Eileen.'

'Edward is very fond of Eileen. He's called to her a couple of times while he's been back in Cambridge. The police won't let her back into the flat, though. He says they're still going through the place.'

'Why?' asked Anni, vehemently. 'They know Minnie was going to kill me. They found your blood on the knife too, and her fingerprints in Maud's office. Why don't the police just get on with charging her!'

'She's refusing to talk. They have to build a watertight case, to send her back to prison.'

'I never want to go back there, Richard. Never, ever. What are Edward and I to do? I won't go back to the flat and he's still so upset that we don't seem to be making any progress. How will it all end?'

Anni turned aside, but Richard noticed that her eyes had filled with tears. He wasn't fooled. Two weeks in the same house was teaching him a lot about his sister-in-law. He liked Anni and saw how good she was for his brother. They sat on in the pale winter sun, with Richard's face becoming more and more set. He rose, eventually. 'Stay here for a little while, Anni. I'm going to have a private word with Edward.'

Anni pulled her coat more tightly around her and sat on as the sun dropped lower and lower. It must have been half an hour or so before Richard returned. She glanced around as his footsteps drew closer.

'Come inside, Anni. I've lit a fire for us.' He took her arm and they walked along the leaf-strewn path into the house. 'I've told Edward that you have a right to know about Lucy's death and that he needs to talk about it. It's the last link in the chain. Maybe there will be peace when we uncover that bit of the past.'

Anni sighed.

'Now don't be worrying,' he said, looking at her strained face. 'I know my brother and I know what I can and can't say to him. Come on, now.'

Once inside, he insisted that she sit on the big sofa directly in front of a large roaring wood fire. He tucked a blanket around her, despite her protests about being warm enough. 'You've been out in the bitter cold,' he said, 'and that's my fault. We have to mind you.' He gave the rug an extra pat. 'Now,' said Richard, 'I've spoken to Edward and I've given him an ultimatum. If he doesn't tell you about the night Lucy died, I will.'

'Gosh, that's a bit radical. Is it wise?' she asked.

'Ah for God's sake you've been far too soft with him and he's not thinking about your suffering in all of this, but too much of his own grief instead. It's time he pulled himself out of it.'

'It's not that, Richard. He does think about me. Something is still eating away at him. Perhaps it is about Lucy.'

'Hmm, but he's not thinking about you in the right way at the moment, and it seems to me that you're far too soft with him. Are you comfy there, Anni?'

'I am.'

Richard looked back at the door, which he had left ajar for his brother. No one was there.

Chapter 40 | *Edward's story*

Edward was sitting at the desk in his and Anni's cramped bedroom. He had returned from another trip to Cambridge the previous day and he felt weary and demoralised. Inspector Grant had discovered the source of the Rohypnol, and the questions he put to Edward, and his guesses about what had been happening were distressing. They had checked CCTV footage from commercial premises on nearby Newnham Road, and Minnie had appeared on camera a number of times. The police were going through Edward's diary with him, checking his movements on the days and times that Minnie had been spotted in the area. It was grim. He knew he would have to tell Anni, but he'd been putting it off. She was recovering, and growing brighter and happier. He hated that he would have to take her back to the nightmare. There was no option, however. The police needed her to help them make their case.

And now Rich was pressing him to tell Anni about Lucy. He knew Richard was right and he needed to do this, but it had all become more complicated and more depressing. The past had been snapping at his heels for years, and he'd tried hard to ignore it, but he understood that he owed it to Anni to tell her the truth, however distressing that would be for both of them.

He wished his father was there. Robert, who was mostly staying in Dublin, had flown to London to deal with a few pressing matters. They were expecting him back that evening. Anni had put a casserole into the oven and Edward could smell it all the way up in his room. The smell was such a homely thing - it reminded him of when his mother had been alive and the smells that had filled their home back then. He remembered Druchsheen too, and how the smell of something delicious cooking would waft out as soon as the front door opened to welcome them.

He almost weakened in his resolve to get the dreadful business over and done with. It was so tempting to stay in a world of lovely people and wonderful food. But... He rose and went slowly down the stairs, hesitating at the door of the living room. He looked through the gap, and saw his wife and his brother sitting by the fire. Just as he went to enter, he heard Richard speak. He stopped and listened.

They had been sitting in silence, Anni and Richard, listening to the spitting of the wood as it burnt. Every now and then, Richard glanced at the door, but his brother didn't appear.

'Looks like I'll have tell you the story about Lucy,' he said to Anni, shaking his head. The mood of this story would be radically different to the stories he'd told her in Cambridge.

'I remember the evening she died,' he began. 'It must surely be burnt into all our minds. It all started out so well. The two families were meeting up to celebrate the engagement. We met at a fancy restaurant in London, Langan's it was, I think. Lucy's parent had travelled to London, and Edward was driving down from Warwick. He and Lucy had found a flat and Lucy had already moved in, so she was making her own way to the restaurant. Both of them were late, and the rest of us were amusing ourselves chomping bread rolls and sipping aperitifs. I remember they didn't give us side-plates, and I was joking with Mum about how appalled Saint Her would have been at this oversight. We chuckled away over that and I got so bold as to draw the outline of a plate by her side and by mine. I told the in-laws a few of the stories about Saint Him and we laughed and laughed and were all in very good form when finally, Edward turned up. That sobered us up a bit, because we realised Lucy hadn't arrived and began to wonder where she was. She was always punctual, that girl. Edward went off to phone her. He came back and said there was no response from the flat. We all assumed she was on her way, and so we carried on for another bit.'

Richard's normal light-hearted delivery was slowing down. 'Fifteen minutes later, there was still no sign of her. And I remember the way we made cruel jokes at poor Edward's expense *standing him up, not even waiting until they got to the altar.* Mum and I could see he was taking it very seriously, though, so we stopped. It just wasn't like Lucy to be late. Ed tried phoning again and again, but still there was no reply. He decided to go over to the flat, and that's when Ed, poor fellow, found her.'

So intently had Anni been listening that she hadn't heard the soft sound of footsteps behind them. Edward spoke, making both of them jump.

'Thanks for breaking the ice, Rich. I'll finish the story.'

He sat down beside Anni. The atmosphere in the room changed. The fire began to hiss and spit. Anni put her hand through Edward's arm, drawing him close. Richard sat on the armchair next to the sofa.

'As Richard says, I was worried. More than worried. It was so out of character for Lucy. I took a taxi to our flat and ran up the steps to the house,' he said. 'The front door was open, but I thought little of that. We were so much less security conscious in those days. My fear was that she might have fallen and hurt herself. I climbed to the top floor, where our flat was, feeling sick with worry. Lucy wouldn't have missed out on our engagement party. She'd been looking forward to it and had spent a fortune on a dress.'

His voice broke. Anni and Richard sat still. They didn't dare speak for fear of breaking the spell.

'The door of the flat was open,' he said, finally. 'I called her name but she didn't reply. I was trembling, I remember. Then I found her.' He stopped again. 'She, she was in the living room, lying on the floor, wearing the lovely long red dress she'd bought.' He turned to Anni. 'She'd spent hours shopping for that dress,' he said, speaking intensely. He fell silent again, and Anni noticed the light was fading. It made the flames from the fire all that much brighter.

Edward sighed. 'Her eyes were open,' he whispered. 'I thought that she'd fallen over and hurt herself. I called out to her, moved closer, but there was no reaction, no movement, and, and I realised she wasn't seeing me That's when I first became aware of the blood. I guess I missed seeing it initially because of the colour of her dress. I saw the rips in the material and the darker shade of red seeping into pools around her.' His voice caught, and he covered his eyes with his hands.

Anni could see it all before her, as though she'd been there too. She could feel her heart beating more strongly. She became aware of a feeling in her belly, soft, as though butterfly wings were touching her inside. The baby! She took Edward's hand and placed it near the butterfly feeling. Would he feel it? This new life growing? Would it help him move beyond the terrible past? He lifted her hand and kissed it, but his face was lined with pain. It would be a very long time before he would forget the past.

Edward looked over at Richard. 'There's something the police forbade me to speak of at the time, Rich. It's the worst part of it.' He tightened his hold on Anni's hand. 'I'm sorry to have to tell you this part, sweetheart.'

Despite the warmth of the fire and the rug, Annie shivered.

'Her finger had been cut off,' said Edward, 'her ring finger, and the murderer had taken her engagement ring. All that was left was a stump. It was awful.'

Anni's heart lurched.

'Oh my God,' said Richard. 'Why didn't you tell us? You didn't have to carry that on your own! Mum could have helped you, I would have, and Dad.'

'I know, Rich. I was close to telling you so many times, but the police didn't want anyone to know because they hoped it would help them find the murderer. They were getting confessions, which often happens after a murder, and they needed to dismiss the false ones.' He stopped speaking, tightened his grip on Anni's hand. The fire crackled. Time passed.

'They never found her killer,' he said eventually, 'and that made her death harder to come to terms with. I blamed myself for so many things that might have made a difference to the police investigation. I used the phone - maybe I spoiled the murderer's fingerprints. I might have destroyed forensic evidence by sitting on the floor and moving her body. Worst of all was the thought that I might have prevented the attack if I'd just gone searching for her sooner.' He ran his hands through his hair. 'These thoughts have looped around my mind for years. For a long time, I couldn't sleep if I didn't have pills. I had nightmares, I kept seeing her body.' He looked at Anni. 'I still have nightmares.'

'But,' Anni began to say, looking intently at the brothers.

'I know what you're thinking,' said Edward. 'Did it ever occur to us that Minnie might have killed her?' He sighed. 'Even now, when all the evidence points that way, I find myself wishing, hoping, that it wasn't so. She grew up as our sister, Anni. There was no reason at all to suspect her. How could someone that close wreak such havoc on us?'

'Minnie?' said Richard. 'But it couldn't have been. She wasn't even in London at the time.' said Richard.

'I know. She was in Scotland. She arrived back two days after the murder. Now, of course, because I'm suspicious, I ask myself if she'd ever been away. There is more to tell about Minnie, but I want to finish talking about Lucy first.'

Anni glanced over at Richard. He nodded. Now that Edward was talking, they didn't want him to stop. Let him tell it his way.

'Back then I suspected nothing. The police were working on the theory that a maniac had been stalking Lucy. Despite all the searching, the door-to-door questioning, the publicity, they found no clues. No one had seen anyone enter the building. No one else had been disturbed. No one was seen behaving suspiciously in the neighbourhood. They found nothing, absolutely nothing.'

'But wouldn't it be better to know who'd killed Lucy?' said Anni putting her hand softly into Edward's. 'Even if it turns out to be Minnie, it would help you to put it behind you.'

'Anni's right,' said Richard. 'Though I don't know how we might possibly prove it.'

'I know,' said Edward, shrugging. 'It would help. I've managed to carry on living and working by pushing it so far away from my consciousness that I almost denied it had ever happened, and out of kindness, no one ever referred to Lucy. But,' and he turned to Anni, 'meeting you and falling in love opened up the emotional side of me again. Don't get me wrong, you're the best thing that has happened to me in twenty years, but I have had to start facing up to the past, and it hasn't been easy.

Anni was close to tears. She laid her head on his shoulder.

'We were afraid to talk about it, Ed,' said Richard. 'The look of pain on your face whenever anyone mentioned Lucy or the murder kept us quiet. We couldn't bear to cause you more suffering. Life went on, and then Minnie murdered Mum.' He turned to Anni. 'Has my brother told you about that, Anni?'

'Yes. I'm so sorry. What a dreadful thing for all of you.'

'It must have been Minnie who killed Lucy, Ed. She didn't like anyone getting close to you. If she was crazy enough to kill Mum...' he stopped.

Edward stood up. 'I now have to relate the latest horrible twist in the tale. Do you remember the police discovered Rohypnol in your blood, Rich?'

'Yes.'

'And they've been puzzling how it got there? Well we know how that happened now.'

Anni wanted to cover her ears. How much worse could it get?

'It was Minnie, of course. She was prescribed it in prison, to help her sleep. She must have saved it up. It can be ground to a powder. It was in the sugar bowl at the flat.'

'The sugar bowl,' shouted Anni. 'I knew something was up with that sugar bowl. It kept appearing on the table or the worktop when I was sure I'd put it away in the cupboard.' She cringed. 'I blamed Eileen.'

'I know, sweetheart. I too blamed Eileen for lots of things that she didn't do. But all the time it was Minnie. She found the spare key to the flat, and she'd been letting herself in for about two months.'

'What?' Anni was horrified.

'She even came in while I was asleep.' Edward shivered.

'How do you know that?' asked Richard, jumping up to stand by his brother.

'The police and I have been putting the sequence together. They have footage from nearby CCTV. They believe she was letting herself into the flat during the day, and at night. As you know, I take lots of sugar. I was sometimes out for the count. That was surprising when mostly I would either have nightmares or lie awake for hours. I noticed the difference, but I was glad to be sleeping through. Now the police suspect the Rohypnol was knocking me out.'

'And I don't take sugar, so it didn't affect me,' said Anni.

'Well I do,' said Richard. 'It didn't affect me!'

'You don't take as much sugar as I do, and you were only in the flat one night. But, actually, it was your blood test that alerted the police.'

'I made you a cup of sweet hot chocolate before you went to catch the train,' said Anni.

'That might be why I have no recollection of being stabbed.' Richard laughed. 'You did me a favour, Anni.'

'I feel ill,' said Anni, bending over.

The brothers sat down each side of her. 'You look so pale, Anni. Should we stop this?'

'It's just the thought of it, that she was coming and going in the flat. Please don't stop. I need to hear all this.'

'Yes,' said Edward, rubbing her hands. 'It's a dreadful realisation. You don't have to go back there, Anni.'

'Minnie!' said Richard. 'What did we ever do to her? She must have killed Lucy too, Ed. It must have been her. Can't we ask the police to re-open the case?'

'I've been thinking about doing just that over the past couple of weeks. Everyone thought she was doing a work placement in Surrey, but all the time she was travelling up to Cambridge and leading a double life. She fooled us all. We may well have been deceived all those years ago. She's mad. Stone crazy mad.'

'Richard is right, Edward. She must have done it. I understand that you might have been fooled in the beginning, but you must have begun to suspect her after your mother's death, when you knew what she was capable of,' said Anni.

'I never made the connection. Perhaps it was just too awful to consider. I don't know. The police said Lucy's murder had been premeditated. Minnie's attack on Mum seemed spontaneous and the psychiatrist said she'd disintegrated into a psychotic state. There was no similarity between the two murders, and when I think back to the time before Lucy's death, I can't recall anything that might have put me on my guard.'

'Not even Lucy's sudden decision to leave London that summer?' said Anni. 'Both of you have talked about Minnie's obsession with Edward.'

'I know,' said Edward, and his voice became strained. 'The whole thing is almost too awful to take on board. If we'd even suspected such a thing, she wouldn't have been living with us, and Mum might still be alive. If I had realised she was that disturbed, I might have saved Lucy, saved Mum, prevented the attempt on Richard and spared you that terrible ordeal!'

'Oh Edward, don't torture yourself,' pleaded Anni.

'I can't help it! Those bad dreams I'm having, I keep walking in and finding Lucy's body but it's your face not hers. What if Minnie escapes? What if she tries to kill you again? The thought haunts me.'

'She won't kill anyone else,' said a voice from the doorway.

'Dad!' Richard jumped up off the sofa and went over to his father. 'We didn't hear you come in. How long have you been there?'

'Long enough.'

Anni saw the look of weariness on his Robert's face. He seemed to have aged in the few days he'd spent away from them. Richard led him to the sofa, and sat him beside Anni.

'I have news,' he said. 'Overhearing your conversation makes the telling of my news easier. It's Minnie. She's dead. She killed herself two days ago. I've been to Broadmoor to identify her body. She's dead. It's over.'

The only sound in the room was the sizzle from the fire. The news had stunned everyone. Robert stood up.

'There's something else, son.' he said, addressing Edward. He put his hand in his pocket and withdrew a ring. A single large diamond sparkled in the light from the fire.

'That was Lucy's engagement ring!' shouted Richard.

'Yes. I found it among Minnie's possessions. The police have re-opened the file on Lucy's murder, son. There can be no doubt about who killed her now.'

Edward took the ring. 'Lucy, Lucy,' he said.

Anni stood and moved to the door, beckoning to Richard and his father. They left the room, as Edward began to sob.

Epilogue

'Maud, Maud? Where are you Maud?'

Tiny little squeals of delight were Edward's answer. Maud's little feet took her off the driveway and in among the trees. Edward followed slowly, grinning, giving his daughter plenty of time to get away and hide. Both stopped their play at the sound of a car coming up the driveway at Druchsheen. Richard leaned his head out of the driver's window as he drew to a stop, calling to his niece.

'I'm back, Maud, I'm back! Did you miss me?'

Little Maud changed course and ran towards the car. Richard jumped out and scooped her into his arms. Her fat little hands held his face and kissed it all over. He laughed delightedly, and carried her up to the house, where Anni was waiting at the door, smiling. He kissed her.

'And how is my favourite sister-in-law?'

'I'm feeling very well, Richard.'

'Mummy having baby!' said Maud, leaning out of Richard's strong arms to put her hands on Anni's stomach. 'It going to be my, my...'

'Little brother,' said Anni, raising a hand to stroke little Maud's curly hair.

'So, there will soon be even more laughter in the house,' said Richard. He sniffed the air. 'Do I smell rock cakes?'

'You certainly do,' said Edward, coming up behind the group. 'But don't go eating them all. Cécile will be here shortly. I'll take Maud out to the swing, while you sort yourself out, Rich.' He hugged his brother and walked off with his daughter.

Richard looked after him.

'He's a different man, isn't he?' he said to Anni.

'I've never known him so relaxed. He really loves it here and he adores Maud.'

'That's the old Edward, the one Maud and I grew up with, the man he was before Minnie brought us so much grief.' He stepped into the hallway, gave another sniff, and put his arm around his sister-in-law. 'Well done, Anni. You've made Druchsheen into a home again. Now do you know what I'm going to do this evening?'

'What,' asked Anni.

'I'm going to draw a family portrait, and we'll frame it and put it beside those terrible drawings I did in Cambridge.'

'They're not terrible, Rich. I love them. But tell me, how will you draw a family portrait if you're doing the drawing?'

They began walking into the house.

'Haven't you seen all those wonderful self-portraits by the best artists?'

'Em, yes, but....'

'Well can't I draw a flattering portrait of myself, on the best paper, and then I could add you all in. We'll have to put a teddy in my chair, and...'

Their voices trailed away.

Also by Siobhán Carew:

Cambridge Rose

Rose Foster meets Ronnie Lyndon when she begins a master's degree in Cambridge. A relationship blossoms. Rose is still reeling from the death of a beloved aunt. Is life now on the up? Just when she thinks it might be, Rose is plunged into a terrifying situation.

DI Harry Meredith has been investigating the kidnapping of a wealthy diplomat's daughter. When he discovers another university student is missing, Harry becomes concerned. Is Rose's disappearance purely a coincidence, or is something more sinister afoot?

This is the third book in Siobhán Carew's Cambridge Crime series. This thriller has humour, a dash of romance, and a little something for cat lovers.

Cambridge Green

When DCI Anne Fountain phones newly appointed Detective Inspector Harry Meredith with news of a murder, he is surprised to learn that his first case will take him back to the Cambridge college he graduated from. A body has been found in the Fellow's Garden of St Benedict's College. Harry and his Detective Sergeant, Ellen Brookes, quickly realise that there is little appetite for helping them among some members of the college. The bursar, Mr Darnton, decrees that no one should speak to the police on college property. Happily for the investigation, Harry and Ellen are willing to run Mr Darnton's gauntlet.

They make a surprising discovery about the murdered

man, who was a visiting scholar to the college, and this takes them out of Cambridge, into the Fens, where they uncover a disturbing crime which shocks them profoundly.

Despite being 'banned' from the college, Harry's investigation takes him there again and again, and he begins to rely on some of the staff to help him tease out the complicated route that led to Dr Chen's murder. Janis, in the Senior Tutor's Office, catches their interest early on; Patrick, the head gardener, whom Harry befriended when he was a student, is a steady source of information and good sense, with a little nonsense thrown in for good measure. The story is peppered with feisty and funny characters, who help and hinder the investigation. No one, however, can avert the tragic conclusion.

Meet me in Hopatcong

A difficult beginning to a holiday in New York, turns into a romantic mystery adventure for a young Irish tourist. She witnesses a man jumping from the Ellis Island ferry just before it docks at Manhattan. Dazed and shocked, she picks up the coat he dropped on the deck of the boat and only becomes aware of it when she is sitting on the subway, halfway back to her hotel. In the pocket of the coat she finds a pencilled note which reads: *Meet me in Hopatcong. Wear Pink.* Other items in the pockets hold possible clues to the man's identity and a mystery beyond the incident on the ferry.

After an unusual introduction, Neasa joins forces with the young man staying in the room next to hers. Alex is an English tourist. They decide to try and solve the mystery together and Neasa is delighted to find a companion to spend time with. Alex, however, is not what he seems. The FBI arrives on the scene and tensions soar. Agent James Fox pursues Neasa and Alex into New Jersey, and their adventure takes unexpected turns.

A chance meeting in New York, leads to a gradual unfolding of the mystery and a very unexpected outcome.

The Pig Shed

Breffni Everingham discovers the body of her Uncle Charles in a shed. He has been murdered. His unexpected death brings relationship difficulties within the family to a head. Simmering resentments explode, allowing shocking personal and family histories to seep out of the chaos.

At times dark and emotional, the novel is full of humour, and it paints a colourful picture of life in a small community, and the interactions of the people within it.

First to arrive on the scene following Breffni's discovery of the body is Garda Malone, a sarcastic bully who finds it impossible to behave either well or objectively. Hidden behind his harassment of the family is the memory of an unrequited love for Breffni's mother, awakened when he sees Breffni for the first time.

Relations and friends gather: Breffni's sister Corry and her brother Henry, who is one of the few calm members of the family; the Bish, Charles's brother and a retired bishop, arrives before Breffni and her sister Corry break the news to him and his anger is almost explosive; Breffni's sanctimonious Aunt Edith sides with him; Aloysius, Aunt Edith's adopted son plays a greater part as the story develops. Mikey Farraher, Charles's ancient neighbour is sure it was tinkers. Hadn't there been a spate of cow-stealing lately? Who else but a wicked, thieving robber could have done such a thing to his old friend?

All are subjected to questioning by Garda Malone, whose inefficient investigation weaves in and out of the story, stirring up anger and strong passions as he conducts his enquiries.

The story gathers momentum, weaving a path through a series of events which finally lead to the murderer.

Siobhán Carew's prose is full of poetry and strong emotions. Her characters are drawn vividly and they move the story forwards, often humorously. This is an unforgettable novel.

(and if you love cats)

CATalogue

All I've ever wanted to do is sleep, eat and have cuddles. Isn't that a reasonable ambition for a cat? But life has treated me cruelly. Why oh why did Angie marry Dick? He's horrible. I'm constantly on my guard. I know just what he'd like to do to me, but he can't, because Angie loves me and she stands up for me, and if only she was perfect, and he wasn't there, it would all be fine. But I have to tell you that she doesn't always feed me what I like to eat, or pay me the attention I need. What is it with humans?

The only good things about Dick are his children. His daughter Celine just loves me, and if I had my way, I'd live with her, but she has a boyfriend and he's a stubborn wimp. He makes up all sorts of reasons why I can't go to live with them. It so annoys me. The world is the wrong way around for us cats. We should be in charge. If I ruled the world, I'd get rid of Dick, then I'd banish our neighbour, Ginger. That may sound like a cat's name, but Ginger is a man, another horrible man. So, I'd banish him, then I'd put a spell on Angie so that she gave me just what I wanted to eat, and I'd make her open the bedroom door so that I could ramble in during the night and curl up on her bed. It would be just her and me. Like the good old days. Dick would be history.

In case you're interested, I've written a few stories about the way I live and the terrible things that keep happening to me. I've added bits about my pals. We're thinking of starting a campaign to change things. I'd like to get rid of Dick, Bumface wants recognition for the Carter kid, Scrotak would like a bit of continuity in his life, and as for The Babies ... actually The Babies are okay. You don't need to worry about them. It's the rest of us who need your sympathy.

Printed in Dunstable, United Kingdom

78884241R00160